BOUND BY DRAGONBLOOD

KENNEDY ANDERSON

To those who believe they are alone, who feel they are not enough . . .
You are not alone. You never were.
There's a fire within you. Let it burn.

For Mamaw, who showed me what falling in love with writing feels like.

CONTENT WARNING

This book contains content/themes that may not be suitable for all readers, including: graphic violence, death, sexual assault, rape, strong language, and scenes of intimacy.
Please read at your own discretion.

CELESTIA
LUMINARA
VELORUM
N
W
E
S
OBSIDIAN SHORE

ASTRIA
SOLARIA
NOVA FOREST
MYSTIQUE

CHAPTER ONE

T HE WAR WAS OVER, but the kingdom still bled.

Everywhere I looked, I was reminded of Solaria's dire state, despite having over two decades to rebuild after The Infernal Siege. The city reeked with decay and despair. People lay motionless in the streets day and night, as if life had been drained from them. The people of the kingdom never fully recovered, and it seemed that would never change.

The stories I'd heard of that time terrified me. People were burned alive in the streets, in their homes, their screams echoing through the night . . .

But stepping through the threshold of our home, my thoughts were buried, replaced with the sight of my father standing from his armchair to greet me. "Valora," he said, welcoming me with a hug that practically squeezed the breath out of me. He chuckled once he realized, then released me. "Your mother is almost done with supper."

I nodded and escaped to my room to set down my bag, unloading the shucking knife and other tools I'd used for work at the fish market today.

Starving and exhausted, I found myself at the dinner table. My mother placed a bowl in front of me as soon as my rear touched the seat.

Stew. Again.

I let out a silent sigh. We couldn't afford much more than this, I'd accepted that fact. But I eagerly awaited the day we could afford chicken or fish for dinner again.

"How was your day, Theos?" My mother turned to my father as she sat on my right at the four-seater table.

He swallowed his bite. "Nothin' out of the ordinary. Blacksmiths don't have much variation between each day, Reyla dear. We go to work, make some tools and weapons, and head home."

She nodded, sweeping the brown strands of hair falling into her eyes behind her ears, blending them seamlessly with the hair tied back into a low bun. We simultaneously took a small bite of stew. "How was the beach today, Valora?"

I shrugged. "It was calm. Quiet. Not much going on except admiring the views."

"I'm glad that you've found a place where you enjoy spending your time."

It wasn't so much the time I liked to spend there. It was more about the setting, the aura of the beach—especially at night—where I could waste away, getting lost in the view. "The stars were gorgeous tonight," I said, recalling how their presence simply scattered across the blackened sky. "And the moon was full and bright."

"That's lovely, Val," my father said with a mouthful of stew.

I'd needed the quiet of the night. The endless horizon before me. The shore was the only thing that reminded me that there were other places out there, other purposes than simply surviving.

The sun seemed to have risen earlier than usual, dragging its heavy rays across the sky, like painting a canvas of endless blue.

My hands moved mechanically as I shucked oysters and wrapped orders of fish. The stench of mollusks and seafood filled the air as I carted my supply through the city.

I'd grown used to the feeling of exhaustion in my bones, the ache in my back that never quite went away. All of this to be disappointed with my wage by the end of the day. That's what a kingdom kept in poverty will do for you.

Nothing. Absolutely nothing.

The crowds seemed louder, the air thicker with every step I took. I felt more disconnected from the world by the minute, like I was drifting through a fog that only I could see. The depressing fact of life—the fact that I wasn't the only one living this way—consumed my thoughts. Consumed me. Why did life have to be this way? It was hardly a life at all.

At some point, the chatter of customers and cityfolk disappeared altogether. This routine was wearing thin, bound by mundane tasks.

The sun dipped lower. Lower. Until the sky told me that the day was turning to night. *Finally,* my shift was ending, and I returned my cart to my booth at the market.

Just like that, I was strolling along the beach. The salty breeze wrapped around me like a cool embrace, and the sound of the ocean's waves on the shore was a soothing balm to my soul.

The sun drifted lower, ever so slowly, casting a golden glow across the land and sea, creating a gradient canvas in the sky of pinks and purples and oranges.

I walked the water's edge for what seemed like forever, the light growing dimmer with each passing second until it was dark outside.

I focused on the way my feet sank into the cool sand with each step, the way the breeze tugged at my hair as if trying to sweep away all other thoughts that swirled like a storm inside me.

Then the stars appeared, brighter than ever, despite the glow of the full moon rising behind me. The light from behind the walls of the city created long, jagged shadows ahead of me. The shadows felt like an extension of me, of my mind, in this moment. Impossible to escape.

But tonight, everything seemed a little different. There was a chill in my bones, a wonder of what else was beyond this shore. What could be waiting beyond the sea? The stars? It had to be better than here.

I trudged farther along the edge of the water, listening to the sound of the ocean's song, allowing it to calm the stress under my skin, in my muscles.

Inhale.

Exhale.

The sharp scent of salt filled my lungs, grounding me in this moment of peace.

Until I was screaming, the ground coming up at me as my toes scraped a rough surface until I found myself face down in the sand.

"What in the hell did I just roll my ankle on?" I asked, knowing no one was around to hear me.

I swear to the Old Powers if I broke my ankle . . .

I knew we didn't have the means of affording to fix it, and so did the gods.

I caught my breath and huffed the sand from my face. Flipping myself onto my back, I wiggled my foot, realizing it moved just fine with little to no pain.

Cautiously, I made my way to my feet and rested weight on it. Stable.

My eyes scanned every inch of the shore's surface searching for the culprit.

I spotted a small lump peeking from under the moist sand.

Stooping over, I gently examined it through the sand, brushing some off to ensure it wasn't anything dangerous. It didn't move. I bent my knees and dusted off more sand.

I'd expected a large rock, a piece of driftwood, maybe. But instead, I had no idea what I was looking at. It was almost too dark to tell. But it was a dark, oval-shaped object, its surface rigid and gleaming faintly in the moonlight.

I rested my fingers on its surface, feeling the warmth of its touch invade my skin. It pulsed, faintly, a rhythm that seemed to echo in time with my own heartbeat.

It looked like an egg, an unusual one, no doubt. The pulse grew stronger, and for some unknown explanation, something deep within me whispered that this was no ordinary thing. It was *alive.*

An egg. It was an egg, though from what creature I had no clue. Various animals and creatures used to roam the kingdom, but many have died out.

I picked it up with ease, and despite its size—being that of a newborn baby—I was shocked that it wasn't heavier than it was.

"This could get interesting," I said to myself as I shoved it into my bag.

I marched home immediately.

Dinner was ready as soon as I stepped through the door. I knew that smell. Stew.

"Did you sell much today, Valora?" My mother started as we settled at the table.

My mind had otherwise been occupied. I'd hesitated to show them what I had found on the beach tonight. I'd nestled the egg within some blankets in my room, hiding it from sight, keeping it warm.

"Valora," my father's voice across from me broke through my train of thought. "Your mother asked you a question."

I turned toward her. "Sorry. Today was about the same as always. Had some insults thrown my way over the prices, but it's not like I'm in control of that." I shrugged. "We've got to make a living, right? And people need to eat. If they don't like the price they have to pay to survive, then they just don't get to eat."

My dad snickered, almost spitting out his drink. "Do you tell them that to their face?"

I laughed with him. "If only I had the courage to do such a thing."

"I hear ya," he replied. "I keep tellin' you, Val, that you should come work with me. I'm looking to hire a new apprentice anyway, so that means more time I'll have to show you the ropes. And you can get that seafood smell off of ya."

"I definitely wouldn't mind that," I admitted. It was a generous offer. I hated my job and the toll it took on me to sell to so many people, having to listen to their rude comments all day long. "It doesn't sound like a bad idea. But I'm a creature of habit," I sighed. "I'm not sure I'm ready to learn something new."

"That's fair," he said, taking another bite of stew, almost finished with his bowl. "It was just an idea. Besides, you'd probably end up dirty all the time like your old man." He sat back in the chair, showing off the dirty rags you'd call clothes, covered in black splotches of ash and soot from his day. I noted that his face still seemed covered in sweat and grime. Even his hair wasn't showing as much gray as usual, just covered up with leftover debris from his shop.

My head lowered. "I just wish we had more money."

"We do too, sweetie," my mother agreed.

"King Altair ruined that for us," my father's voice deepened, his fists clenched. "If he hadn't brought a damn *dragon* with him to burn our city to the ground and take the throne, we'd be prospering."

"Correction," my mother interrupted, "it wasn't *his* dragon that burned the city."

"Right. King Polaris aided *him* instead of us," he shook his head in defeat, heat growing in his eyes. "Some High King he is."

I thought back to all the stories I'd heard about the war. How the king of Mystique, King Altair, decided to conquer Solaria through bloodshed. Somehow, the High King of the five kingdoms of Luminara, King Polaris, had been convinced to aid Altair in the war, and sent his dragon over to slaughter our people and our own king.

"Hun, you can't change the past," my mother said, reaching for his hand to calm him down.

"You can't, but it doesn't take away the fact that our King Jesper is dead, after all he did to help this city and our farmlands prosper. Now our current ruler neglects his new territory and the people he left to starve on the streets."

My father's voice and his anger grew louder with each word. My mother hushed him softly, trying to keep his rage at bay.

Now, King Altair chooses to reside in his home territory of Mystique. I didn't blame my father for the way he felt, but I did wonder how a king could rule a kingdom without even being present in it.

"Why didn't anyone help us during the war?" I asked. "Didn't other kingdoms have dragons, armies that they could have sent over?"

"King Polaris had the last dragon known to the realm," my mother started. "The other four kingdoms hadn't been so lucky in raising dragons. We left that to Velorum and their magic there, and focused on our armies instead. But the Eclipse Guard here was still no match for Mystique's guard, and though they put up a great fight—somehow taking down King Polaris's dragon—too much damage had already been done. I'm afraid this would have been the outcome whether another army assisted us or not." Her gaze reached the ceiling as she thought back to that time over twenty years ago. "To see dragonfire in person," she shook her head, lowering her gaze to her lap, "I'll never forget the destruction it caused."

So many questions swirled in my mind. "But why would King Polaris choose to aid King Altair instead of us? What could Mystique give him that we couldn't?"

"I'm not sure, Val. Velorum is already a wealthy kingdom, so I don't think money would have been a factor," she sighed.

I'd heard about our capital, Velorum, and how its kingdom was a city of gold that was said to gleam so brightly it could be seen for miles on end. The High King and his family had ruled for generations, honing magic and dragons, while remaining the richest territory in Luminara. Yet, the High King never sent ships with supplies, at least not to Solaria. He never sent over soldiers to help protect our borders and guard the gates that led to the castle. Neither did King Altair. Not one ship sent, not one extra guard handed over from Mystique. We were nothing to him. Nothing to them.

"But I thought King Jesper and the High King were good acquaintances?"

My father's knuckles were white. "No one knows why Polaris did what he did. *Our* king is dead. Maybe the High King is a spineless, traitorous prick like King Altair."

"Calm down, Theos," my mother whispered, running her fingers along the top of his hand. The tension in his shoulders eased. She looked back at me. "This is why we don't discuss the happenings of the war with your father. He gets all riled up."

I shifted back to my stew. "I just had questions, that's all."

The small talk drifted to other conversations, but my mind returned to the egg I'd found today.

Then, it clicked.

No. It can't be. Dragons haven't existed for decades now. The last dragon died during The Infernal Siege. Surely this egg had come from another creature that lived in the forests long ago.

"Valora. . ." My name echoed in my head. "Valora!" It was my mother's voice. I met her eyes. "You seem more distracted than usual today. Are you feeling unwell?"

By now, all sets of eyes were on me. They knew me better than I knew myself, and they knew that I was internally occupied more than normal.

I should tell them.

No.

Yes.

The words scattered inside me from one side to the next.

"I think I found a dragon egg."

My confession was met with deafening silence.

CHAPTER TWO

Someone gulped, yet no one spoke for many seconds. A minute.

"I think I found a dragon egg," I repeated.

"We heard you," my father finally broke their silence. He shared a nervous yet perplexed glance with my mother, then looked back to me with an inquisitive stare. "What makes you think such a thing?"

"I can show you." I rushed to my room before they could argue, unwrapping the egg from its spot, its iridescent glow from the candlelight chilling me to my core, and returned to set it before them on the table. Their eyes flared, flashing to each other before returning to the egg.

More silence. I sat in my chair and waited impatiently. "Why are you both acting so odd?"

My mother sighed and seemed perturbed. "It looks *exactly* like an egg, Theos."

He sat back and nodded, folding his arms in each other across his chest. I could practically see the gears turning in his head. "Dragons haven't been around since before you were born, Valora. How did you come about finding this thing?"

"It was buried in the sand along the shoreline. I tripped over it and thought I'd broken my ankle at first," I gestured to my foot, which was completely uninjured.

"Well, a dragon won't be kept in this house, I'll tell you that," he laughed it off as though he'd expected this thing to hatch right here, right now. "That thing would have to be in . . . in . . ." He reached for the right word.

"Incubated," I said.

"Incubated in order for it to hatch. We can't afford to do all that. We don't have the time to waste or the money."

"Also, Val, we can't keep a dragon here, and we have no need to keep an unincubated egg," my mother locked eyes with my father. "Honey, we could always sell it . . ."

My pulse quickened at the words.

"Now that's an idea, Reyla."

"No," I interjected. They looked back at me.

"Excuse me?" My father's brows furrowed.

"How can you decide what to do with it when *I* am the one that found it?"

"Valora, when the stars align, that's when you can have whatever your heart desires. But until then, you live under our roof, and we aren't keeping a dragon here. The money we could make off this egg could be life changing."

Part of it tempted me. No more stew every night. More than two meals a day. I could quit my job at the market. It was all so tempting. But . . .

When the stars align, my ass, I thought.

"No." I said again, standing up from my seat. Their faces lost color. "I don't care if it hatches or not. I don't care if it is truly a dragon egg or not. There is no harm in finding out. I found it, and I can feel the life inside of it. I can *feel* it, father. Mother. Like it's calling to me. It's as though the gods placed it there to be stumbled upon—literally, in my case." I shook my head. "I'm not letting you ruin this rarity for me, the first nice thing we've had in a long time, by selling it!" I stormed off, retrieving the egg on the way.

My parents' baffled looks were etched into my brain. I never talked back to them. Never. But the way they'd acted so strangely as soon as I told them and showed them, made me wonder if I should have kept this information to myself.

I plopped on my bed, staring at the object in my hands, its faint glow echoing off the walls from the candlelight and the moonlight filtering through the window.

Whatever creature had lost their egg that I had the pleasure of finding, it didn't matter to me. It was a precious find. It was like a question that had gone unanswered for so long that I finally understood. There was more out there than the hustle and bustle of working your ass off every day only to afford one meal. There was so much more than I knew about.

Whispers in the next room cut through the previous silence. I had no choice but to listen harder through the walls.

"An egg? Does that not ring any bells to you, Theos?" "Absurdly, it does. I'm concerned as to what this means. For her. For *us*. What are the chances of our daughter finding this so long after dragons have been known to be extinct." My father paused, stumbling over his words for a moment.

"Does this mean that it's time to tell her?"

I could hear his sigh from here. "I assume so. It's only the fair thing to do. But let's wait for tomorrow. I don't want to rush into it while she's in this mood. She'll be worried all night wondering."

The shuffle of footsteps down the hall and the closing of their bedroom door told me that the conversation was over.

I relaxed back onto my bed, more concerned than I'd been before I stormed in here. I thought at first that they were just worried about the egg, about possibly having a dragon present, or whatever other creature might come of it. But it's apparent that there's more to it than that. There's no possibility of them having experienced this before. If they'd found a dragon egg before they went extinct, then someone would have known about it, or maybe they'd have told me about it. Then there would be a dragon in Solaria. But clearly, that didn't happen.

I'd just have to wait until tomorrow.

"Fresh seafood! Straight from the market!" I called out as I made my way past Fisherman's Square and through the gates of the city to lure customers. "Oysters and trout for sale here!"

My mind raced as soon as I began my monotonous route, thinking about that damn dragon egg. I hardly slept last night, just *wondering* what had my parents so worked up over it.

"Dragons . . ." I huffed under my breath, my voice a whisper. "So what if it is a dragon? I'm not selling it. I am *not* selling it." My head low, I shook my head at the thought of getting rid of it.

It was eating at me the way it spoke to me solely with its presence. I was meant to find it. It *means* something. There was a connection there, somehow, someway. Maybe it was simply in my head, and the egg was just something new in my life meant to keep me fixated on something other than reality. Whatever it was, maybe it was working.

A man whistled to my left, snapping me out of my trance. I came to his beckon.

"Would you like anything, sir?"

"Oh, yes, I would," he said, leaning back in his rocking chair outside of a worn down house, shutters hanging next to the windows by a single nail. "Just some oysters from ya, m'lady." He tipped his head down slightly and gave me a grim smile.

I returned a soft smile. "How many for you?"

"Four sounds just right."

Removing the shucking knife from my belt, I turned to the wheelbarrow I carted behind me and cracked open the first oyster, exposing the raw mushy inside that everyone seemed to love. The man's eyes were pinned on me, I could feel it, but I continued on without a word.

He was at youngest my father's age, but with thinning dark hair, and was unbearably thin. Too thin. He was draped in a large brown rag that you could barely count as a robe. It seemed he could hardly afford food for himself, let alone afford oysters. But it was none of my business.

"So," he began, "what's a pretty thing like you doin' sellin' seafood? You could belong in a castle, never havin' to work again." His voice drifted off as he moved closer to me, still seated.

There it was—the sly comment I had been waiting for. Men tended to do this to me, and it was one of the many reasons I'd begun to loathe this job. According to them, I was blessed by Iana, the Goddess of Beauty. And they never *stopped.*

"That black hair would be beautifully styled with a crown atop it," he said, running his fingers lightly down the single braid I wore. "And those eyes, that striking green. I never seen no color like it."

This was exhausting.

The man's dirty, sunken face grew so close to me I could faintly smell his last meal still between his teeth. I kept my composure and shucked the rest of his order.

"That'll be two silvers, sir."

"Two silvers? That high? Ya sure it's worth all that, darlin'?" He sat back against the chair and cocked his head. His brows furrowed as he waited for my response.

Gods, I wish I had the nerve to slap these arguers with a fish.

It took every bit of willpower to not chuckle at that subconscious thought. How I so badly wanted to go through with it, though I knew I couldn't do it.

He gave a slight shrug, reached for his pocket, and handed me two silver coins that seemed as if he'd just fished them out from the mud of the nearest river. "Here ya go, darlin'." The smile had wiped clean from his face.

I thanked him and handed him his tray of oysters in exchange. He reached out, giving me another full-face smile, his eye contact never breaking. His hands brushed gently against mine before he grabbed the plate, as if he'd "reached a little too far."

"Thank ya, darlin'. Come by again tomorrow. Maybe someday I can pay you in other ways." I caught an unwanted wink from him and quickly snatched my cart to leave.

When the sun finally eased behind the city walls, my shift was finally over. I hauled my cart back to my station at the market. I glanced at the money I made today. Hardly enough to pay for a full meal for my family. Not surprising.

A wave of regret washed over me on my march home, like I was suddenly being trampled with despair. I wasn't sure what caused it this time, but it stopped me right as I reached the West Gate.

Then, a realization struck: I didn't want to go home. Perhaps it was the embarrassment of not making much money today. It couldn't be. I was used to it by now. But deep down, I wasn't sure I was ready for whatever information my parents had waiting for me at home. I was afraid of the consequences. Of the truth. Whether the truth would be good or bad, there must have been a reason my parents hadn't told me.

I assumed the worst.

And I had a feeling they wanted me to sell the egg. I couldn't live with that feeling. I wouldn't do it.

Without a second thought, I spun and made a run for the beach. My second home, where I could isolate myself from the harsh realities of the world and free my mind. Where I could look out onto the horizon and hope that there was more out there than what I was living.

The life that the ocean breathed into me slowed the rhythm of my heart, and the grit of sand beneath my boots grounded me to something bigger than me. Something alive and real.

I took in the view in front of me. Ships lined the horizon, coming and going from our ports. This was the same shoreline I found the egg on, only a farther way down. If I could make it far enough, maybe I could get a clue as to how this egg appeared here. If someone left it. If *something* left it to be found.

Before I could take another step, a solid pressure wrapped around the midline of my body, and my feet were no longer in the safety of the sand. The last thing I could see before my eyes were covered with a cloth was the waves on the shore getting smaller and smaller.

CHAPTER THREE

"Ugh . . ." I grunted as I gasped for a breath. I had been dragged through the streets for countless minutes until I ended up here . . . wherever I was. I kicked and screamed the whole way, but it was no use. Whoever had taken me was too strong. And for some reason, no one intervened for me.

My boots were loose on my feet, like the force of dragging them on the ground while I flailed had ever so slightly pulled them off.

The cloth covering my face snapped away, leaving my eyes to adjust to the lack of light in the room. The space had no furniture, no candles lit, and only one window to my right. We were solely relying on the light of the dimming sun.

In front of me were the silhouettes of three men: two large beasts—I assumed one of them was the strong brute that carried me here—and another man stood behind them in the middle, just out of reach of the light.

"What do you want from me? Who are you?" I asked, attempting to keep my voice as steady as possible.

"We've heard a rumor about you . . ." the man in the back murmured, his voice vaguely familiar, but I couldn't quite place it.

"I don't think you have the right person. I'm a nobody. There's nothing to hear about me," I rested my hands at my sides and leaned tall against the wall behind me.

A soft chuckle filled the room. "You're the right one, 'ight. I wouldn't forget your beauty for a moment." The man took a step forward, and my heart jumped to my throat when I recognized that too-thin face. It was the man I had sold oysters to today. I knew I'd had a weird feeling about him, how uncomfortable he made me in those few moments we interacted. My stomach dropped.

"What did I do?" I held my head high. Maybe if I didn't show weakness, if I held my ground, it would keep the tension at bay.

"It's not what you've done. It's what you're *gonna* do." I was certain that he read my puzzled expression. "We want somethin' from ya, girl."

"Fuck, Judah," one of the large men interrupted, his voice a low roar. "Stop trying to be so mysterious and get to the damn point." He turned back to me before allowing him to continue. "We want your dragon egg."

My brows raised in disbelief. How in the world could they already know about it? I *just* found it, and I know for sure that no one was around when I nearly *died* tripping over it. I gulped, unsure of how to respond.

"I was getting there, you bastard," the smaller man, Judah, snapped back, his voice raspy. They waited for my response, eyeing me up and down. "Well?"

"I'm not sure I know what you're talking about," I lied. It was my only option. They couldn't possibly *know*.

"I can see right through that lie, girl. If you don't want people knowing your business, you should start keeping your pretty little mouth shut when you're out and about. We heard ya say today that you had a dragon egg ya didn't want to sell."

My eyes flared, and by the venomous smile that tugged at Judah's lips, I knew I'd just given myself up.

"Spoke a little louder than you meant to, huh? That's why I called you over to me, darlin'. You grabbed my attention with those words . . . and in other ways, too." He looked me up and down, sending a shiver straight down my spine.

Why didn't I stay quiet? I should have known better. But how was I supposed to know that this scum was listening in on me, and I would end up in this situation? I didn't.

There was no use lying now.

"You can't have it. Besides, it's not even a real dragon egg—" Before I could say another word, Judah's callused hand was around my throat, and all of my thoughts went to keeping myself breathing.

"Listen here, little girl. You will come back tomorrow with more seafood, that we *won't* be payin' for, by the way. And that egg? That'll be comin' with ya, and that will be ours. Understood?" His shove forced the stray hairs loose from my braid, and I puffed them out of my eyes as best as I could, despite his death grip around my windpipe.

"Or what?" I croaked, though I probably shouldn't have said something so bold.

"There will be consequences."

"What consequences?" I choked out through his constraint as his grip tightened. "Fuck!" I exclaimed as the back of my head was forced into the wall behind me. My vision blurred for a moment as I scratched and clawed at the hand holding me captive. For such a scrawny man, he was rather strong. Soon enough, I was staring blankly back into Judah's sunken face.

"Do you understand how much that egg could be worth if sold, let alone how much a dragon could be worth? If ya refuse to sell it, then someone else should be worthy of that money." He scanned me from head to toe, then his eyes landed back on my face. "Ya know, I could be doin' a lot more do ya right now. Things that ya probably wouldn't like. Maybe you'll heed my warning before it comes to that. For *your* sake."

He released his hand from my neck, and I gagged at the sudden influx of oxygen, nodding in understanding. They laughed in unison as they turned to each other, finally deciding that I was no longer worth their attention. Good.

Where. Is. The. Door . . .

To my left, I caught the faint glint of a near-rusted doorknob. I stumbled that direction, the wall my guide, before they changed their minds about letting me leave. I heaved open the door and took my first step out, falling immediately into the dusty road. I gasped for more air so I could gain enough strength to stand up and run.

I had to get out of here.

But I had no clue what part of the city I was in. It had only taken a few minutes to get here—I think—from the West Gate, though at the time it had felt like an eternity of struggle and panic. But I knew if I could find that gate, I could find home.

Staggering to my feet, I shuffled my way down the road, my vision slightly blurred. Everything resembled a painting of endless swirls, and I hardly knew which way was up. Despite that, the more air I mustered in and out of my lungs, the easier it became to walk.

The people passing by gave me odd looks, yet did nothing to assist me. The fact that no one reacted to a girl of twenty-one, stumbling down the street with her hair ragged, and most likely with a red mark around her throat, was rather surprising. I could have been raped. Or murdered. I expected more from these people, seeing as though everyone was struggling in their own ways, but now, it felt like I was simply on the wrong side of the city. Where criminals and folks with no morals roamed freely. This street gave me the gut-wrenching vibe that this was a common occurrence around here.

I made my way into a clearing where I could see the sky better around me, the streets branching in various directions around me. The sun was to my left, which meant I was facing north. The castle was behind me, so my home should be straight ahead.

So I ran.

I only wished I would have gone home and faced whatever truth my parents had waiting for me instead.

"There you go, dear," my mother said, placing a steaming bowl of stew in front of me.

I couldn't be upset. Not tonight. I nodded in thanks.

The fact that this had been the same dinner we'd had all week was the least of my concerns. I could've died today. I didn't, but I could have. They didn't know that, but it was a truth that would haunt me for a while. I could have *died*.

I thought through every possible option. What if Judah had been bluffing? He thought he knew about the egg, but what if he really didn't know? Unless he knew something about dragons and their eggs that I didn't, how could he be sure it was even real? He seemed to be going through a lot of trouble to take this thing from me. But then again, if I showed up tomorrow without it, they could hurt me worse than they did today. Or if I didn't show my face in the city at all tomorrow, I could blame it on illness, but what would happen then? I'd have to face them eventually, whether they believed my lies or not. They would find me no matter what.

"Valora?" My father grabbed my attention, eyes narrowed on me. "Your mother asked you a question."

"How was your day?" She repeated.

"Just the usual." I sipped slowly on my stew, careful not to expose too much of my neck. I was worried they'd be able to see the red marks around my throat through my high-neck tunic. "I put today's pay in the bowl," I told them, gesturing to the small wooden bowl sitting on the end table by the door.

"Thank you," my father said, his filthy hands grasping his bowl of stew as if it were going to fly away.

"It will be rationed out at the end of the week," my mother started. "Maybe we'll have a little more for next week so we can splurge on another meal. A few extra orders came in this week for me to sew, and hopefully it was worth it. Besides, with cooler weather approaching in a few months, quilt and coat orders should be coming in soon."

"Hopefully so," I agreed, though I really needed to stop talking. My throat felt like I'd swallowed a hundred needles, and I was afraid they'd start to wonder why I was getting raspier with every word.

"So . . ." my mother began, dragging out the word. "I was thinking about the egg all day today. Your father and I have discussed it at great length."

Oh great, here it comes. The moment I'd been dreading all day.

Her eyes met my father's, and he gave her an assuring nod. "We believe it would be best to sell it."

"What?" I yelled rather than asked, raising myself from my seat again. "No! Please!"

"Valora Emberlyn. Sit down." My mother spoke in a voice calmer than I was expecting. I obeyed, but I did not break eye contact with my father, waiting for his explanation.

"Why? Why do you feel we need to sell it?"

"Val, we don't have a *need* for a dragon egg, or even a dragon. It can't hatch unless it's kept in the proper conditions, and we can't accommodate that. And who in the world would want, or be able, to keep a dragon as a pet anyway, besides the Polaris lineage? We aren't Polaris's. We aren't dragon riders." He laughed it off, but I wasn't smiling.

"Val," my mother turned toward me, "we could really use the money."

"I'll work harder. I'll work extra hours. I will. I don't care. If it's not going to hatch anyway, then it shouldn't matter whether we keep it or not. It's special to me. It means something to me." I dropped my head to stare at my feet, and after a heavy breath, picked it up again.

They exchanged concerned glances, and then they both sighed.

"Okay, Valora. Here's the not-so-simple truth," my mother stated, adjusting herself in her chair as though she were growing uncomfortable. "When your father and I were younger, *we* found a mysterious egg."

I opened my mouth, starting to interrupt, but she cut me off. I shrunk in my chair once more but kept my ears open.

"This had happened after the war, and the entire surviving city was trying to regain their life back. We were rebuilding from scratch with what we had. The work never stopped. Your father and I took a rowboat along the shoreline just outside the South Gate to take some time away from the work of cleaning up all the destruction. We ended up venturing down a little river. It was a mostly sunny day, and we were so thankful for it, but as we reached a cove, a storm hit. We weren't prepared for it. We ran for cover in a small cave under a cliff. And then, we spotted a strange object in the depth of the cave, just out of the light's reach. It looked so similar to the one you found, and the iridescent glow is what had caught our eye . . ." She paused to clear her throat, but it seemed hard for her to keep going.

"We had always wanted kids," my father continued for her, reaching for her hand. "We could never have any of our own, despite our years of trying. We were growing older and knew that it was now or never. We wanted a kid before another war could start. But, we came to the realization that this egg would be the perfect opportunity to raise something from birth, even if it wasn't a child of our own.

"We sent a message to the castle to ask for guidance from the council. After conducting their research, they allowed us to take it to them and keep it in the laboratory in proper conditions until it hatched for us. There, it could be observed at all hours. No one had seen a dragon for a year or two . . ."

He paused, and I patiently waited to say anything. That wasn't the ending to the story. There was definitely more information to come. My eyebrows raised as my mother cleared her throat.

"One evening, there was a quake in the earth, and the city began to panic. We thought another war was upon us so soon, and knew we weren't prepared. But some of the Eclipse Guard found us and told us to come immediately to the laboratory. We were escorted as quickly as possible to the castle. We thought the egg was destroyed in the quake, or that a dragon had hatched . . . only to find . . ." A singular tear fell from her face, landing right next to her bowl of stew. My brows furrowed in anticipation. "Only to find that it wasn't a dragon that hatched. It wasn't *anything* we were expecting."

"So, is it not a dragon egg that I found? Is it some other creature?"

They shook their heads side to side.

"What hatched from yours?"

"You, Valora."

CHAPTER FOUR

I STOOD IN THE midst of a chaotic, fiery war scene, the sky an ominous shade of crimson, filled with thick, black smoke that choked the air. Flames leapt from the ruins of buildings, casting eerie shadows that danced along the ground around me. The heat grazed the hairs of my arms as I eased forward.

Shouts echoed all around me, and the ground trembled as the Eclipse Guard marched through the streets. The scent of burning wood from homes filled my nostrils, mingling with a trace of smoke—and decay.

I watched in silence as people scattered from their homes, leaving behind a burning memory of what had been theirs.

As I continued forward, the shouts were heard more as screams. People were everywhere, frightened and panicked. The sky grew more colorful as the flames danced closer to me. There was a strong heat around me, as if I were inside the blazing homes, but nothing hurt. I wasn't in any sort of pain. Looking down, I found my own skin on fire, yet undamaged by the flames . . .

"Valora!" The voice of my mother woke me from the next room.

"I'm awake, Mother!" I sleepily exclaimed, a yawn soon escaping me. I drove myself out of bed, pondering over the dream I just had. It had felt so *real* at the time. I felt like I'd really been there, watching people run frantically for their lives. Had I stepped back in time to envision the war? The Infernal Siege was a war I was never a part of, yet it haunted me every day I lived. Everywhere I turned in Solaria was a reminder of what happened. My heart jumped into my throat just thinking about it. *Reliving* it.

"Valora, your food will be cold soon! And you'll be late!"

I dressed in my everyday work clothes: my tan tunic with brown accented stitching (made by my mother, herself), brown pants, and brown boots. I tied my hair into a quick messy bun at the base of my nape and hurried to the kitchen, where my mother and father were already seated.

They didn't bother to wait for me to eat breakfast. That was my own fault for sleeping too late. I sat down, taking in the plate in front of me, the serving not quite as large as it usually was. In fact, it wasn't large at all.

"I'm sorry, dear," my mother began as she stood to clear away the empty plates in front of her and my father. "We were running low on eggs, so I could only ration out two each this morning. I used an extra gold to buy a chicken for today." She gave me a weak smile and continued on.

I didn't complain. I couldn't. Actually, I was grateful to have three meals today. Some days we didn't have enough money to have lunch during the day, only dinner in the evening. I knew that if I complained about anything, I would get another lecture about how we should sell my dragon egg in exchange for extra food on the table. I wasn't ready for that conversation again. I would do everything I could to avoid it.

I still wasn't sure how to take all the information I'd heard last night. After my parents told me how I was born—or how I *hatched*, rather—I couldn't grasp it. A part of me refused to believe them. There was no way that story was true. No way it was possible. I'm a human. I always have been. Humans aren't born from dragons. Or eggs, for that matter. So if the people that were standing before me, the people that have raised me my entire life weren't my parents, then who *were* my parents?

Some might think they were being delusional—creating a story to cope with not being able to have children. The thought had crossed my mind—had they been thinking and seeing what they wanted to?

Or they could have been telling me a story just to make me want to give up my egg, in case I'd have the same experience? I doubted it, but I wouldn't be surprised if they tried to manipulate me into selling the egg. It wouldn't work on me like they'd think it would. And, although I loved them, I couldn't let them talk me into such a thing.

I shoved the entire story into the back of my mind in an attempt to forget about it. I didn't want to think ill of them anymore.

My head hung low as I scarfed down my breakfast.

Midday came before I knew it. My voice didn't carry well above the murmurs of the townspeople this morning, so I'd hardly sold any seafood. A few people would look up from their tasks, but none would call me over.

So I continued on, until I was so distraught from this morning's work, I felt I needed a break. I parked my cart against the inner wall of the city in a quieter part of town, and propped myself up against the wall, allowing the coolness of the stone to seep through the thin fabric of my clothes.

Slowly, I shrank to set my rear on the dusty ground and let out a heavy breath, resting my head between my knees. I took deep breaths to calm my nerves, trying not to let in the depressive thoughts.

They still seeped through.

I hated how poor we were, how the whole city was in poverty. I hated how boring our lives were, that we never had enough money to do anything other than eat, sleep, and work, and most days we could hardly afford to eat. I hated that years and years of work are going to waste with no progress. No hope of becoming any better.

After a few moments to myself, the growl of my stomach grabbed my attention. It always did.

I reached into my satchel I had attached to my cart and pulled out a wrapped piece of chicken—a helping of chicken hardly larger than the palm of my hand was all I'd have for lunch, but at least it was something. By only giving my mother, father, and me a small portion each, we could all have another serving to hopefully last one more day.

I picked it apart with my fingers, savoring each and every bite I put in my mouth for as long as I could, whilst observing the chaos of the townsfolk ahead.

Soon enough, my lunch was gone, and I was left with an empty napkin on my lap. I folded it up and tucked it back into my satchel, dusting off my filthy shirt and pants as I stood.

My ears practically shot up as I heard a voice a few buildings away. I knew that voice.

Judah.

He didn't sound angry in any way, like he was seeking me out somehow. In fact, it sounded like he was talking and laughing with someone. But his voice was growing louder, coming closer, and I had to get out of here. Fast.

As far as I knew, he didn't know I was here. I'd honestly completely forgotten about him. He should have been my main priority to avoid, but my mind had been so occupied since the flood of truth last night.

As swiftly as I could, I took off with my cart of seafood, which wobbled back and forth behind me as I hurriedly moved onto the bumpy streets. Hopefully my tracks wouldn't be left in the dirt for him to find. Then, he'd know I was here.

After a few winding turns down some old, withered streets, I felt that I was out of his path. There was no sign of his voice. No sign that he'd be getting closer anymore. I was definitely out of earshot.

Now I was back in a busier part of town where I felt safer trying to sell, and I hoped I could stay out of his way.

I took a deep breath in, then exhaled, and continued on with my day.

When work finished, I went home immediately.

It had been a slower month for me profit-wise so far. Maybe it had something to do with the warmer weather, as spring was quickly approaching its peak. The hotter it became, the less people wanted smelly seafood in their homes, and I honestly couldn't blame them. Whatever the real reason was, I was just relieved that I did not run into Judah or the other two guys today.

However, the sinking feeling in the pit of my stomach reminded me that there was always tomorrow.

Dinner tonight was no surprise. Stew. I was praying to have some grilled fish soon, but I knew that my mother had spent the extra money to have the chicken this week, so there was only wishful thinking for next week.

There wasn't much speaking at the table tonight, only eating. Animosity still lingered between the three of us since our conversations the previous night. I had shown them that I didn't like what they told me. Could I have gone about it in a more polite way? Yes. But what did they think was going to happen when I found out the very *important* information they'd hidden for over twenty years? Just accept it and move on as if nothing happened? Like it doesn't change the way I feel about myself?

Finding out that I'm not really my parents' child, but some sort of monster instead, didn't sit right with me.

I had a right to feel the way that I did.

Once everyone finished their meal, I shut myself in my room for the night.

I carefully collected the egg from amongst the pile of blankets I'd set aside for it. I examined it as though it was the first time I was seeing it, admiring its pure beauty that it possessed.

It was absolutely a magnificent thing. The purples and greens and reds reflected on its surface when the light hit it *just* right.

"There's no way I would give you up," I whispered to no one but myself.

Reluctant for the next day to come, I sat in silence with the egg cradled on my lap, staring out the window at the gleaming full moon.

CHAPTER FIVE

The air was thick with smoke, the stars that were once present now invisible through the eerie orange glow against the sky. The acrid smell of burning wood filled my senses. People were panicking, scrambling in every direction, their faces masks of terror and desperation. Some were running from the flames, while others were running into them, trying to save what little they could from the inferno.

Amidst the chaos, soldiers were hollering, trying to keep order. It was doing no good. There was a hellish landscape as far as the eye could see. The fire was steadily consuming everything in its path. I stood calm, watching in silence, then with no warning, the fires ceased to exist . . .

"Have a good day at work, Valora," my mother said as I rested my satchel on my shoulder. "You too, honey," she turned to my father, who was also on his way out the door for work, and gave him a peck on the cheek.

I ventured over to the fish market, reflecting on the dream I had earlier. That was the second dream I'd had involving that setting. Panic. Homes. Fires. It seemed to have picked up right where it had left off the time before.

Something about it made me uneasy—like deja vu of an event that I hadn't even been around to experience. I could vividly remember every scent, the heat that revolved around me, but when I woke up, nothing was burning.

I brushed it off and gathered my belongings and cart from the market, filling it to the brim with seafood, and icing it down. I attached my shuck-ing knife to my belt loop and began my route through the city.

The morning flew by like a breeze, and I received more business than usual. If it continued like this much longer, I would have to return back to the market for a restock. But—

"Hey, girl!" I stopped in my tracks, recognizing the voice immediately.

Shit, shit, shit. There's no way.

It couldn't be.

"Yes, you!"

Slowly, I turned my head toward the man, then allowed my body to follow. Sitting outside of an old cottage was Judah. One of the large men stood next to him, with thinning brown hair and a jaw of pure steel.

"Are ya gonna sell to us or what?"

With a hesitant gulp, and a wobble in my knees, I began toward him, my feet reluctant with every step. I picked up my pace, although fear was an understatement for this moment. I didn't want to show it. Perhaps if I showed some confidence, like nothing was wrong, then they wouldn't hurt me. Maybe they forgot what they'd told me a few days ago.

"Girl," Judah began as I approached, leaning in closer to the air I breathed until we shared it. His gaze followed me up and down until it finally landed back on my face. "Where's that egg we talked 'bout before?"

Well, there goes the hope that they'd forgotten.

"I told you, I don't have it." My eyes probably told them otherwise. Or maybe the quiver in my voice.

Judah chuckled, glaring over at the larger man next to him. "We have a liar upon us, Jovis."

So that was his name. Jovis.

Judah turned back to me, his smile quickly fading, and his face looked more drawn than ever before. Darkness glinted in his hazel eyes. "I'm gonna ask ya one more time. Where is the dragon egg?"

I choked on my own saliva, buying myself time to think of a quick excuse. "I was sick this week. I couldn't come by."

"Liar!" He shouted as he stood abruptly. My heart beat out of my chest and my bowels began to swim places I wished they wouldn't. "You cannot and will not lie to me, girl. I told you there'd be consequences." His hand was around my wrist before I could react to his words. I tried to yank it away, to free myself, but his grip held strong despite his meager size.

While focused solely on escaping from his grasp, another force, stronger, placed itself on my other wrist. Jovis. I was now trapped between them.

"Help—" I made an effort to shout, to call for someone—anyone—but there was no hope. Jovis covered nearly my entire face with his hand, and it took all my energy to try to breathe.

My feet rose slightly off the ground as I was swiftly moved into the cottage, my shouts going nowhere. It was as though I was being led into the only cottage, the only *building*, in the entire kingdom, and there were no other people remotely alive to hear me scream. All at once, the hand moved from my face and a cloth was shoved into my mouth. I coughed, gagging, in hopes of dislodging it from my throat, but there was no use.

"Please stop!" I cried, and the words echoed through my mind, but through the rag stuffed in my mouth, they were nothing more than muffled sounds.

Jovis shoved me down onto a bed, where another pair of hefty hands immediately clamped down on my wrists, pinning them above my head.

That's where that other guy had been. Waiting.

They had this planned the whole time. They had been waiting for me.

Judah approached me, his movements deliberate as he slowly released the buckle of his belt, his pants sagging against his scrawny stature with each motion. "I told you there would be consequences," he repeated, his voice cold and detached.

Jovis yanked off my boots with a single, brutal pull, and my pants were gone from my body before I could even blink. No matter how much I thrashed at their movements, they continued their assault.

Like I was a game to them, and they were winning.

I felt Judah's presence, inching closer, while Jovis stood at my side, spreading my knees apart with a sickening ease. I squeezed my eyes shut as tightly as possible, hoping deep down that somehow one of my eyeballs would pop out and scare them off. I knew it was a futile thought, but anything to distract me from the horror that I knew was about to occur was welcome. The darkness behind my eyelids was as comforting as it could be at this moment.

A loud, ugly groan escaped me as a searing pressure bore down on my groin. My pelvis was on fire. Not in a literal sense, but it may as well have been. I almost wished it had been.

The pain was *excruciating.*

I had never had a man inside of me, and this was far from how I had ever imagined it going. Each of Judah's thrusts brought a fresh wave of agony, and I choked out groans through the cloth gag.

It hurts. It hurts. It hurts.

The thought consumed me.

I reached out to the wolves of my mind, the ones that were almost always there taking over my being. The ones normally there that occupied my every thought. I searched for any distraction. Any thought that could make this moment better.

Nothing was getting any better. There was only one thought taking over my mind right now.

Pain.

Agony.

I whipped my legs in every direction, desperately trying to slip out of Jovis's grasp, but it was no use. With every movement, my strength waned. Judah's hands pressed into the insides of my thighs, and the weight of the other man behind me crushed my wrists, sharp pains fleeing up my arms.

"You'll learn to do as we say next time, won't ya, girl?" Judah's throaty voice cut through the haze, each word like a jagged knife. I groaned again, wishing desperately for it to stop. The fight was beginning to slip away from me, each of his thrusts sending shockwaves of pain throughout my body.

Tears streamed down my face, soaking my hair at my temples, turning into a damp, tangled mess. My eyes ached from being clenched so tight, but opening them offered no relief.

For a brief moment, I had seen them—all three men, their eyes gleaming with cruel satisfaction.

Judah's movements were relentless, each one a reminder of my helplessness.

But now, I couldn't shut my eyes. The vision of their faces was already seared into my brain. My vision blurred, but I didn't even bother to clear it.

Thrust. Thrust. Thrust. The rhythm of my torment.

I laid on the bed, my body a ragdoll devoid of resistance. My tears flowed freely, merging with the sweat and blood that stained the sheets around me. My limbs were leaden, my spirit crushed. The adrenaline that had fueled me moments ago was gone, leaving me a hollow shell of who I was.

The ceiling above was the only thing in my focus as I laid there in the most vulnerable state of my life.

Thrust. Thrust. Thrust.

I pictured the stars overhead, looking down on me just as I looked to them for comfort.

I prayed silently to Phobos, our God of Fear, to save me. To help me. I was scared . . .

Judah continued his assault, and I suddenly had nothing left of myself to give. Not like it made much of a difference . . . He would take it anyway. I waited for the pain to subside, and in turn, be replaced with numbness. The fire and pain between my legs dulled to a distant ache. My senses retreated into a protective fog, drawing me out of this very moment. My face, my body, felt lifeless, as if my soul had fled to some distant place, watching from afar.

"C'mon, girl. You can't give up without a fight," the man behind me taunted with the same booming tone as Jovis, as though I had a chance against them. He shook me roughly, but I was beyond his reach. Beyond caring. The gods had numbed me, physically and mentally.

I was done.

It's like I'd crossed into another realm, where my body was the battle-field, and my spirit was a silent observer.

"Aw man, I liked you better when you were fighting," Judah sneered, his voice dripping with venom.

My legs went tingly, the sensation of a thousand tiny pins prickling my skin, and my arms felt the same. Heavy and numb.

I wondered if this was what death felt like. Or if it was just some twisted form of torture, a cruel game played with my senses.

Then, in an instant, the relentless pain and the brutal movement ceased. Everything fell into an eerie calm, the sudden silence almost deafening. I could feel the tension in my legs and arms release, as if invisible chains had been unlocked, but my muscles refused to respond.

I laid there, limp and unresponsive for a few moments, my mind still struggling to comprehend the shift from agony to stillness.

One minute? Five? I wasn't sure how much time had passed.

The only thing that pierced through the fog of my daze was the sharp sound of a belt buckle being fastened, followed by the malicious laughter of men.

CHAPTER SIX

HAD DEATH TAKEN HOLD of me? If this was anything near what being dead felt like, I never wanted to die.

The walk back to turn in my seafood cart was the most dreadful thing I've ever had to do. More dreadful than telling my parents about the egg in fear of their reaction. More dreadful than hearing the story of how I was born and completely changing the way I looked at myself. And now, I realized that it was so much worse than I thought seeing those men again.

My legs quaked underneath me the entire way back to Fisherman's Square, hardly holding me upright. I was just a fawn attempting to stand on its feet for the very first time, learning to walk again.

Looking around, the city didn't pay me much attention. But when they did, they weren't really looking at *me.* They were looking at my clothes.

My garments were practically rags now, or they at least felt like it—stained with sweat, tears, and my own blood from between my thighs. My tunic hung halfway off my collar, stretched out from my movements. My pants had been shoved loosely back onto my legs and my boots were barely halfway up to where they normally sat on my calves.

I was falling apart at the seams.

I'd been scarred from the inside out. I wasn't myself. What would I tell my parents when I got home? How would I even go about telling them? No doubt, they'd notice something was wrong with me, especially once I walked in with a nest of hair and red blending in with the brown of my pants.

I'd finally made it to drop off my cart without speaking a word to anyone.

I didn't so much as look another soul in the eye.

At least I still had what little money I'd made today. Thankfully, they had left my satchel alone. They only wanted me.

It was still the late afternoon, and even though I had refused to continue working, I couldn't go home. Not yet. If my mother saw me in this state, that would be the end of her world. And I didn't even want to imagine how my father would react. He'd probably end up being taken in for murder after what he'd do to my attackers.

Rather than confide in them just yet, I decided to head to the only place I felt comfortable.

It seemed to take an eternity to make it there, but I eventually stood on the beach, as far away from the commotion as I could travel, before plopping myself down against a large rock close to the water's edge and shoving off my boots.

The sand between my toes grounded me and made me feel like there was at least one thing going right today: the fact that I was right here, right now, and alone.

The sun would set in the next couple of hours, so I had plenty of time to regroup myself and think about what to say to my parents before heading back home.

If I could just . . . rest . . . my eyes . . .

I awoke to the sound of a scream. No. Not just one. Multiple screams. And they occurred in a sequence, one after another after another.

I shot up from where I'd been laying down against the rock and looked around at the darkness surrounding me. The sun had already set, and the full moon shone overhead, much bigger than I could ever recall, and I've seen many full moons during my walks out here.

I must have slept for hours.

I dusted off the sand from my clothes and looked toward the city. The uproar resonated somewhere within the walls.

As quickly as I could, I pulled my boots on and began a swift walk until I reached the bridge at the fish market. From there, I picked up my pace, travelling through the West Gate and pushing right past the people in front of me that seemed just as clueless as I was.

There was no telling what time it could have been. My parents were probably worried sick about me. Surely it was after dinner by now. They were probably furious that I hadn't come home.

There was more commotion once inside the walls of the city. The farther I progressed, the louder the shouts.

If I could just get home safely to my parents, I would be at ease.

Farther and farther I went, and the shouts began to sound more like screams. Many screams sounded all at once.

My heart leapt into my throat, my breathing heavier by the second as I witnessed stragglers of people run by with only fear fixed on their faces.

"Ouch," I stumbled as a passerby nudged me without a care. They were running *from* something. Another person was running in my direction. "Hey, what's going on?" I tried to stop them, but got no answer. They kept running and refused to turn back.

I marched on ahead, picking up the pace as best as I could despite the soreness overtaking my muscles from the events of today. Around each corner came more and more people, running and shouting, though I couldn't make out a single word they said.

My trek home seemed to be taking a lifetime.

I turned down the main road, the screams becoming more animated, and clusters of people began to flood in my direction. The sky ahead of me was suddenly a vivid shade of crimson, and I could smell a burning stench that choked the air. Burning wood.

A fresh wave of anxiety took hold of me. I'd had this feeling before, because I had *seen* this before. Twice.

But this time, it was real.

The closer I moved toward the uproar, the more my breath trembled. The harder my pulse thumped in my chest. People kept flooding toward me with no plans of stopping. They scattered around me.

Over the top of a roof, I spotted flames.

I stopped in my tracks. This was my street.

Thud. Thud. Thud. Thud.

The ground shook under my feet as a steady rhythm rang through the street. The Eclipse Guard came marching down the road, attempting to stop the chaos of people running amok.

They took a chance at trying to calm them, to lead them away from danger, but not me. I had to make it through. To find my parents.

Suddenly, the only thing in my line of sight were flames; fire was every-where, and it was spreading. Fast.

Our neighbors ran from their burning homes, children in hand. A few soldiers held a man back from going back into his home.

With a series of heavy breaths, I ran.

"Hey, girl!" a soldier yelled behind me, knowing it was directed at me. He reached for me as I passed, but I quickly dodged his grasp.

I was almost home.

It was a nightmare. The shouts . . . they were terrifying. It was exactly like the dream I'd had, only worse. This was real life. These were people's homes, their livelihoods, their belongings. These were the lives they had built over the decades, vanishing before their eyes. Burning to the ground.

Reminders of the war.

But there, in the middle of the blaze, was my home, the roof engulfed in flames. I halted before it. Before I let the moisture forming in my eyes escape down my cheek, I spotted my parents on the opposite side of the street from the house, cowering in each other's arms against the wall of another home.

"Valora!" they shouted in unison, and I ran to embrace them.

"We didn't know where you were. We thought . . ." My mother's trem-bling voice faded as a tear trickled down her cheek. She gazed off at our home. Everything would soon be gone.

The memories. We would have to rebuild from scratch. Again.

"I know, I'm sorry. I fell asleep—" My ears perked. I heard laughter. Familiar laughter. Who in their right mind could be laughing in such a terrible moment? I shot a look past my parents toward the next block over.

Standing there was Judah, Jovis, and the other guy, whatever his name may be. I didn't care to know. They were cackling to each other like young schoolboys, staring in awe at the flames.

Judah glanced in my direction, doing a double take before locking eyes with me. He wouldn't dare harass me here, not with my parents right next to me. Instead, his lips curled into a malicious smirk, and he carried on.

My heart dropped at the sudden influx of thoughts that raced in my mind. Did he do this? After everything he'd already done today? Did he purposefully set my home, and all the other homes here, ablaze? I wanted to know. I wanted answers. But this very moment wouldn't give them to me. Right now, my parents were in distress—heartbroken at the sight before them. With the shadows dancing all around us, they had no way of noticing my mangled clothes or the stains that covered them.

"The heat is growing, Reyla," my father sniffled. "Let's move down a ways." He lifted her from their stance and began down the block, stopping to turn back to me. "Valora, let's go."

But someone called my name. It wasn't my parents.

"Valora, what's done is done. Don't get burnt, dear."

But I was stopped in my tracks. Someone *was* calling my name, but it was coming from the direction of the fires. The flames grasped at my gaze, pulling me into a hypnotic state.

"Valora . . ."

It whispered again.

I was mesmerized by the blaze, intrigued as it pulled me in. I couldn't let go. My mind was free from everything but the flames ahead. Something was there, pulling me like a magnet.

My vision changed into something that was no longer mine. I saw my dragon egg, nestled within the blankets that were finally being engulfed in the flames. I closed my eyes, soaking in the moment, letting the orange and red light dance in the darkness behind my eyes.

The egg was there, lying in the same corner I always kept it in.

It moved, quivering against the fire that enveloped it.

With a deep inhale, I opened my eyes, and with one swift *whoosh,* the fire ceased.

CHAPTER SEVEN

It happened so fast—like a black hole sucking all of the air from the flames and making them disappear.

You could choke on the silence that clouded the street. The townsfolk once scurrying about stopped immediately, and the guards turned now to face the homes that were *just* doomed to burn to the ground. Confusion painted their postures.

I looked around to find my parents. Fright took hold of their faces. I glanced at Judah and his men, the same looks on theirs. The mess that they had caused was . . . gone. But how?

"Valora . . ."

It called to me. A rustling sounded from inside of our home.

I cocked my head, and eased forward, inching closer to the noise that grew louder with each step.

"Valora, please come back," my mother called after me. "We don't know what's in there. You'll burn yourself. Valora!" As she called out my name, an ear-piercing shriek echoed through the street. Its origin was, once again, my home.

Though everyone around was startled by the cry, cowering as though it was a threat, I ignored my mother's request. I stepped through the singed door of the house, resting my hand against the frame. It didn't burn me.

No one's calls mattered right now. The only thing that mattered was the thing in here that was calling my name.

I cautiously turned the corner to my room, and my breath instantly left my lungs. A vivid pair of green eyes stared back at me from the floor. Ash laid everywhere, painting the room black, but there was an iridescent glow along the scales of a creature. With a sharp lift of its wings, it let out another screech, no doubt heard by the people outside. It eased my way.

I started to step back. But why? I wasn't actually afraid. *This* is what was beckoning me inside.

The creature waddled up to me, and the light of the moon beaming through the window illuminated it more clearly. The most captivating part was its eyes—those green eyes that could probably light up the room on their own. Its scales were a deep black, yet they shimmered with a kaleidoscope of colors under certain lighting. From snout to tail, it was adorned with spikes, and a small array of horns, two on each side, jutting out from the back of its head.

"It's alright, little guy." I bent my knees and slowly lowered myself to the ground, gesturing my hand out toward the creature. Without a second thought, it nudged up on my hand, taking in my scent and then climbing up my arm and onto my shoulder. Its tail wrapped around the opposite shoulder as it held onto me, burying its head in my neck as if claiming me. Marking me with its own scent.

"I've been waiting for you," a small, boyish voice spoke to me, though his mouth never moved. He was in my head. *Speaking* to me in my head.

"So, I'm not crazy," I smiled. "I knew someone was talking to me, I just didn't know it was you."

"It was me," he confirmed.

Something about the feel of him on my shoulder, the sight of him in our home, kept me at ease. Most would be scared, but I was not afraid. Not in the slightest.

The faint sound of my name being called outside made me stand up and turn to leave. I made my way back to the door, trudging carefully in hopes that he wouldn't fall off my shoulder. But he was locked onto me; his body and his tail and his eyes were all in sync with my every movement.

I eased out of the doorstep to find an audience of curious faces. All in unison, they gasped.

It was dark, the moonlight barely reaching me from behind the house where it sat in the sky.

"Valora . . ." my father started, his grip firm on my mother's arm. "What in the gods is that?"

I knew he knew the answer to that question, but for the sake of the people gathered around, I simply grinned.

"It's my dragon."

"He has your eyes," my mother chuckled as she looked between me and the dragon the very next morning. It was true. I had abnormally green eyes, a more vibrant color than any eyes in Solaria. The dragon, who now sat on the table gracefully watching me eat my breakfast, had an identical eye color.

"What do dragons even eat?" My mother turned inquisitively to my father. He shrugged.

"Meat," he said in his childlike voice.

"Meat," I said. "I plan to take some fish home from the market today. I'll bring home any leftovers or scraps for him."

"Maybe he can stop scrounging around for bugs, then," my father added.

"Hopefully."

I finished my eggs and headed to my room, or what was left of it.

I was quite shocked that we even stayed here last night, but some families had it much worse than we did.

Every board and brick was intact, but the fires had unequivocally done damage throughout the house. It took quite a bit of time to clean up the ash and soot from the floors and walls to make the space *liveable* again. But we made do with what we could, and thought it best to sleep last night's events away before acknowledging how or why I now had a dragon companion.

"You know," I said as the dragon followed me to my room, "if we hadn't made . . . whatever that connection was that we made . . . at the exact moment we did, these houses may not be here."

"You're welcome," he chuffed at my heels.

After a few hours of labor, I was able to spare two fish from the stock, and I wrapped them in a napkin, stuffing them in my satchel. Then, I took off toward home, wheeling my cart with me, pretending I was on my normal route just in case any one of my bosses came looking.

I'm almost home to my dragon. The thought made me smile.

I was found face to face with a dirty man and a thin face. I stopped in my tracks as my breakfast threatened to greet me from the way it went in.

"Runnin' away from somethin'?" Judah said with a devilish smirk. That voice sent a chill down my spine.

Then the world slowed down as I felt a presence to my left—footsteps approaching.

Quickly.

I ducked and took off at a sprint just as Jovis's hand launched behind me at the space I'd been standing. He tumbled forward in a cloud of dust.

I would not be a victim today.

I had to get home.

And in a flash, I was there.

I stumbled through the door, locking it behind me, and raced to my room. After heaving open my door, I found my new little friend comfy on my bed, the sheets dusty and burnt. He cocked his head at me. I smiled, easing forward, and I saw the light glint in the depths of his green eyes.

His head shot up, peering toward the door behind me.

"Someone is coming," he said.

"I know." I looked back at the front door. Their footsteps could be heard, growing louder with each passing second that I was wasting. "I need you to stay quiet." I gestured my index finger vertically over my lips. He nodded once, and I tossed the two fish from my satchel onto the floor and closed the bedroom door.

I was light on my feet as I made my way to the kitchen—a lot quieter than I'd expected to be given that I walked these floors every day, and now that they were half scorched, they creaked even more.

I reached for a knife on the counter, coming out with a long, thin blade. I lowered myself behind the cabinets. They'd have to look dead at me to see me.

I would have planned on going to my parent's room and snatching one of my father's prized weapons he made, yet never used. But the approaching footsteps told me there wouldn't have been enough time as they grew louder and slower.

They were here.

I steadied my breathing, releasing a long and slow breath. My heartbeat ventured to my ears. Everything slowed. Everything was calm, and for a moment I thought time stood still. Despite my history with these men, my heart rested at a steady pace, and I was fully in tune with it.

My front door was heaved open, revealing the dark silhouettes of three.

"Runnin' from somethin', little girl?" Judah repeated himself. He took a step through the doorway, scanning the room up and down, and then he stopped. His eyes landed on me.

The silence was deafening.

Shit.

"I see ya, girl. Where the fuck is that damned dragon egg?"

"Please help me, please," I prayed to Aesis, our God of Hope. But maybe I should be praying to the God of luck instead. I prayed to Tyche.

Then, I stood.

If they had weapons on them, I'd assume they would've used them by now. Or at least unsheathed them. I kept my knife concealed behind my arm, ever so slightly out of his view, as I quartered my shoulder toward them.

"What do you want?" If I held my ground now instead of running, I may have a fighting chance.

They let out a mocking laugh. "As we have said to you *many* times, we want the dragon egg."

"Is she stupid?" One of the taller men said to the other, the one with less hair and more scruff on his mega jaw.

"Shut up, Javie," hissed Judah.

I took a mental note of their names. Judah, Javie, and Jovis.

"I'm not stupid. And you aren't laying a hand on my dragon."

Their faces went blank, then Judah smirked. "A dragon, eh? No egg?"

Damn it.

"It hatched?" He continued, easing forward.

"Get away from me."

Judah snatched at my throat. I backed away before he could touch me. He marched forward again as I retreated. The other two stood back, realizing that soon I'd be cornered in the tightness of our kitchen.

My instincts were heightened. He was fast. I was faster.

"I guess I'll have to lay another hand on you instead, pretty girl," his tongue brushed his lips as he approached. I was almost out of room to back up.

"You will not," I retorted. "And you're the stupid ones for seeking me out, and coming into *my* home."

His arm reached out to my neck, and while his torso was exposed, I plunged my knife deep into his side.

CHAPTER EIGHT

JUDAH GASPED, HALTING BEFORE he laid a hand on me. I pulled the knife from his side and watched him stumble back, his hand covering the wound. Blood dripped onto the floor, and I realized from the sudden warmth spreading along my hand to my fingertips, that I'd shoved it deep enough to taint my hand. It flowed steadily from my fingers to the ashy floor.

Judah mumbled some swears under his breath. "Who do you think you are?" He choked out the words, his eyes growing deep with worry. His two men began to approach and I stood taller, holding my blade farther out into view. Dark red droplets trailed down the steel. Judah held up his hand opposite his wounded sight, and Javie and Jovis stilled. "She's not worth it. Let's go."

He retreated with a wheeze, his entourage behind him. I followed them out of the kitchen until they were out of the house. Once their presence vacated the street, I let out a heavy sigh.

There was a good chance that I killed him . . . I knew that much. His wound would ooze steadily until he'd realize that he wouldn't be able to stop the bleeding.

I may have rid Judah from my life, though I hated the way it happened. I didn't want to have to kill him.

Maybe I just injured him enough to where he will never approach me again. He would never seek me out, and it would buy me time from their harassment.

I ran to the kitchen sink and scrubbed my callused hands as vigorously as my muscles would allow before the blood dried to my skin. I rinsed the nearest towel I could find under the water and then flung it to the floor. It landed with a rather loud thud. Running my boot along the top as a guide, I mopped the floor where the drippings of blood had started to seep into the wood, and I followed it all the way out the door.

There was no way I'd let my parents know about this. I had to hide the evidence that any intruders were here, and I had to hide the fact that I outright *stabbed* one of them in their own home.

They had no idea this side of my life existed. They had no idea that these men even existed. I hadn't told them about their threat. They had no idea that I'd been kidnapped—twice—violated and raped, and then left to fend for myself like a stray dog. They didn't know that these guys had caused the fires from last night.

Only I knew.

They wouldn't be able to handle it. They wouldn't know how to handle the fact that these things happened to their only daughter—one they'd prayed to conceive, yet ended up with even more in the end. I had to protect their innocence, or all hell could break loose. They'd for sure lose their minds.

Once I was confident in my cleaning work, I dried the knife and placed it back into its holder. The towel I threw in the trash bins outside in the street.

"Master," a young voice whispered in my mind, snapping me back into focus. My brows bunched upward as I turned toward my room, forgetting that he was in there waiting for me.

I inhaled deeply, feeling every ounce of oxygen fill my lungs and released it, slowly calming the rate of my heart.

I approached the door to my bedroom and opened it with trembling hands. My little dragon beamed up at me with such wide, innocent eyes. His tail flicked softly on the floor beside him.

"I did a terrible thing . . . I really did," I said to him. He was my only confidant during this time.

"You saved me," he responded, the calmness of his little voice wrapping

around my mind.

But I couldn't stop shaking. I sat on my bed, staring at nothing ahead of me. "I was just going through the motions before, instinctively, but I truly have done something terrible." I looked at my dragon. He stayed silent. "I stabbed someone."

"You saved yourself."

That was true.

"You saved me.*"*

The confidence in his tone, his untroubled stature, brought a sort of tranquility to my body and mind. He was why I did what I did. The pulse in my chest slowed, and I sighed heavily.

"I did," I replied, "I saved both of us. And I will continue to do so." I knelt down from my bed and reached down to pet him, his scales sliding warmly against my fingertips. "It's a promise. We will be safe now. Together."

His green eyes sparkled as he nudged his snout under my hand. A vibration tickled my skin. Is he . . . purring?

Deep down, I knew this ordeal wouldn't be a secret forever. If Judah lived, there was a high probability they would come back. If I *had* killed him, then the other two may seek revenge. It may not be tomorrow, or even next month, but when they do come, their plan may include not leaving me alive.

I needed a plan from here on out.

I wasn't sure how fast dragons grew, but if I was lucky, he'd grow quickly and help me defend our home and my parents from future attacks from them.

But until then, it would be my vigilant duty to protect us all.

Working every day was a cost to my body and my mental health, but the pros outweighed the cons. It ensured us more money for the week. Every coin counted meant securing extra food for the dragon we now raised.

Well, the one that *I* was now raising.

I figured the more I could feed him, the faster he would grow.

The conversations between me and my parents stayed casual, as usual. Work. Food. Money. *Lack* of money. It was all about our survival. I tried to ignore it, to not let the thoughts drown me into a state of depression where I no longer wanted to eat or socialize. But having a dragon helped a lot with keeping my mind busy—not to mention staying exhausted from the endless days at work.

As far as I knew, my parents had no idea about what happened a few days ago in our home. They didn't know what I'd done.

A week had passed since the occurrence, and dinnertime was approaching. The aromas of seared trout with various herbs and spices filled the air.

We settled at the table with our plates. "Thank you so much, Mother," I said, my nose never having smelled anything better than this meal. "This is my absolute favorite."

"I know it is," she winked, and we began feasting. Having stew every day for a week or two straight really makes you appreciate a meal like this.

My dragon sat next to me on the corner of the table, his eyes married to the fish. I gave in to that precious face, tearing off a bit of trout and tossing it toward his corner.

It vanished in mere seconds.

Without a second thought, my mother fetched him his own serving and sat back down. He feasted, his wings flared and his tail flicked in excitement.

"So, Valora," my mother began, sipping her water to clear her throat, "you finally have a day off from the fish market. Your father and I were wondering if you wanted to try anything new?"

It was rather a statement than a question, but I looked between them with raised brows and my eyes met my father's as he spoke. "I need some help at the shop tomorrow. I got extra orders coming in, and I could use another set of hands."

I swallowed my bite. It was my only day off, and I thought I would be able to spend it with my dragon and bond with him. Though we already seemed to have a trustworthy bond established, I wasn't quite sure what he and I would be able to do other than simply speak to each other. He was still young, barely forming complete sentences.

Working with my father would be productive, helping him while also keeping me busy. Not to mention, keep me out of Judah's reach, if he was still alive. He wouldn't dare come mess with me with my father around.

"I believe I could manage a day helping you," I winked. The dragon next to me chortled in approval, flapping his wings softly and bouncing his head up and down. "Can I bring him?" I gestured his way, his eyes locking with mine. "It may be good for him to get out of the house. He hasn't ventured out or been exposed to anything since he hatched."

"I don't see why not," my father answered, cleaning his plate and pushing it away. He sat back in his seat with an inquisitive look etched on his face. "Say, does your little friend have a name yet?"

I hesitated. I hadn't even begun to think of a name for him. My mind had been elsewhere, focused on work, family, and protecting us. Protecting him.

I shrugged, and the silence lingered on like they were thinking of names for him like I was.

"Zorath . . ." a whisper invaded my mind.

"What?" I said out loud, a tingle surging through my body.

"Zorath . . ." it said again.

"Valora, are you alright, sweetie?" My mother cocked her head.

"You guys can't hear this?" I retorted. They both shook their heads side to side.

Then some sort of realization hit, some type of confidence grew within me. My dragon was in my mind and my mind only. He was *mine.*

I glanced at the dragon next to me, and he stared back with intent.

"Zorath."

CHAPTER NINE

I VISITED MY FATHER a few times at his shop when I was younger. His business was a lot smaller back then than it is now, and it has fascinated me to watch it grow, though it still had a long way to go.

I dressed in my usual working clothes: dirty white tunic, brown pants, and matching boots. It was the most comfortable outfit I owned that I didn't mind dirtying up.

I was there to help my father, not sell seafood. Maybe this would make for a good day and a nice change of pace from my usual.

Zorath chirped in excitement on my bed as I tied my hair into a braid at the back of my head and let it fall behind my back. He hadn't stopped annoying me about how happy he was to leave the house today. I was happy for him, too.

He was like my sixth sense. Before him, I never would have been able to avoid Jovis's grasp on the street just over a week ago. I wouldn't have had the nerve to stab someone in my own home. But because of him, I had the confidence in doing so. *He* gave it to me, intentionally or not. Before his existence, I would have over-thought every move.

But there was no doubt now that I'd done those things for a reason. I protected me and my dragon.

The smell of freshly cooked bacon brought me back to reality, and Zorath followed me into the kitchen, where breakfast was waiting for us. All four seats had a plate in front of it. We gobbled down our bacon and eggs in no time, hardly even discussing our upcoming day, and after fetching some leftovers for our lunch, my father and I made our way out the door.

I trotted half a pace behind my father as he led the way through the crowded roads. People hustled in every direction to go to work. My father's satchel hung securely over his right shoulder, while Zorath sat on mine, his tail wrapped around the back of my neck reaching to my other shoulder for more stability. I admit, he wasn't very heavy, but the weight of carrying him on my shoulders would take some time to get used to. I could only imagine how sore I would be after today.

We received a few odd stares from passersby, mostly from those who hadn't been around when Zorath hatched and I'd emerged from the fires with him. No one had finished refurbishing their homes, the singed roofs a blanket of darkness as we passed by. It was like an endless cycle here in Solaria that no one could ever afford to rebuild.

My ear closest to Zorath twitched like a cat's when I heard him purr, nuzzling his head closer into mine. I could sense his anxiousness, his want to be close to me for comfort. I didn't blame him. I saw the looks on some people's faces as they passed. He hadn't ventured out of the house yet. He was foreign here.

"It's okay, Zorath," I whispered softly, "you're safe with me." He knew he was. I reached my hand up to run my fingers along the spines of his back.

He'd calmed down once we made it to the shop. My father set down his satchel and handed me a brown apron, another one for him grasped in his other hand. Once donned, he pulled some documents from his bag, followed by our lunches that he placed on a separate side table.

Finally, he pulled a knife from the bag: the knife that he had had for years. It was one of the first ever pieces he created in his shop, and though he always told us he brought it with him for protection, my mother and I both knew it was simply a sentiment. If it was his lucky charm to have it at work with him, then I was glad that he had that hope to hold on to.

I stared in awe as he unsheathed it and rested it on a corner of the table. The blade spanned about six inches from the tip to the cross-guard, curved in an elongated angle that gave it a sort of elegance. The hilt was formed with Moon Hazel wood, the wood from the rarest tree to ever exist in

Solaria. The cross-guard separated the wood from the steel of his blade, draped in solid gold.

Looking at it up close, it was no wonder it was such a special item. It was the perfect blade.

"Okay, little guy," I looked at Zorath. "This is where you get down." He chuffed in obedience and crawled down my arm onto the table beside me. He made his way down to the floor of the shop and began to wander around. "Stay close and behave, please." I called out to him with an emphasis in my tone.

"Yes, Master," he responded.

I pulled the apron over my head and tied it around my waist. "How did you come about having Moon Hazel wood, Father?"

He cleared his throat. "Before the war, when King Jesper sat on the throne, the forests outside of the city walls were filled with magic and rarities, animals and plants, and that included the Moon Hazel." He thumbed through the ticket orders for today. "We thought it was a rare wood then, but now, it is nowhere to be found. I just got lucky to have it gifted to me one day before they disappeared."

I nodded as I looked toward the furnaces. They'd been lit prior to our arrival. I would have questioned who had done it until I noticed a figure turned the corner ahead of me. A tall, blonde young man stood before us, his brown eyes matching the dark brown of his apron and boots. Ash and soot already gathered on his clothes and had even invaded his hair.

"I hope you didn't mind that I got here a little early today, sir," he spoke to my father with a respectful tone, his voice like silk.

"Of course not," my father replied as he finished reading and organizing the orders. "Oh, Valora. This is my apprentice, Jameson."

His eyes finally met mine, and I reached a polite hand toward him. He gladly accepted it and shook it gently. "I have heard much about you in just the short time I've worked here, m'lady." He tipped his head forward, a thin gold chain falling from his collar, and took a step back, a mannerly smile creeping onto his lips. "I should get to work." He stated more toward my father than me, though his eyes still held firm on me until he was out of sight in the next room.

"You ready?" My father asked me with a grin, and placed a hand on my shoulder. "It's going to be a good day. I've got my favorite daughter with me, after all."

"I'm your *only* daughter, you weirdo." I gently jabbed his elbow with my own, and we laughed as if it was the funniest thing we'd ever said.

"You know, my business has grown almost overnight. Ever since I got Jameson startin' to work for me, I'm able to put out a lot more orders than I would if I were by myself."

"That's really great," I replied.

It really was. More money equaled more food on the table.

"We could do really well with *you* here full time."

I entertained the thought as I familiarized myself with the forge, touring the entirety of the shop with my father.

I stayed within arms reach of him through the first few orders, mostly observing every step of how he worked. Zorath kept himself occupied, entranced most often by the smells and the noises that surrounded us. Jameson wandered around helping us, then would head to the next room to sharpen the forged metals. Every so often, he'd walk by and give Zorath a scratch under the chin.

I'd initially been afraid that my dragon would scare people. Though he was a small creature, he was foreign to this kingdom. Most people haven't seen a dragon in over twenty years, and the last time that they had, it had burned their homes to the ground. I wouldn't blame them for being a little apprehensive.

But they weren't. Of course, some people gave us some worried glances, but thankfully, most seemed more fascinated by him than anything.

An hour or so passed, and I was doing basic tasks by myself. I heated the metal to forging heat in the furnace to give to my father and Jameson as their next orders to work on.

Zorath was mesmerized by the burning coals and the glowing iron I pulled from it.

Another hour later, and I was at my own station in the shop, catching on quicker than my father had expected. As the scent of hot metals and coal filled the air, I picked up a hammer and began to strike the glowing metal on the anvil. There was something intensely satisfying about this feeling. As the weight in my hand crashed into the iron, a sound rang out, vibrating through me, and bringing a smile onto my face.

It took doing it to realize it, but this was the kind of work I'd wanted to do all along. Keeping to myself. Working alongside my father. I was using my hands and my mind for something good, not pestered by the outside world.

I hammered more precisely.

I wasn't expecting this piece to be absolutely perfect. It was only the first one on my own, but the more I struck the metal, the more it took form. I was sharp, precise, and my hammer clanged the piece over and over again until the iron stopped glowing and it was simply a well-shaped sword lying before me.

There was an airy chuckle behind me. "That's nice work for a first-time blacksmith!"

I looked over my shoulder, my braid swinging around with me, to find Jameson standing there with a smile on his face. His arms were folded across his chest as he beamed, looking between me and the sword. I returned a light smile and turned back to my creation.

"I didn't mean for it to sound insulting. That wasn't my intention," he clarified. "It really is good. It took me a fair share of tries to forge one that looks like that." He eased to my side. "I can take it to be sharpened if you'd like."

I wasn't used to the kindness, the manners. I was so used to conversing with rude and entitled customers. The way he spoke to me and my father with such respect was something that baffled me.

I handed him the sword, still unable to take my eyes off of my first piece of work. I noted the size and length of the metal, and how it would have been perfect for me to use against Judah, Jovis, and Javie for defensive purposes that day. Or even if they were to somehow walk in here and attack—which would honestly be the dumbest thing they could do with all the weapons around and the two men that work here with me—the blade still needed sharpening.

Hours passed, and before I knew it, the growling of my stomach outshined the crashes of metal upon metal. By the look I received from my father when we shared eye contact, he felt the same way.

"Allow me to warm up our lunch," my father offered, and gestured toward the empty bench on the back wall. I sat and waited while he warmed it over the fire, even taking Zorath's serving of fish into consideration.

I normally was forced to eat my lunch straight from the wrapping as I had no place to warm it while on the go. That is, if I *had* lunch that day.

Silence stretched into a quiet peace as I looked around the shop, taking in every sight before me. I belonged here. This was like a second home. Whether it was solely the fact I was working next to my father, or if it was just a trade I had liked doing, I wasn't sure. It just felt natural being around the fire, the steel, and the atmosphere.

"I really should have been doing this all along," I said with a mouthful.

Zorath gulped his food down in almost one bite right next to me, and my father laughed. He turned to me. "I told you, you'd be good at this. I know my daughter." He drank some water from a nearby pitcher, replenishing the sweat that was cascading down his face. "Much better than selling that smelly seafood, right?"

I nodded with a giggle.

A few moments later, we were back to work. I was mostly working on swords, while my father handled swords, horseshoes, daggers, and whatever other variations of orders would come in. He would take orders as needed at the front of the shop when people stopped by, and once done with each piece, I sent them over to the sharpening side where Jameson was.

Sweat ran down my back and dripped from the crown of my head, but

I admit, I was having a lot of fun doing the dirty work. My hammer beat down with a rhythm, *my* rhythm, over and over again until I was onto my next piece.

"Valora, hun," my father glanced between me and the furnace behind me. "Would you mind tossin' some more coal into the fire? My hands are a little tied." He sorted through orders, a set of daggers laid in front of him ready for sharpening.

I turned around and sure enough, the fire was dimming with each passing second. Zorath sat stationed in front of it, watching it with intent, growing bored with each moment the flame died. He flicked his tail, and his green eyes darted to me as I approached.

"Fire," he whispered to me in my head.

"I know, buddy. Let's give you some more fire to watch." I marched to the other side of him to grab the shovel for the coals. Before I could scoop any from the pile, Zorath screeched at me, sending me a step backward.

That was not in my head. That was out loud.

His wings flared wide as he crouched his head down, facing me. I wasn't afraid of him, but this was the first time he'd shown any aggression. Whether he wanted me to replenish the flames or not, I had to for the purpose of the shop. I had no choice.

I took a step closer, easing the shovel into the pile of coal.

He screeched again.

"What is wrong with you?"

By now, my father had stopped hammering at his station, and Jameson's head peeked out from the doorway of the next room.

"Fire! Master!"

"I'm not your master. We've been over this. Now let me get this fire going."

He screeched again, and I shot him a devilish glare. I could feel my father's eyes burning as he looked between me and my dragon.

"Do *not* threaten me," I warned him.

But Zorath turned toward the fire, and let out a powerful screech, almost a roar. But it wasn't just sound that came out this time. A jet of green flames burst forth from his gaping mouth, startling the three of us that watched him. I retreated a step, my eyes widening as the embers were reignited and the flame grew as normal. The green faded out and an orange glow was left painting the inside of the furnace.

I returned the shovel to its home without taking my eyes off of Zorath. I knelt down next to him.

"You're just full of surprises, aren't you?" He was so young, and though it wasn't a massive flame that he breathed, he still produced it. He breathed fire. And it had been the perfect day and time for him to do it for the first time.

"I've never seen a green fire before," my father trailed off and he stood mesmerized at what he'd seen. Anxiousness laced his voice.

"It was a first for me, too."

Jameson stalked forward. "Me, too."

"I'll say, it's pretty useful for a place like this, though." Everyone nodded in agreement, and I turned back to Zorath. "Don't screech at me like that again. Don't yell at me again unless necessary. Understood?"

"Sorry, Master. Was just excited."

The rest of the day continued on as usual. Zorath kept by the fire, and every time he sensed it growing dim in the slightest, he showcased his new power, and reignited it for us.

By the time dusk fell upon Solaria, all three of us felt satisfied with the day's work. I'd never imagined before today how busy my father's shop could be. No wonder he always came home exhausted. When I was younger, his shop was hardly a business, hardly growing. He had to build it from the ground up after The Infernal Siege.

There was a deep sense of fulfillment that came with today's events, knowing that I've finally found happiness in a new skill set and how Zorath could breathe fire now.

We packed our things and prepared to close up.

"I can finish closing, sir," Jameson offered.

My father's eyebrows raised. "Are you sure? It's getting late. We don't mind helping."

Jameson simply nodded. "I'm positive, sir."

"Well, if you don't mind, that would be wonderful. That way I can get my daughter and the dragon home." My father rested his hand on my shoulder as he slung his satchel over his own.

"Not a problem. I'll see you tomorrow," Jameson nodded, and we headed out the door.

"Successful day today, huh?" My father stated on our walk back home. Our bellies grumbled the entire way back, ready for whatever dinner my mother would have cooking for us.

"I'd say so." I glanced up at Zorath as he perched on my shoulder.

Gods, I may have my work cut out for me when it comes to him.

CHAPTER TEN

"I APPRECIATE ALL THE help you've given me the past few days," my father told me on our way to the shop. "My days have been much easier having a third set of hands available."

"I'm glad I could be of service," I replied. Taking these past days off from my normal job benefitted not only him, but me. I didn't have to sell seafood. I didn't have to risk seeing either of the two guys that I *hadn't* stabbed.

I had been happier over the span of these days than I had been in a long time. My work was growing better by the day. Each piece of iron I forged grew more consistent than the last. My edges were cleaner, and I worked faster and faster with every order. Before long, I may be a necessity around there regarding productivity.

Jameson was there every day, opening and closing for us without complaint. He mainly sharpened while we forged.

The swords and daggers we made were truly magnificent. At least, *I* thought so. It was only proving what I already knew: My father's shop could no doubt be the best in the city, if it wasn't already. His shop may not be the most popular yet among the vanguard, but his kindness, his consistency, it would all lead up to it one day. It was a shame he didn't make more money for his talents.

With my help, it was only a matter of time before the higher ups found out how well the business was fairing, and he could progress in this field. Perhaps even charge more for his work.

Zorath accompanied us every day to the shop.

One day, I told myself, I would grow used to the stares I received by having him with me. He was a daily part of my life and routine now, and it was hard to remember that he didn't exist in other people's lives like he did in mine.

But he thoroughly enjoyed roaming about the shop, mostly fascinated by the fires. I noticed the way his eyes glistened every time we pulled metal out of the flame, a burning glow of pure red. I could have sworn that every so often I'd hear in the distance of my mind him whispering *"flame . . . flame . . ."*

Whenever he wasn't enthralled by that, he would stare at the fire, cooing and trilling every so often in excitement. When the fires died down, he'd relight them again for us. The flame would begin as green, and eventually fade back to orange as it settled.

"Ya know," my father started, "every time that he lights that furnace, it saves us money on coal."

"That's true." It would definitely be worth it in the long run for his business.

"Say, where is he anyway?"

I glanced around, and he was nowhere to be found. But it wasn't anything out of the ordinary. "He's probably off scavenging again."

"What do you think he's going to bring us back this time?" Jameson popped in from the other room, taking an armful of horseshoes my father had completed.

I shrugged. "Last time it was a rat. I'm going to be optimistic and say he was able to catch a bird this time."

Not very likely, though.

"I heard that," he said.

Damn it.

Part of me didn't mind his adventurous personality, but the other part of me worried heavily when it took him a while to return. What if Judah, or one of the other guys, made their way to this side of the city and spotted him? They'd steal him away from me in a heartbeat, and I likely wouldn't know until it was too late or until the screams invaded my head. What if he got hurt and he couldn't get back to me? Or I couldn't find where he was? The thoughts spun in my head, beginning to consume me until I shook them away.

At least he was learning to hunt on his own, though. He was gaining life experience, and the more he ate, the more he could grow.

And by the gods was he growing. It hadn't been long since he hatched, yet there was a noticeable size difference. He seemed a little heavier on my shoulder each day, and the objects he'd perch next to at the shop and at home seemed to grow smaller next to him.

I turned back to my father. "I am glad he's able to get out of the house more. Being cramped up in my room, or even in the house, for hours on end, just isn't good for the little guy."

"I can see that. He needs to hone his wild instincts. Hunting. Breathing fire. Flying. There's no doubt there's no room for him to fly cooped up in the house."

Hopefully, one day he'd fly. His wings were still too small, too weak right now for his body. Once he had the chance to strengthen those muscles and mature into them, I'm sure he would be ready.

The day dragged on until our bellies miserably ached in hunger. My father and I sat at our usual bench to eat, my father first heating up some chicken for me, him, and Zorath. Just in case Zorath made it back from "hunting" without a catch.

The chatter of people in the markets outside drowned out the crackling flames of the furnace beside us.

"May I sit with you?" Jameson made his appearance from the sharpening room and approached us.

"Sure," my father said, scooting over, allowing room on the other side of me for Jameson to sit.

He found his spot next to mine and began to eat a sandwich stacked with meat and cheese. My gods, it looked heavenly.

"So," I started, "how long have you been working with my father?" I realized that I'd been so focused on Zorath and my own productivity at the shop, I hadn't even spoken much to him in the past few days. I didn't even know him, really. Conversation had been the last thing on my mind, but not anymore.

"Only a couple of weeks. Mr. Theos has really been a great mentor to me, and I look up to him a lot." He peered around me to my father and smiled brightly, his dirty-blonde hair falling into his deep brown eyes. "I have heard a lot about you, m'lady, and I'm glad we finally got to meet, let alone work together! You have a real talent for this, you know."

"I've been telling her to come work with me for a while now!" My father interjected.

I smiled, but took a sip of water to hide it. Compliments weren't often given to me. None that really mattered anyway, as they usually came from perverted older men trying to get me into their bed.

"I'm happy to be here, with both of you, and so is he." I pointed at Zorath, who let out a cry of happiness as he approached from the room next door, lighting his serving of chicken aflame and swallowing it in a single gulp. "Where are you from? What's your family name? Since you know mine, I assume." I chuckled.

He laughed with me. "I do know yours, m'lady. Miss Emberlyn." He winked. "But you wouldn't know my parents or any of my family, for that matter. They don't originate from Solaria, and . . . and sometimes, I don't really get along with them. So, I try to keep that part of my life a little private."

"Oh, I'm sorry. I didn't mean to pry."

He shook his head. "Don't be sorry."

A moment of silence stretched between us as we ate. "You don't have to call me by any sort of title. I'm not a Lady. Valora will be just fine for me."

"Well, Valora, I am glad that you made it here to work with us." He raised up his glass of water as though he were giving a toast for a speech. I wiped the sweat from my brow with the sleeve of my tunic in an attempt to hide my smile.

"You know," my father began as he folded his empty napkin wrapper from lunch. "You could work with us full time, and I think in a matter of weeks we could grow this business twice as fast. After all, the last few days have been more productive than any other day *I've* had. With your hands helping us, it's a lot easier for us to keep up with orders and get ahead." With a soft pat on my shoulder, he went back to work.

I mulled it over a few moments, and Jameson's soft touch on my knee broke my train of thought.

"He's right. We could make a hell of a profit if we had you here to help us every day. We could make so much more happen in a day." He finished his sandwich, and stared into my eyes, as though searching for my answer in them. When I hadn't responded, he smiled. "Just think about it." He patted the top of my knee in a friendly gesture as he stood, and followed my father back to work.

I thought about that touch the rest of the day.

"I quit my job today," I announced at the dinner table the following evening. My mother's soup almost spewed from her mouth. My father simply sat back and grinned. I made eye contact with him. "I want to come work for you. *With* you."

"I knew you'd come to your senses, dear."

My mother cleared her throat beside me. "What made you do this so . . . spontaneously?"

I wasn't one to do or decide things on a whim. They both knew that as much as I did. I was always an over-thinker that weighed every option imaginable to know if it was the right way to go. "My market job pretty much chewed me up and spit me out. The hours are long and hard on my legs, the people are ruthless to me, and there's so much commotion." I took a bite of my dinner before continuing. "It's just too much for me.

It's not good for me mentally, and somehow it took me this long to realize it. It took working at the shop for me to realize what's good for me. That's where I want to be."

Their smiles reached their eyes as they continued with their meals.

"The thought of leaving Zorath at home while I'm outside all day makes me sick to my stomach. I've grown used to the job without him, but now that he's here, all I can think about is him, and the time we spend together at the shop." Zorath chortled next to me in approval. "Though I love the ocean and the smell of the salty wind that comes with being at the fish market, I love the forge more. I crave the heat of that furnace, the embers that glow redder by the minute. I love watching Zorath's eyes light up when he realizes the fires are dimming, and he gets to breathe his green flame to keep them going."

"He's saving us money by not having to use so much coal, that's for sure."

I nodded in agreement.

"Well," my father started, leaning back again in his seat, "you chose wisely, my dear. I thought my apprentice was good when I hired him because he caught on fairly quickly. He always offers to open and close the shop without a complaint, and he does it well. But you have a real talent for this, Valora. You could have a strong future in this trade."

"*We* could have a strong future in this," I corrected him. "I am here to help *your* business succeed."

He simply beamed at me. I knew I'd made his night. My heart warmed in my chest.

A weight had been lifted off of my shoulders. No longer did I have to listen to disgusting mens' comments about me—men that clearly couldn't woo a woman their own age so they opted to settle for the nearest young woman.

Now, I'd have Jameson for *me* to steal glances at during the day, who was a rather handsome man that was *my* age. The tables had turned. Now, I just wanted to get to know him better.

I had to lean over and take a bite of stew to hide my growing blush. *What in the hells was wrong with me?*

I glanced at Zorath to distract me. He once perched at the corner of our dining table to eat his food with us, but now, he was able to sit in the empty chair at that spot. His head just peeked over the edge, but he'd definitely grown multiple inches since he first hatched. He'd be a grown, human-sized dragon sitting in that seat soon if he kept it up.

He gnawed on some leftover chicken and its bones, and when he finished, his eyes cried into mine.

"I'm still hungry." He whimpered out loud, shifting his gaze between me and the chewed bones.

"You can go scavenge for something else." He leapt from the chair and began to roam the house, light on his paws.

Our little exterminator. I giggled at my own thought.

"It's like he can understand you completely," my mother observed.

"Well," I started, trying to find the words to truly explain our connection. "He does speak to me."

"Speaks to you?"

"He quite literally speaks to me. I can hear his voice in my head when he talks to me. It's a little weird, but I'm getting used to it."

"Definitely a little weird, I'd say," my father agreed, cleaning out his bowl. "But I'd been wondering what was going on with you two when you weren't speaking. You can't talk to him the same way?"

I shook my head. "No, only outloud. Though I think sometimes he can hear my thoughts, but I'm not actually speaking them *to* him."

"Maybe there's a way you can talk to him in your head. Or his head . . . I'm not real sure how all that works." He scratched the back of his neck.

I cocked my head at the thought. "I usually just speak out loud and it works just fine. But maybe you're right. What if I was too far from him to speak one day? I could mentally call him then."

"Could be useful for you two if you could do it," my mother said, standing to take her and my father's bowls away. I finished my last bite and handed mine graciously to her.

It was certainly an idea. Since he'd come into my world, I've felt like a different person. It was like he invaded my being and just made me even better. I am better *because* of him. My senses were heightened; my primal instincts were elevated, just as they would be naturally for him. It's as though we were cut from the same cloth.

But the evening drifted onto other conversations while we mingled by the crackling fire in the den. All the lively chatter of the night filled the room with so much joy, I wished it would never end.

The crash of metal hammering metal vibrated through my head, an oddly satisfying sensation that fulfilled me. Sweat ran down my back, dripping from my forehead and my arms as I worked on a set of large daggers that a hooded man ordered yesterday.

I finally felt that I was doing something good for me, rather than having to approach my customers, they came to me. They buy from me because they want our products, and I don't have to force them to pay a price they didn't like.

Once those customers realized they no longer had to wait a week for their order to be completed, they came more often, and new faces appeared with them. Working with Jameson and my father was really paying off.

Many that approached us were younger men, aspiring knights, wanting their own tools and weapons for their practices.

We were definitely kept busy, and work seemed to flow like a wave on the ocean.

Zorath's happiness meter constantly stayed full now that he could leave the house every day. He kept the flames in the furnace bright, and kept his instincts sharp by hunting the occasional roaming rat, or by spotting and growling menacingly at a stray cat. But he was rather tame and very intelligent for a wild, and supposedly, extinct beast.

"I'm not a beast. I'm a dragon."

But sometimes he could get a bit of an attitude. "Sorry, Zorath." He chuffed back in response, resting in front of the furnace. I set the shaped daggers off to the side in the ready-to-be-sharpened pile. "I'm taking a quick water break," I announced to my father, who nodded back at me. I made for the empty bench and the pitcher of fresh water that Jameson prepared for us this morning. My hand brushed against something as I reached. A hand. I looked up to meet a pair of startled brown eyes.

"My apologies. Allow me." Jameson poured a cup of water and placed it in my outstretched hand, and served himself next.

"Thank you."

"You're welcome, m'lady." He settled down next to me on the bench. We'd spoken on and off throughout each day, having friendly conversations to get to know each other. I was close to being able to consider him a friend. I'd never really had friends—an attractive one, especially.

"I hope you realize you don't have to refer to me as a Lady. I don't have a title. Never have and never will." I laughed it off, keeping the mood light. Ladies were typically of noble heritage and belonged in a king's court. That was not me.

"My apologies. I guess it's just a habit."

"A habit?" I asked, taking a sip from my glass. "How many *Ladies* have you met?"

He drank down half his glass. "Not many, to be fair. I suppose it's the manners that my parents originally taught me as a kid and I've adopted it."

That's right, I remembered. He said that his parents were from a foreign land, not from Solaria. It made sense that he would have taken on different lifestyles, culture, and language from them. But the subject of his family seemed to strike a nerve within him, so I reminded myself to steer clear of conversing about them.

"So, why don't you tell me more about this dragon of yours?"

I glanced at Zorath, then back to him. And so I told him.

I quickly confided in him about how my mind tended to wander, consuming me as a person, and how it kind of closed me off from other people. I was always distant. The only thing that seemed to calm me was the ocean, the beach, and the mysteries that lay beyond the shore. It all intrigued me, and gave me something else to wonder about other than the life I lived. I told him that I found his eggs one of those afternoons on the beach, and the moment he'd hatched, the growing fires tearing our street apart ceased completely.

I left out the minor details I'd learned along the way. I left out my parent's story about how I was born, as it didn't seem necessary information to share for this conversation. We were talking about Zorath, not me.

While on the subject of Zorath, I made sure to leave out the details of the men that wanted to take him. My kidnapping. My rape. The home invasion, and everything else they'd done just to get their hands on him. I wasn't ready to relive that yet.

When I finished my story, he sat in awe, his face a mask of wonder. "Wow. That's a crazy story. Just think, dragons have been extinct our whole lives, and you were able to find his egg just sitting *there* in your favorite place!"

"It's definitely ironic when you put it that way. Where he washed ashore from, I have no idea. But, a part of me believes that he was waiting for me there . . . somehow. Maybe it was fate. But maybe I was just in the right place at the right time."

"Aren't we all?" Jameson's brown eyes met mine for a heartbeat, and a smile crept onto his lips, revealing a pearly white row of teeth that I'd never paid attention to until now. He had a lovely smile.

My gaze shifted to my feet, feeling heat rising to my cheeks. Surely, it was the warmth from the fires around us that was doing that.

"I don't necessarily believe in fate. We choose our own fate—intentionally or unintentionally. You chose to go to the beach, walk that path, and there he was. It was all you." He leaned in half an inch. "And I chose to be here."

My breath caught, and his eyes bore into mine for a moment. "Perhaps you're right." It was the only thing I could think to say as his smile held firm, as did his eye contact. My cheeks tingled.

"Hey, Val," my father shouted across the room, "the fire is going out." I looked at the furnace to find that sure enough, the flame had almost dissipated completely.

Well, it hadn't been the heat from the furnace that made my cheeks flush.

I scanned the room. Zorath was nowhere to be found.

"Just when you think Zorath was here to be useful," I snickered as I stood, shaking my head. I reached for the handle of the shovel.

"I've got it," Jameson intruded, standing to take the shovel from my hands. He scooped, and as the pile of coal made its way toward the fiery hole in the wall, I caught a glimpse of something within it. I stalked forward a step to get a better look.

I recognized what it was immediately. A blade, with a Moon Hazel wood handle and gold cross-guard. It had somehow been misplaced.

"Wait!" I screamed as Jameson released the coals into the pit, the flames rising almost immediately.

Within an instant, without a second thought, I dove toward the fire, my arm engulfed within the walls of the blaze.

CHAPTER ELEVEN

"Valora!" My father cried out.

But it was too late. My body hit the ground with a breath-catching thud, and my arm had reached elbow-deep into the pit of the fire.

Instantly, a green flame wrapped around my arm. My mind and soul sat captivated by the sight in front of me, the fire swarming my skin, until my body was heaved upward by another force.

"Are you alright?" My father blatantly yelled rather than asked. I was still in a trance from the vibrancy of the flame that had wrapped around me in the short time my arm was engulfed. My gaze shifted to the furnace, then back to my father, and I held up my hand.

In my palm was his blade. His lucky charm. His prized possession. And I'd retrieved it on instinct.

His eyes darted to the dagger, and I spotted tears near the corners of his eyes, but they never fell. They didn't have time to, because his eyes soon darted to the arm holding the blade and his expression altered fully from relief to pure astonishment.

"You're unscathed," my father breathed, not believing his eyes.

He was right. My arm was intact. Sure, later on I may have some bruises appear from the fall, but my arm was completely normal. The green flame seemed to act like a shield, protecting me.

"At first I thought it was the adrenaline rush," I started, "like I was in shock and just couldn't feel the pain. Or that my arm had burnt to a crisp entirely and I didn't have an arm left."

"But you're okay."

"But I'm okay," I replied. No burns, no cuts, no bruises to be found.

"How in the . . ." Jameson's words drifted off.

I stumbled to find my words, because I had no idea how to explain how it happened.

Maybe my heightened instincts knew that I would be okay. Maybe that's why I'd had the urge to walk into our home after it was ablaze merely moments before, and I came out without a burn or a scratch on me. The heat, the smoke, it hadn't affected me.

No one else had said a word until my father spoke. "Thank you, Valora." He reached for the knife still in my hand and inspected it. The heat never had time to alter it. "I don't know how you did it, but thank you. Just—" he cut himself off. "Try not to do it again."

Clearly, he was still in shock and didn't know what else to say. I would be too if I'd just watched my only child stick her hand in a furnace. He slowly drifted back to his workstation, leaving me and Jameson alone.

I faced him, his eyes still bouncing between my arm, the fire, and my face. "The fire was green."

I nodded. "The fire was green."

I inhaled deeply. They deserved to know more since witnessing this. So, I gestured to the seats we were occupying just moments before the incident. Jameson followed me, and I released a heavy sigh.

"I wasn't entirely truthful with you earlier. I didn't lie to you. Everything I'd told you was the truth, but I left out some major details." I looked at my father, who could very well be listening from his station, if he still wasn't in shock. "I wasn't truthful with either of you. But now that we are all experiencing these new things together regarding me and Zorath, you both should probably know everything.

"I've been a different person since Zorath came into my life. More specifically since he hatched. I found his egg, and I was kidnapped shortly after. Somehow, the men that captured me had found out about him, and they wanted to take the egg from me. They threatened me, telling me that if I didn't turn it over to them, bad things would happen to me. They knew

I'd refuse, but their threat stood strong. I had no idea what their plan was at this time, but now I felt even more inclined to protect my egg."

I lowered my head. "I tried to evade them as long as possible, and I succeeded for a while. But the next time that I stumbled upon them, they took me into what I assumed was one of their homes against my will. They . . . violated me. They did things that I never thought I would say out loud or talk about. Unspeakable things. I didn't stand a chance against all three of them. I had no defense. Their mission was to destroy me, to teach me a lesson, and I had to let them." A single tear fell from my cheek.

The rustling of papers at my father's station stopped, but he didn't interrupt. He listened harder and let me continue. "I came home that night to our house up in flames, and all the others around it. The fires seemed to be their final warning to me, as if they hadn't already done enough to me."

I shook my head, reliving the moment. "I saw them there that night, standing on the street and cackling like little boys teasing each other about a girl or their first crush. They were certain they'd get what they wanted now. But, I felt Zorath's aura tugging at me from inside our house, before I'd even set eyes on him. He was calling me in. And then the moment he hatched, the fires disappeared, sucked away into some other realm. I ventured into the house that was engulfed just seconds before.

"Once inside, the residual heat didn't bother me, though I didn't recognize why at the time. You know the rest of that story."

I let in a breath, and let it out slowly.

"I saw those horrible men again after some time had passed. But this time, I refused to let them win. I dodged every attack they threw at me as if I'd been training my whole life for it. They tried to lay their hands on me, but I was quicker. It's like my brain knew what they were doing a moment before they did them. They followed me into our home, and when the leader of the three neared me, I attacked. I stabbed him, and they ran off. They finally saw that they had a right to fear a young woman. And I pray to the gods every day that they don't make the mistake of coming back for me."

When I had finished, both of their faces met mine, mouths slightly parted in disbelief, with stares as blank as a clear sky.

I gulped, hoping that my father wouldn't be angry that I withheld this information from them.

Zorath trotted in from behind the shop, a fresh rat in his jaws.

"I say all of these things because ever since Zorath hatched, I believe his powers intertwine with me, and whatever he can do, I can do. Dragons are immune to fire. So am I. He speaks to me through my mind. Maybe that's one of the reasons I love the forge so much, because he does. The flames and the heat give me a rush I can't explain. Joy. Happiness. I'm not sure. I don't know what other powers he will have, but there's a good chance we all may be surprised again."

I left it at that. I'd released all the information that had been weighing on me. No more secrets.

I waited for a response that seemed like it would never come. At last, my father finally spoke.

"Let's not tell your mother about all this."

"I promise, I didn't do it!" Zorath yelled back at me, flaring his wings.

"I don't care what you say," I seethed between my teeth. "That dagger got into those coals somehow, and you've been around the fires all day."

"Why would I put a blade into some coals?"

"I don't know why you'd do it, I'm just placing blame on you, because what happened could have ended badly."

"What are they doing?" Jameson asked my father behind me.

"They're arguing. They do that," he retorted, getting back to work. "Got to leave them be."

"I'm sorry, Master."

Zorath's emerald eyes softened . . . I just couldn't stay mad at that face.

"It's okay. I'm sorry for yelling at you."

He purred, and then left to feast on his dead rat.

Today could have been a lot worse. I could have lost my arm, not knowing that I was immune to fire. But I didn't, and I am a lot stronger than I realized I was. I was glad that I spilled my heart. I couldn't keep bottling up all the things that happened to me. It wasn't a healthy way to get through it.

The sky was fading to an ombre of purples and blues. I took a short break to drink some water, and Jameson came over to me with urgency. I hadn't really seen him or heard from him since the incident. And the confession.

"Valora," he started, leaning in close to me, his proximity forcing slight heat to my face.

"Yes?"

"I've been thinking all afternoon. I have an idea for some bonding time," his eyes met mine. "For you and your dragon, I mean."

"Yes?" I repeated, drawing out the word, intrigued by his comment.

"There's this old cottage in the Nova Forest. No one knows about it. It's hidden and enchanted with some sort of ancient magic. anyway, it's a very useful place, and I think it could benefit you two. It's not attached to a path off the main road, so you'll have to venture off to find it yourself, but I've got directions that I can give you."

I didn't respond. I wasn't sure how to.

"The cottage is filled with old books. I've spent a lot of time there. Whoever goes in will be taken care of and will be given everything they need. I was thinking it may be a good place to go to test your powers and your bond, and strengthen it. Read up on it, maybe."

A lot of information had just been thrown at me. I looked at Zorath who had been awaiting my response the whole time. I simply shrugged.

"Just think about it," he said as he turned to leave with a grin in my direction.

CHAPTER TWELVE

"Tell me what you think about all this," I asked Zorath as I laid belly-down on my bed, my hands lazily propping up my head. He rested his front claws on the foot of my mattress, peering wide-eyed at me over his rapidly growing paws. The moonlight reflected the vibrant pattern of his scales in perfect harmony across the walls.

"About what, Master?"

"Stop calling me that," I ordered. "How do you feel about venturing into the woods? To find this mysterious hidden cottage? What if Jameson is lying and it isn't real, or he had his facts wrong and it serves us no purpose?"

"I wouldn't think he would harm you."

I sighed.

"Do you think he would lie?"

My gaze dropped to the comforter. "No."

Zorath leaped to accompany me on the bed, the mattress pressing toward the ground under our combined weight. He nudged his nose against my hand, and I sat up to pet him.

Ever since he began breathing fire and we found out I had a partially shared power with him—my immunity to fire—he's been conversing with me more often in my mind. Like our bond had grown astronomically just from sharing these traits.

"It would just be me and you there, you know that, right?"

"I think we can manage." He chuffed.

He was so optimistic. He wasn't afraid. It was exactly what I needed in my life. As anxious as I was about leaving home on my own for a while, he kept me grounded and kept me from worrying too much.

I took a deep breath, then released it slowly, the tension falling from my shoulders. "Okay. Let's do it, then."

Zorath flapped his wings in approval.

"But before we go, I have to ask," I continued. "Why in the realm's name do you keep calling me 'Master'?"

Zorath cocked his head slightly. *"Because one day, you will be a Master."*

Whatever the hell that means. I rolled my eyes and hopped from the bed.

I opened my bedroom door to find my parents to tell them about Jameson's offer and what I'd decided. My father was in his usual spot this time of night: his chair by the fireplace. He sat across from my mother, who worked on the dark quilt she was crocheting for my bedroom.

"I have an announcement." They turned their attention to me. "Father, if it wouldn't be a problem, I want to take some time off work. Jameson told me and Zorath of a place we can go in the Nova Forest to learn more about ourselves and our bond. There's a private cottage. I will have one-on-one time with my dragon, and can hopefully get some answers to some things we've been seeing from him. And *maybe* find out if Zorath has any other powers and what other things I may be capable of."

My mother snapped her head to my father. "Theos, did you know about this?"

He shrugged. "I'd heard him mention it."

"And you didn't tell me?"

"Guys, please," I cut in. "I didn't say anything earlier because I've been reluctant to go. You know how I am. I'm still nervous if I'm being honest with myself, but excited at the same time. This is the only opportunity I may have to gain information about him. About *us*." I gestured to Zorath, who sat tall at my heels. "There are no archives or bookstores that we'd have access to that would allow me to learn about him. The *true* last dragon. This is my only shot."

They shared a look.

"You know that we'll be worried about you," my father stated.

"Always," my mother added.

"I know."

"Well, I guess since you've been helping us for a while, and our profit has increased, I could spare you for a few days." He winked, inviting a chuckle among the room.

"Where will you be?"

I turned back to my mother. "At a cottage in the Nova Forest. Jameson knows of it."

"When will you leave? When will you return home?"

"Tomorrow, and sometime at the end of the week. Or whenever I feel I've accomplished what I've wanted to accomplish."

"She lacks faith in you," Zorath whispered in my head, and I shot him a warning glare.

He seemed to be right, though. She was worried about me, and she had every right to be, but she didn't seem to have any trust in me. Or in *us*, for that matter.

"I believe in myself and Zorath, and you should too," I said calmly. "I'll be alright."

She nodded, though I know she didn't want to believe it. "Will Jameson be there?"

I stilled. Heat rushed to my face causing chill bumps to scatter my arms. "I . . . I don't know. I wouldn't think so. He made it out to be like a thing for me and Zorath to do."

"Ah. I see." She blinked. Or did she wink at me? Whatever it was, the concern stayed marked on her face the rest of the night.

The next morning came too quickly, and I was already overwhelming myself thinking about everything that could possibly go wrong. I could get hurt. Zorath could get hurt. What if we couldn't make it back home safely? What if we got lost? What if we starved because of it?

Stop.

I stopped myself. *I believe in myself.*

I'd repeated those words to myself all night long while I laid wide awake thinking of the next day.

I packed a bag full of extra clothes, each item feeling like a small piece of home coming along with me. I donned a pair of sturdy brown pants, my half-sleeve tan tunic, and laced up my well-worn boots, somehow feeling comfort in them.

I twisted my hair up into a messy bun, allowing the short pieces in the front to fall around my face and ears. I shouldn't be too hot for travel.

Then I was ready . . . I think.

"Oh, Valora," my mother hugged me tightly as soon as I stepped out of my room. "Please be careful."

"I will. I promise." I assured her, my voice steady as an arrow, though my heart raced like wind. "This is what I need to do right now. For us." I glanced at my dragon.

"And you know to be careful if you and that boy . . ."

"Mother!"

"Alright, alright," color flooded her face, as did mine. "Sorry."

I nodded to her and tried to hide the embarrassment in my expression.

"You won't be alone on this journey, Master." Zorath peered up at me, ready to go.

"I'm not your master," I reminded him. "You are my friend, you are my dragon, and we will always have each other. No ownership here."

I'm not the girl I was before him, no. Prior to his hatching, I would be a nervous wreck if I attempted to do something like this. *Actually,* I wouldn't be doing it at all. Everything that would've told me that something would go wrong would haunt me until I'd decide completely against it. But now, I was slowly becoming eager. We would make it. We would find what we needed until we were the greatest dragon-human companions to ever exist.

"Here," my mother turned to grasp something from the table behind her. "This is for you. In case you can't catch, or *kill*, what you need." She shuddered at the word "kill".

She placed a rather hefty bag of dehydrated meat in my hands. The weight of it, despite our poverty, was a clear testament to her love.

I set my bag on the table, and noticed a spread had been laid out. Not one of food, but a variety of gear. A belt with a sheathed knife, a fishing pole with a line, and a thin, but sturdy rope.

"I won't let my little girl go unprepared." I whirled around, finding my father in his chair, hands behind his head, a grin wide on his face. He stood to approach me, and nodded toward the table. "You see everything I got for you there?"

I took another scan at what was in front of me, and when I saw it, I couldn't believe my eyes.

It wasn't an ordinary knife that was sheathed in its scabbard. No—I'd recognize that golden cross-guard a mile away. I had just saved this knife from melting.

I unsheathed the blade, its unused silver edge gleaming in the morning sunlight. I spun back around to face my father.

"Are you sure you want me to bring this?"

"If this blade has been my lucky charm for so many years, and you dove into a fire to save it for me, then yes. I'm passing my luck to you, hoping it'll keep you safe in your time of need."

I had no words appropriate for this moment. Each of these items on the table were meticulously chosen for this trek, and I didn't know how to properly thank him for the love and kindness.

I simply embraced him tightly. "Thank you," I said into the sleeve of his tunic, my voice barely above a whisper.

"You're welcome." He pulled back.

I wrapped the belt around my hips, securing the knife at my right hip in its sheath. I packed my bag with the food and supplies and strapped it over my shoulders, the weight settling comfortably. "I'll be back by the end of the week." It was Sunday, the only day off my parents had during the week, unless my dad was back up at the forge. It would be up to me whether this trip would take a few short days or the entirety of the week. Hopefully my father's good luck charm would pay off for me.

Emotion bottled up behind my eyelids, and to avoid causing a scene, I hurried out the front door, Zorath following close behind me.

Why was I so emotional? It's not like I was going off to war.

I couldn't help but to glance back to see the longing on my parent's faces until—

My body thudded into another. "*Hey!*" I screeched, my frustration bubbling up, until I looked up to the face of who was in front of me.

Jameson.

His brown eyes glowed amber in the dawn's light, and his blonde hair shone a solid gold when the usual ash and dirt wasn't muddling it.

"Hey, m'lady," he began, an awkward smile taking over his mouth.

I frowned at him in acknowledgement of what he'd just called me.

"I'm sorry . . . Valora." He corrected himself, scratching the back of his neck.

"Much better," I teased.

"Much better, m'lady," Zorath mocked him in my head. I lightly kicked his leg beside me. I could have sworn I heard him snicker in the depths of my mind.

"I knew you'd be leaving today, so I uh . . . I brought you a gift." I noticed that he'd had his hands behind his back this whole time. I raised my eyebrows in question.

Revealing from behind his back was a sword. But it was rather short. Shorter than a blade you'd see the Eclipse Guard wielding. This one was more petite. Its hilt was solid black, while the cross-guard and pommel glistened with gold. A small green jewel sat in the center of the cross-guard, catching the light at every angle.

"Why are you giving me this?"

"This was the very first blade you made as a blacksmith. I could see what this piece meant to you as soon as you finished it, so I wanted you to have it. I matched the gemstone in the center to your eyes. And Zorath's. Don't worry, I made another one for the client that ordered it." A light chuckle escaped from his lips. His words were laced with sincerity, and I took the sword from his grip.

It brought back a flood of all the memories from my first day there. The sweat. The determination. The hours spent learning this trade. It all culminated in this blade. Now, I could take it with me on this journey, as a part of me.

"I'm not sure what to say," I admitted. I caught his eyes shifting between me and the blade, then me and Zorath, then finally landing back on me. I sheathed the sword in the empty spot of my baldric on my left side. "Thank you."

"You're welcome. I hope you don't need to use it, but it's yours. It can be *your* good luck charm, like your father's blade is for him." His smile widened.

"Thank you," I stupidly repeated.

"You're welcome, Valora." He reached a hand out in front of him, awaiting a friendly handshake in exchange for the gift he'd just given me.

But for some reason, I grabbed his hand and pulled him in for a hug. He stumbled forward a bit at the motion, his gold necklace nearly slapping me in the face, but then I felt the gentle touch of his hands on my back. I slowly pulled away, embarrassment flushing my skin.

"I'm sorry. Thank you," I said again, my brain obviously unable to find any other words. "Let's go, Zorath," I commanded, and he squealed with excitement.

I left Jameson behind me, my heart thudding with adrenaline.

The East Gate would lead me outside the walls of the city.

Solaria was, indeed, a vast territory, but the kingdom sat on the western border, while the rest of the land was occupied by a colossal expansion of forest, jungle, rivers, and farmland—but mostly forest. It used to be home to many creatures, and had been known to harvest some type of magic within the woods, but this was before the war when the land was prosperous, and the carnage brought extinction to the forest it used to be.

I'd only been outside the city through this gate a handful of times. When I was much younger, my father would take me hunting in the Nova Forest—usually an unsuccessful trip. In the early years after The Infernal Siege, the presence of wildlife was few and far between. You just had to know where to find the game. The lack of animal life was possibly a huge reason the city still lived in poverty today. We relied on the farmlands outside the city, and even those didn't prosper as much as they used to.

As soon as the massive wooden doors led me and Zorath past the towering stone walls, the world seemed entirely different.

The path ahead was a simple dirt road, but where it led to had my head spinning in awe. I'd never seen this much greenery existing in one place.

The city had always been a palette of browns and grays, painted by the dusty streets and the stone buildings that lined it, and the ocean was simply a vast stretch of blue that merged with the sky.

But this was different. Trees grew thicker and more abundantly here, and stretched as far as the eye could see. They were *everywhere*, their trunks tall, and their branches swaying gently in the breeze. I didn't remember the forest being so vibrant when I was a kid.

We trekked past the treeline and onto the dirt path, the songs of birds echoing along the treetops.

Even the air out here seemed different compared to within the walls—crisp and filled with the blending scents of pine and earth. Sunlight filtered through the lush canopy above. The forest felt more alive than anything I had ever been around . . . Like I could feel it moving and breathing around me.

Zorath trotted alongside me, his eyes wide with the same sense of wonder that I felt. We moved deeper into the forest, and the farther we went, the more the sounds of the city faded away.

I remembered the instructions Jameson gave me to find this cottage:

Head down the main road until the brush begins to thicken around you. An ancient Oak Tree will be nestled into the woods on the right. From there, follow the deer trail around the tree that winds through the forest. Once you reach the stream, cross it, and look for the trail marked by broken twigs and dead grass. This will lead you straight to the cottage.

I had recited these words over and over again in my head. My memory seemed stronger than ever, and it wasn't entirely as difficult to remember his instructions as I thought it would be.

The road continued to stretch before us. Zorath pranced at my heels, sometimes running ahead with pure excitement.

"Stay close by," I called to him. He halted twenty or so feet ahead of me and waited for me to catch up.

"Sorry," the little voice intruded my headspace.

"You're just growing so fast. If you exhaust yourself on the way over here, I won't be able to carry you the rest of the way." I shifted the bag on my shoulders. "Not with all this gear on me and the weapons on my hips, at least."

About thirty minutes of leisurely strolling had passed before the brush began to grow more densely, and the trees began to cascade overhead, almost encircling us completely. We had to be getting close. I kept my gaze drifting toward the right, searching for any sign of this large Oak Tree that Jameson said I "couldn't miss".

Within a matter of minutes, I found he was right.

Its trunk rose like a pillar, twisting and contorting with the weight of centuries. Its bark was rough, weathered brown, and moss clung to the base of the trunk, creeping its way toward the lower branches.

The branches stretched outward in every direction, a hard sight to miss. We ventured around the tree, the earth surrounding it thick with roots that I was careful to not trip over.

There was no doubt in my mind, with all the stories I'd heard about magic existing here, that this tree held that magic at one point. Its presence was breathtaking and undeniable.

We pressed on through the narrow deer trail, and the forest enveloped us. The trail twisted and turned. Every so often, I thought I'd heard a rustle of leaves or the snap of a twig around us. But I reminded myself that we were in the wilderness, and I was certain that if there was a threat nearby, then Zorath would sense it before I did.

We continued forward.

After what felt like an eternity of wandering through the trail, Zorath keeping close by, the faint sound of running water tickled our ears.

"The stream."

"Yes. The stream."

We quickened our pace, and soon enough, a creek lay before us, its clear waters bubbling over the stones.

We crossed carefully, so as to not lose our footing, testing the sturdiest rocks before pressing our full weight down onto them. Then, we landed on dry soil, stepping right into an arrangement of flattened, nearly-dead grass.

"Do you think they're just making it easy on us?" I asked my dragon who pranced in the grass ahead while I laughed at my own remark.

"Too easy," he agreed.

We walked farther, the bag on my shoulders beginning to rub me sore.

The trees started to part. More. And more.

Until the light from a clearing ahead could be seen.

Upon stepping into it, we found a cottage at its center.

It was just as Jameson had described it.

CHAPTER THIRTEEN

THE COTTAGE WAS OLD and worn, its roof shielded completely in moss. The stone walls were covered in entangled ivy. Bushes lined the outskirts of the building and wrapped around each wall, and seemed relatively taken care of despite the place's status as supposedly abandoned. Though the windows appeared dark and dusty, the blue shutters and door welcomed me, seeming to call my name.

There was an undeniable charm to the place, and it made me wonder if this had been a cozy home for someone at some point.

What could have happened to them?

Zorath and I stepped forward cautiously, taking in our surroundings. We noted every scent, every sound, every aspect of this clearing that we could before we reached the door. No one was here except us.

I eased inside as I pushed the door, swinging open with a light creak. Zorath stayed right behind me as my eyes started scanning the room. Shelves lined every wall, and on them, were books. Every nook and cranny was covered in books, journals, artifacts, and antiques. Like whoever may have lived here before had a hobby for collecting. There was no space left behind. I'd never imagined so many books in one place. The air was thick with the smell of old parchment, yet with every step I took, I felt something new. It felt like this place was meant for me at this very moment.

There was a buzz of magic, charm, and *life* in this cottage.

Zorath perched himself near the doorway, looking around the room the same way I had been.

I ran my fingers along the rows of books, familiarizing myself with every edge of this place. But something stopped me about halfway down the first wall. A twinge in my gut pulled me back, like tugging a fish on a line. My sixth sense tingled in my head, but it was a little different than anything I'd felt before. Different from when I avoided Jovis's attack on the street by mere inches and made a run for it. No. This one was *pulling* me somewhere: over to the next shelf.

I stepped forward, the feeling growing stronger.

My eyes met a large dusty tome, slanted in its place, with a cover adorned with intricate symbols. I flipped through this book until I landed on a random page and studied it.

Inside were lists of instructions, various diagrams, riddles, poems, and I even caught the word "spell" mentioned a few times throughout the pages.

"Zorath," I turned toward him at the door, but I didn't look up from the pages, "we will start with this book. There's a key to our powers somewhere in here, I know it."

"Okay!" His eyes gleamed with anticipation and he danced in circles around the room, knocking over a nearby stack of books in the process.

I laid my bag and weapons belt down against the nearest wall and made my way to the desk that sat in front of the right wall, and cleared off a space. Empty parchment and writing utensils were scattered across the desk and floor as if someone hadn't cleaned up after themselves from studying.

"Alright, Zorath. I admit, I'm not the fastest reader." Zorath was approaching the tiny fireplace along the back wall.

"That's okay, Master," he replied.

I ignored the title he gave me and rolled my eyes. I wouldn't keep having the same argument with a juvenile dragon that clearly chose to not listen to me.

But he reared back, and blasted forth a line of green flame, igniting the dried wood in the fireplace.

I knew how to read thanks to my parents, who continued to teach me what they could even after pulling me out of school. It was a necessary skill in life, and it was one I used at my jobs. At the market, I needed to know what the seafood was that I was selling, and what price I was selling it for before I loaded up and took off with my cart. I had to read orders, and sometimes take orders, at my father's forge.

I opened the book and settled in, thankful for the rest I'd have from journeying here this morning.

I began to read. Page by page I turned them, searching for anything useful regarding dragons, green fire, even being *immune* to fire and heat. If I could find any information at all that would give us answers, then this would be a successful trip.

I read for hours, only stopping to take a break for water, which I'd found fresh in a well outside. Zorath kept himself busy and out of the way.

My eyes burned. My head was beginning to throb, and my jaw grew sore from clenching it in thought.

Page after page, I read. In this book, I mostly found recipes for potions, diagrams on how to build things, and some intellectual riddles, which I didn't dare take a chance at solving.

I heaved a sigh and sat back in the chair, only to notice that I wasn't even halfway through this book.

The sunlight was creeping beneath the treetops, painting an orange and gold picture across the sky.

My stomach growling is what finally pulled me away from the books. "I guess let's get settled in."

I set my backpack on the bed provided in the room at the back of the cottage. I began to unpack, laying all my extra clothes on a nearby bench and taking out the hefty pack of dehydrated meat my mother had prepared for me. I grabbed a handful and began to eat.

This cottage was amazing in its own unique way, and it's nothing like what I'd pictured when Jameson described it to me. It was made liveable to whoever needed it at any time, and I was skeptical until I stepped foot inside. Plates and cups for eating, and towels and soaps for bathing were ready for use, even though no one actively lived here. It gave me an odd, but satisfying feeling. How was this place still existing when magic seemed to leave Solaria so long ago?

I ate slowly while strolling amongst the remaining shelves I had yet to explore. Books of every genre had a home here, and if I knew I had the time, I would love to read them. Maybe if I find the information that I need by the end of this trip, then I could bury my head into one of these mystery novels or romance novels.

I smiled at the thought.

The sun was setting, and I had much more that I wanted to do.

The cottage was dark now, save for the glow of the fire that Zorath provided us for warmth. Well, for him it was for warmth *and* entertainment. A candle sat atop the desk I had been reading on, but it wasn't lit. Not yet. Then I realized I had no way to continue my readings at nighttime without candles.

"Use the fire," Zorath suggested.

"Good idea." I released the candle from its stand and brought it with me toward the fireplace. It helped that I was immune to the heat of flames. It was possible that I could stick my entire arm into and the only thing that would come out burning would be the candle.

Though I'd done it before, I wasn't doing it again.

I shoved the candle into the fire, watched it spark, and pulled back. The candle was lit.

I could have easily just let Zorath light my candles for me, and the thought did cross my mind as I lit another one in the fireplace, but I shut it down almost immediately. This cottage, pretty much made of books and parchment paper, would cause the realm's greatest bonfire if I wasn't careful.

So, I sat back down at the desk and continued to read.

The sky was wrapped in an eerie green, casting an unnatural glow over the

land. Below, streets and towers were engulfed in emerald flames, the intensity lighting the night. The fires danced and swirled. Explosions rang from one side of me to the next. The fire was hungry. And it grew. And grew. The flames below danced into the shapes of dragons, and it called me forward . . .

I awoke with a sharp gasp, sweat pouring from my temples. The sheets underneath me were soaked from my sweat, leaving my skin slightly pruned and moist.

I let out a heavy breath as I tried to calm the rate of my heart.

"Are you alright?" Zorath lifted his head from where he slept next to me on the comforter. He yawned widely, teeth gleaming in the low light.

"Yes. It was only a dream," I replied, convincing not only him, but myself, that there was nothing to worry about.

But I couldn't be sure that there wasn't. Yet again, I had another dream of things *burning*. But on the outskirts of those flames, the scene was so faded, I couldn't see where I was. Could it have been my home? No, not again. Could it have been Solaria? Solaria couldn't take anymore destruction, and there was no possible way that Zorath's flame could accomplish such a massacre.

Either way, it was just a dream, and there was no way of knowing its meaning. I heaved myself out of bed, Zorath leaping down beside me.

The rising sun brightened the room as I drew open the curtains. Orange and yellow beamed through every crevice of the windows, heating the cottage with each passing minute.

I changed into my clothes from yesterday until I could get myself properly cleaned up. Digging through the bag I'd packed, I found the rope my father gave me. This morning would be the perfect opportunity to try and catch some food so I wouldn't have to rely on dried meat all day.

Some fruits and vegetables rested on the end table near the doorway, and I snagged them on my way by.

"Stay here until I return. I won't be long," I ordered Zorath. He huffed a loud breath, but sat by the front door as I stepped outside, closing the door behind me.

"Hurry back," he whispered.

"I'll try."

He sat perched in the windowsill on top of a pile of books, following my every step with his eyes until I was out of the clearing and headed into the woods in front of the cottage.

Any other time, I would have taken him out with me, but I didn't want him to disrupt the woods and risk us not catching anything. Animals could probably smell him easier than they would me.

I moved quietly through the dense underbrush, careful not to disturb the silence of this forest. There had been magic in these woods long ago, and the cottage was the closest thing I would get to magic now. But I could still feel its life buried deep in the soil, in the roots under my feet.

I trudged on, the peace of life in the air bringing me comfort, until I found a small clearing between a few trees.

Perfect.

I knelt down and readied the rope that my father provided for me, and my hands began to work. I tied a series of intricate knots—knots I hadn't realized I could tie so well until right now. I'd only practiced it a handful of times when I was growing up, and hunting was an occasional hobby with my father, but we were hardly ever lucky enough to come back with a harvest. That's the reason we'd stopped hunting. However, for some reason, at this very moment, I seemed proficient at it, as though it *hadn't* been years since I'd attempted it.

A nearby sapling stood at the edge of a tall trunk, young and flexible enough to accomplish what I needed it to do. I bent it down low, securing it to my cord and opening up a small loop on the ground. Carefully, I arranged the trigger mechanism with some twigs, ensuring that the slightest touch would spring the trap.

Finally, I placed the fruits and vegetables from the cottage in the center, hoping an animal would be oblivious enough and come across it soon.

I stepped back to examine my work.

"Not too bad, Valora," I told myself, smiling for whatever reason. I headed back to the cottage quietly.

Zorath was pleasantly excited to see me return. I freshened up, bathing myself in the deep tub provided in the small room connected to the bedroom, washing the sweat from last night from my skin. Fresh towels were waiting for me on a nearby shelf by the time I was finished.

A few hours went into reading the same book I'd started on yesterday, partially because I found it interesting, but the other part of me had high hopes that I'd find something useful in the first book I tried.

Besides, my brain began to rattle me with a question I couldn't take my mind off of: what if I stopped reading a book just before I found some useful information? The knowledge of that possibility haunted me.

But as time went on, I realized as intriguing as this book may be, it wasn't for me, so I set it aside. Maybe that was a book for some sort of witch or sorcerer, but not me. I stood to examine the other books along the shelves. Most were solid neutral covers of blacks and browns merely collecting dust, but then one in particular caught my eyes.

A dark green tome sat on the top shelf. I reached for it, and noted its intricate detailing.

It was trimmed with swirls of gold lining all across the cover, and flakes and specks of gold were scattered along its spine, retreating onto the front and back. The book looked rather new, at least compared to the ones around it. There was no doubt it was coated in less dust.

The ache of my growling stomach halted my examination, and I remembered the snare. Lunchtime. I replaced the book back in its original spot on the top shelf and trekked outside to see if I'd gotten lucky with my trap.

To my surprise, a rabbit was waiting for me, hanging limp just above the ground. I untied it and carried it home along with my rope, its body still warm in my grasp. Now, it was time to feast on a real meal.

After I returned, I skinned the rabbit outside with a hunting knife from my pack, steam rising from its freshly deceased body, and placed it above the fire that Zorath had graciously lit for us.

Zorath began to nip at the raw meat.

"We have to wait." I told him.

"I'm impatient," he said, sitting on his hind legs to keep himself from snatching at the food again.

"I don't care. You can always go outside for some extra food if you need to. You don't always have to wait for me to eat."

"Yes, Master," he replied, and scurried off to leap out of an open window.

I rolled my eyes, refusing once again to respond. He's incapable of listening—like a real child.

The remainder of the afternoon I invested in another book as I ate my rabbit. While I let it cook, I noticed a book with a dragon symbol embossed on the spine titled *Luminara: The Dragons' Awakening.* The first few pages were about the history of dragons in our realm and where they came from. I kept reading.

The capital of Luminara, Velorum, is where the winds hum with magic. This magic is called Illumae, and it is the breath of the realm itself. It flows from the core of the earth to the farthest edges of the continents, but it flourishes like a wild garden in Velorum. It is here, within this radiant city, that the marvelous creatures we call dragons, are born. These dragons are born from the very essence of the Illumae, and in turn, dragons create Illumae, keeping Luminara thriving. When dragons mate, the abundance of this magic gives life to each egg.

There are a variety of dragon breeds known to Luminara.

The Amberclaw is a beast of flame and fury. Their breath is not merely fire, but an inferno of pure energy, capable of turning forests to ash and splitting stone with the intensity of their heat. But their claws are primarily what they are known for: long and sharp, they are like molten iron, able to slice through the toughest of armors, even those made of Diamondtail scales. Amberclaws are fiercely territorial, and only those with an unshakable will and strength can hope to form a bond with them, and even then, they are a stubborn breed to connect with. The riders of this species must learn to control their own inner fire, for if not, the dragon's overwhelming heat can consume them entirely.

The Stormscale is as silent as a breeze. Their wingspan is the largest of the known species, allowing them to ride the wind with grace and swiftness. Their scales shift in subtle shades of silver and blue, making them hard to find in the sky on a bright, sunny day. While they do breathe fire, their strength relies on their intelligence and cunning. While they are not as powerful as other breeds physically, they excel in speed, agility, and trickery, often using wind or weather to outmaneuver their foes.

The Diamondtail is a creature forged in the heart of Luminara's deepest caverns. As dark as night itself, its scales portray an inky black that seems to absorb the light around them. These scales are not only a beautiful sight to see in person, but they are incredibly strong. Diamondtail's scales are often sought after by blacksmiths and artisans. When properly forged, they create armor stronger than any metal. Armies have wielded these scales for shields and breastplates, and no weapon can pierce its surface other than the talons of an Amberclaw. But their scales are resistant to magic, a feature that no other dragon possesses, making them the most coveted resource for those who seek invulnerability in battle. Its tail is long and adorned with jagged, diamond-like protrusions, and the force of its blow can shatter stone. In the rare occurrence a Diamondtail chooses to bond, it chooses its rider carefully. It seeks someone whose heart is as strong and unyielding as its scales.

The rarest of them all is the Nocthale. They are as rare as a comet's passing. Their scales are an array of never-ending colors, flickering like the light of stars scattered across the night sky. Ancient texts speak only in whispers of their origins, suggesting they are a manifestation of the Illumae itself. They only hatch under specific circumstances, when the alignment of celestial forces is just right, usually under the light of a full moon.

To encounter an iridescent is to be chosen, though for what exact purpose the elders cannot say. What is known, however, is that the bond between such a dragon and its rider is unlike any other, especially in this breed. The last known rider of a Nocthale is King Polaris III.

When a dragon bonds, it is not a bond of mere loyalty or companionship, but a shared consciousness. It is a link that allows for the exchange of thoughts and feelings. With practice, a rider can communicate directly with their dragon without having to speak aloud. To the untrained mind, this bond is imperceptible, but to those who have lived with dragons, it is the most natural of things.

To form a bond with a dragon is a privilege few can claim, and it is a bond that cannot be broken. Once formed, it lasts a lifetime. A dragon is not merely a companion; it is a reflection of its rider's heart and soul, its strength and resolve.

I sat back, my brain whirling. So much information had just been crammed into my head, yet it was the most useful, most intriguing thing that I had read so far on this entire trip.

Zorath was a Nocthale, the rarest of dragon breeds. I found him the night after a full moon. He hatched on the night of a full moon. I still had no idea why he came to me, or why he chose me, but he did.

And King Polaris, our High King, used to ride one. *Ride* one. I could only imagine that it would be years before I would be able to ride Zorath, if he grew large enough to carry me before I died, that is. The physics of his size versus mine just wouldn't work for quite some time.

"Zorath, did you know I could learn to speak to you?"

"You're speaking to me now."

Sarcastic ass. I huffed. "In your head. Just like you do with me."

"I suspected it," he replied, munching on the rest of his rabbit as he stared into the fire.

"Fair enough. I'm glad you could help," I said with a roll of my eyes.

I sat back and recited what I had just read. With practice, a rider can communicate directly with their dragon without having to speak aloud.

I skimmed the next few pages, and stopped when I saw a paragraph that mentioned the bond.

The bond between you and your dragon exists always, though it may not always be felt. It is like an invisible thread between your very beings. You must reach for that thread with your mind to speak internally with your dragon.

"Sounds easy enough, I suppose." I shrugged.

Straightening my spine, I allowed myself to sit with perfect posture to relax my mind. I visualized Zorath, his scales shimmering distinctly in the moonlight. I saw the way his eyes gleamed at me with every breath he took. I *saw* him. *I felt* him.

Within only a minute or two, the string that connected us appeared, an iridescent sparkle linking us together. It vibrated softly in my mind.

The fire crackled in the fireplace, breaking my concentration, and the string disappeared. And then, Zorath left with it.

"Try again," he ordered. *"I felt you there, but I didn't see you."*

That was the only motivation I needed. He *did* feel my presence through the bond, I just wasn't close enough. So I tried again.

I failed, unable to find a way to pull on that string. It was a difficult feat trying to become a physical being in a mental realm.

I tried again, seeing his little body standing there, waiting for me. I reached for the thread, and my real hand hit the underside of the desk with a hard *thud*.

"Ouch," I whispered as the image faded again.

I tried once more, and failed again. And again. And another time. Until my temples pounded and my muscles grew rigid. A bead of sweat prickled my forehead. I couldn't get closer to him for the life of me. My bones began to tremble under my skin. I knew I was dehydrated . . . and tired. Tired of trying with no success.

A bundle of frustration bubbled up with every breath, consuming my being. My blood ran boiling hot through my veins. The bead of sweat ran down the bridge of my nose, and fell onto the open book in front of me. I felt the agitation in my blood as it grew hotter. And *hotter*. It needed to come out. Sweating it out wouldn't do.

So, I let it out. I yelled, and my fists slammed down onto the table.

From each fist, a spark of green flame burst upward, and then it was gone.

CHAPTER FOURTEEN

THE NEXT MORNING, I awoke on my own. No bad dream present. And yet, I'd hardly slept.

When I saw the flames in my hands last night, I jumped up from my seat. It was there so briefly, and then it was gone. I would've believed that it was my tired mind playing tricks on me if Zorath hadn't leaped up at the same time. He was just as startled as I was.

So I laid in bed the majority of the night, sleeping here and there in short spurts. My mind raced with questions.

How had it been possible for me to conjure *fire?* I read almost all of that book two days ago regarding spells and conjurings, and remembered every word. None of them pertained to what I had just done, only witches and sorcerers with their conjured spells and hexes.

What I'd done, I didn't instigate it. Not on purpose. No series of incantations were spoken, and I hadn't done anything specific that I knew of to conjure fire to my palms, so it was truly a mystery to me.

I began the same routine as the previous day, setting up the snare with fruits and vegetables as bait in the woods outside. After Zorath and I both split that rabbit yesterday, we didn't have any leftovers for last night or today.

I made eye contact with my dragon. "Today is the day that I figure out all this mind-to-mind shit with you."

"Good morning to you, too," he replied.

I summoned him outside as I kicked off my boots, the daylight peeking in behind the treeline. I sat down and crossed my legs, my pants immediately soaked in the dewy grass, but it was the least of my concerns. Zorath settled on his back legs in front of me, wings folded in, and his attention focused solely on me.

"Alright, let me know if you see me," I told him, closing my eyes.

"*I see you right now.*"

"Shut up," I chuckled, then regrouped myself.

The morning air around me was crisp, and the sunlight filtering in casted long shadows along the forest floor that surrounded us. The scent of damp earth and pine filled my senses, grounding me, and I began to breathe deeply.

In through my nose. Out through my mouth.

My body relaxed in its upright position, the tension from last night finally easing up.

Minutes passed, the concentration on my surroundings unwavering. Zorath sat completely still, waiting for me to find and tug at that invisible string between us.

I wiggled my toes, the grass and the dirt under my bare feet seeping into my skin.

The sun climbed higher, warming the air around us. Sweat retreated from my hairline and down my temple.

Then he was there, sitting in front of me in my mind just as he sat in front of me in real life. The string glistened, like rays of sunlight on the ocean's waves. It called to me. I reached out, not with my physical hand, but with my mental one, and I drew nearer to him.

The string tightened, and it pulled me forward some more.

"*I felt you strongly, there,*" Zorath confirmed.

I tugged again, yanking him closer to me. He was just in front of me now, and I could feel his soul connected to mine. Any closer, and we would become one being.

"*I see you, Master.*"

"*I see you, too,*" I responded, but the words did not escape my lips. They were in my head. "I did it!" I exclaimed, this time out loud as I opened my eyes. I hopped to my feet, and Zorath copied.

"You should try again. Try to make a stronger connection this time."

I closed my eyes once more and searched for him in my mind. It wasn't just the sense of the string that tethered us together, or the sight of him in my head, it was a feeling deep in my soul where he and I were connected. That's what I reached for.

"How are you, Zorath?" I spoke.

"Great!" He shot up and let out a cry as he hopped through the grass, wings flared as wide as they could go.

I couldn't help but chuckle and let out a heavy breath filled with relief. I reached down to pet him, his scales gliding smoothing under my fingers.

I was on the right path with figuring out our bond. No. *We* were on the right path. Here. Together. A healthy combination of relief and excitement was building within me as thoughts rushed through my mind. Not only did I have a dragon now, but I was *bonded* to one. I could be a rider one day.

One day.

"I'm drained," I announced out loud as I took a break from reading about dragon lore to snack on some dehydrated meat for dinner.

We hadn't had luck catching a rabbit today, so the feeling of malnourishment was hitting me like a brick to the head. My energy levels had crashed, and it was difficult to keep my eyes focused on the pages in front of me. Everything ran together. After the mental energy that it took to learn how to communicate with Zorath this morning, sleep felt like the only thing that could possibly help me at this point.

The sun dipped lower beyond the trees, various shades of light streaming through the windows. We hydrated and we ate and we tried a little longer to make it through this book.

But it felt like a chore. My eyelids would hardly stay open. My head pounded harder and harder with every page I turned, like thunder was rumbling through my brain. I had found a book on the shelf that I thought would have been more interesting than it was, yet after a few hours of skimming page after page, nothing was sticking.

"Are you okay?" Zorath propped his front paws on the edge of my desk and stared up at me with curious eyes.

"I'm drained," I repeated through our bond as I closed my eyes.

At least this trip wasn't completely useless. I did learn how to talk to my dragon, though I still needed more practice for it to become effortless, and I learned about dragon breeds in the process.

I washed up before bed and climbed into the sheets slightly discouraged. I could somehow sense Zorath growing bored, though he never complained to me.

"I'm not bored," he blurted into my head.

"Thanks for reading my thoughts," I said aloud, a bite in my tone, not bothering to find the energy to speak through our mental bond right now. "I'm still sorry I dragged you here. I thought this would be easier and more relaxing for us."

He found a place on top of the comforter to nestle in. *"You didn't drag me here. I am with you, always."* His voice was hardly above a whisper as he closed his eyes.

There was always tomorrow.

Two days had gone by in a flash, my time primarily spent indulging in that book about dragons and learning about their breeds and their history. Though only the Nocthale pertained to me—as Zorath *was* the last dragon alive—I wanted to be well-read in every subject regarding dragons that I could.

The grumble in my stomach lifted my drooping eyelids.

I blew out the candle next to me and stumbled my way through the dark room back to the bedroom, where Zorath slept soundly on top of the comforter. The dim break of dawn peeked through the window panes, allowing just enough light for me to find the bag I'd come here with. I'd only been here for a few days and I was already running out of clothes. Clean clothes, at least.

As though the cottage had read my mind, a small armoire sat tucked away against the far wall of the bedroom. If it had been there this whole time, I never noticed it. Inside was a top. A long-sleeve, dark green tunic that once I put on, flowed down past my hips and cinched tighter around the waist with an intertwining gold belt etched into the fabric. The gold detailing weaved through the sleeves and ran up from the belt around the neckline in various shapes and patterns. A fresh pair of brown pants were next to it, and they fit me like a glove—a very comfortable glove.

The top was easily the most beautiful piece of clothing I'd ever worn, one I wished we could afford to buy more of at home.

I pulled the top half of my hair back into twists behind my head and secured them with clips, then laced up my boots. Once I finished, I rigged up the fishing line securely to the fishing pole that my father provided me.

Zorath rustled against the sheets and yawned into a stretch until his sleepy eyes met mine.

"What are we doing?"

"We're going fishing."

His eyes widened to twice their size, and he leapt from the bed, the sounds of his claws against the wood floor trailing all the way to the front door. He needn't say more. I snatched my bag, some dried meat, and an empty basket and shot for the door, buckling my belt with the dagger attached on my way.

Stepping out into the morning light, the crisp chill in the air filled my nostrils. The trees swayed with careful practice in the soft breeze as the dawn began to touch their leaves.

I had a feeling it would be a good day today. No bad dreams last night. I had a beautiful new top to wear today. And, I was finally starting to learn something from the books here. I had a streak of good luck going for me.

My ears twitched as I focused all of my senses into listening for a nearby source of water. We had to cross a creek to get here, so I knew there had to be a river or a pond or a lake nearby.

As though it were right under my nose, the faint sound of running water tickled my ears.

"Let's go," I gestured to my dragon and nodded toward the treeline. Then, we left the comfort of the cottage.

It took us no more than twenty minutes of walking to find the stream. It would have taken less time if we didn't have to trudge through dense brush and around thick trees. I snacked on some of the packed meat to keep my hunger at bay until I could catch some fish for the potential feast later. The sounds of gushing water grew louder as we approached until we were met with the sight of a steadily flowing creek. The sun's rising flame reflected atop the trickling water.

My bag fell to the ground with a thud, and I crouched low to take out all of my necessary supplies. I set the wicker basket from the cottage onto a dry, flat patch of dirt on the bank in preparation to hold the fish we caught.

I glanced at Zorath, whose eyes sparkled with nothing but curiosity and excitement. His scales glistened in shades of green and gold as he eagerly stretched out his wings behind him. He was such an animated little creature, and had such a unique personality. I was so thankful to have him by my side. He was *my* dragon. His mind flowed with mine just as effortlessly as this stream did.

We settled in, Zorath climbing on top of a small boulder as I propped up against a larger one next to him. Any anxiousness I may have had eased away as the soothing melody of water babbling over the smooth stones filled my ears. It's like I was at the beach listening to the waves lapping against the shore. It was peaceful.

I carefully baited my hook with a worm I found buried in the dirt under some nearby stones. Zorath, meanwhile, began fluttering toward the water with every fish that he spotted near the bank. He dipped his claws in in an attempt to catch one, but of course, the fish were much faster and darted from his grasp.

I casted my line, and the rod arched ever so slightly as the worm plopped into the creek. The water ran just clear enough where the fish could be seen swimming in from upstream. Their silvery scales couldn't stay hidden under the surface as they caught the light from the sun.

The peace of the moment enveloped me until I felt a gentle tug on my line. My eyes widened, and I tightened my grip on the pole. Zorath focused in along with me. Another tug, this time a little stronger, and so I firmly pulled upwards and began to reel. The fish put up a good fight, but I won. It flailed out of the water, and somehow ended up right in Zorath's mouth as it reached the bank.

"We were supposed to be keeping that for later, you know."

"Sorry."

I laughed and casted my line again once I found another worm in the moist dirt.

We immersed ourselves in the solitude and the quiet of the moment. Zorath splashed into the water, occasionally catching small fish that ran into his grasp. He'd indulge immediately, but I didn't scold him because the more he ate, the more he'd grow. If he was hungry, he should eat.

I started reeling them in. We caught fish after fish, the glow of the day rising higher above our heads with each passing moment.

"How many animals do you think died in this forest during the war?" I asked Zorath down that bond—that invisible string—in my brain. Just for practice.

"I'm not sure. Probably many."

"My father and I hardly ever had luck hunting out here when I was a child. It's like the magic that held this kingdom together was lost and never returned. The Illumae.*"*

The fish were plentiful, but the other wildlife seemed scarce. I hadn't seen a deer since we'd been here. Only squirrels and rabbits and birds.

Almost two hours passed since we'd come out here to fish, and the heat of the day began to beat down on my skin. I eyed the basket I'd brought for the fish and found that we had at least six trout there waiting to be cooked. That should be enough for today and possibly some for tomorrow. That is, if Zorath actually got full from his endless feast and wouldn't be stealing all the fish that I cooked.

We packed up quickly. There would be a lot to do to get these fish descaled, filleted, and cooked for lunch.

Zorath extended his wings behind him the whole way back. That usually meant he was happy. There was a hum of excitement building up in my blood that must have been spilling over from his mind into mine.

Was sharing emotions like that even possible with our bond?

"Yes."

I looked down at him ahead of me. "What's got you so chirpy today?"

"I love fish. It was the first food I ever ate."

The first food I'd ever fed him was fish from the market, so now it made sense that it was his favorite food. This had by far been his favorite part of our trip.

The break in the trees showed the clearing growing closer, and my eyes stayed locked on my dragon as his energy levels soared. His wings flapped behind him, he cooed and galloped head. He'd stop for only a moment to allow me to catch up, and then he'd take off again.

I don't think he realized that *I* was the one carrying the backpack of supplies and the basket of fish.

But as we approached the clearing, he calmed down and tucked in his wings. That hum of joy in my veins settled down with him. He fell back to my side.

I only realized why when I looked up the stone pathway that led to the cottage and the basket of fish fell from my grasp.

Jameson stood at the door.

CHAPTER FIFTEEN

JAMESON. THE ONE THAT had informed me of this cottage's existence. The one that had been my father's apprentice and helped me in his shop. He was standing at the doorway.

I wouldn't be at this cottage if it weren't for him.

He slowly turned to face me as I stumbled up the walkway, the basket of fish now back in my grasp. His tan tunic with golden stitching shone in the light, and neatly matched his clean hair and the necklace at his throat.

"Valora," his lips curved into a smile at the words, "I was just coming to check on you." A lump grew in my throat as he looked me up and down, staring at my green and gold outfit that wasn't really mine. "You look beautiful."

I gulped, but no words came to my head. How could this ordinary man make me speechless? It must be because I'd never heard those words from anyone but inappropriate men that only wanted me for one thing. My lungs felt so small and heavy.

"Breathe. Use your words." Zorath appeared beside me, and focused his attention on me. He was right. I had to breathe. I had to say something. *Anything.* I took a deep breath as I finished my ascent and stood in front of Jameson.

"I'd ask you how you got here, but you're the one that told me how to get here," I chuckled, and he only grinned in response. "I caught some fish. Do you want some?"

"Sounds delicious," he nodded, allowing me in the doorway ahead of him. At the desk I'd been reading on, we descaled the fish and filleted them for cooking. Once they were settled over the fire and roasting, we settled on a bench against the wall outside the cottage that I'd never even noticed before now. Well, I hadn't really walked to that side for any reason, but still. Flowers and bushes surrounded us, perfuming us with fresh scents.

"Your shirt almost matches mine," I pointed to the golden fabric of his tunic then gestured to mine.

"Well, look at that. It sure does."

I met his eyes. "What are you doing here?"

"I was just coming to see you and check on you. Your parents miss you dearly. Your father won't stop talking about you, and bragging about how grown and strong of a woman you've become."

A blush grew to my cheeks, and I lowered my head as I played with the cracks of my fingernails in my lap. "Did *you* miss me dearly, Jameson?" I lightly nudged his knee with my own.

"Yes," he said whilst beaming back at me, the tanness of his face bringing out the glow of his smile.

My face neutralized, not expecting the short and sweet response. "How do you know about this place anyway?" I changed the subject as quickly as possible in hopes to not make things awkward.

His gaze drifted off into the trees, like the answer was out there ahead of us. "This place is actually an old family heirloom. It's always meant the most to me, though. No one has hardly used it except for me and you." His eyes landed in his lap. "It's quite a long and complicated story as to how this place possesses the magic it does, but it always makes me feel at home."

His words strangely resonated with me. This place had made me feel at home while being here, and it was comforting to know that if I ever came back, that it would continue to provide me with what I needed to feel at home. It was comforting to know that someone else felt the same way I did about it.

"Well, I hope I haven't overstayed my welcome here."

"Of course not. I wouldn't have told you to come here if I thought you would."

I smiled. "You want to go check on lunch?"

He nodded and we ventured back inside. It was almost done cooking. Zorath was curled up for a nap next to the fireplace.

"Our little fishing adventure must have worn him out." I whispered to Jameson.

He snickered as he led me toward the walls of books that lined the cottage.

"I grew up reading this one right here," he pointed to a small book on the second shelf from the bottom. "It's a fairytale, but a good one that describes all sorts of monsters that attack kingdoms and a hero that destroys them all. And this one," he pointed to one on the opposite end of that wall, two shelves up. "This one is a cute love story of how a princess and a knight fall in love. Two people that you wouldn't expect to fall for each other, fall hard. It's a good one to read if you find the time." His eyes met mine with a softness I hadn't yet seen from him.

I responded to his book remarks by showing him a few of the ones that I'd read so far, or tried to read.

"This one had so many spells and potions in it, but I knew I'd never be able to use them, as cool as it sounded."

"That one has always intrigued me," he replied. "But I felt the same way about it."

Once we finished our walkthrough, the cottage began to smell of freshly roasted fish, and my stomach grumbled again. Jameson stepped over to the fire and plated it for us, setting some aside to cool to be wrapped up for later.

We stepped outside to the bench to eat. The chirping of birds and the wind drifting through the trees made this the most peaceful meal I'd had in a long time.

Jameson offered to tell me a little more about his childhood as we ate, and about this cottage being necessary for him to spend his time. I tried to ask him about his parents again since he never spoke about them at work, but he dodged the question and moved on to another topic when I asked. I took the hint. His family, whatever kind of people they may be, may have been the sole reason he liked to escape here in the first place. I noted it as a touchy subject.

The fish tasted magical. The blend of seasonings Jameson had smothered them with was so delectable that I could put up against my mom's trout recipe.

I'd never tell her that, though.

We headed back inside after our plates were cleaned. The midday sun glistened through the windows, illuminating every surface. Zorath had just woken up when we stepped through the threshold.

"Oh, here's a book that I meant to show you. I find this one fascinating." Jameson wandered over to the left wall, scanning the shelves until he picked up a book that triggered my memory. He turned around to unveil the green book that I'd seen just days ago. The gold spread throughout the cover caught the light as he brought it over to the desk.

"I'd seen that book before, but I'd forgotten about it, I suppose."

He didn't respond. Instead, he smiled down at me with his chocolate-brown eyes and motioned for me to sit at the desk. I followed him.

He pulled up a nearby stool that seemed to appear out of thin air, and started to flip through the pages as he sat down. My eyes darted back and forth between the book and his blonde locks falling in front of his brow, his features laser-focused.

"I found something in here one day recently that I think you'd find intriguing." I continued to watch the book until he made it about halfway through and stopped. "I think this is it. Yes. Here, read this to me and tell me what you think." He nudged the book closer to me, and I read the series of lines out loud.

Beneath the moon's full, guiding light,
A child of scales and fire bright,
From dragon's egg, they will arise,

With emerald eyes and fierce ties.
Their hands shall hold the realm's fate near,
To save or destroy, their path unclear,
With heart of pure or vengeance bold,
The story of the realm unfolds.
If noble thoughts and deeds they bring,
Peace and magic their power sings,
But if their soul turns dark and cold,
Ash and ruin shall take hold.
The choice within their heart will lie,
To lift the realm or see it die,
For in the dragonblood's flame,
The realm's destiny finds its name.

When I'd completed reading, I made eye contact with Jameson. "What does this mean?"

"That's why I wanted to show it to you. It sounds to me like some sort of prophecy. When I first read it, it meant nothing to me and I didn't think much of it. Then I met you, and it started to make more sense." His hand brushed a stray hair from my temple to better view my face. "The emerald eyes. The dragonblood. It all clicks."

I looked back at the words on the page and skimmed it once more. "It could just be coincidental. I'm not sure—"

A sudden knock at the door accompanied by the shuffling of footsteps broke me from thought.

CHAPTER SIXTEEN

Silence sucked the air from the room.

Jameson said himself that he and I were the only people that have used the cottage.

I shared a look of concern with Jameson, and his face reciprocated it. He straightened up, his face hardening into confidence, and quietly went to the bedroom, emerging a moment later with the sword he'd gifted me before I'd come here. *My* sword.

He placed it carefully in my hand and closed my fingers around the grip for me, his eyes locking with mine. "Stay behind me. I don't think you'll have to use this, but no one should be here, so be prepared. I'll try to handle it myself first." I nodded, feeling the cold weight of the sword in my palm growing heavier by the second.

He approached the door and opened it with purpose.

I couldn't believe my eyes. Judah, Jovis, and Javie all stood at the door, their silhouettes dark against the afternoon sun, peering in with malicious intent. Judah's eyes were glossed over with a sinister light as he spoke. "We're here for the girl. *And* her dragon." A deathly smile crept to his lips.

Jameson straightened up, his stance protective. "She's not yours to take."

"She owes us an apology. We won't have to take her if she confesses she done us wrong." Judah lifted his shirt, a gnarly scar appearing where I'd stabbed him just weeks before.

"Too bad you didn't kill the guy," Zorath said.

"I was thinking the same thing." He should be dead. He should have bled out.

"She doesn't owe you anything," Jameson retorted, his voice steady as stone.

Rage trickled through me as the men bantered back and forth—one trying to protect me, the others trying to take me, harm me. But the devastating thought ran through my head: Jameson wouldn't be able to protect me against all three of them. Not while I was the one with the sword in my hand.

Zorath growled from behind me, a low, menacing sound that filled the small space. I turned to shush him, but it was too late.

"I hear that dragon of hers. Give them to us." Jovis spoke up from the back, his voice dripping with contempt.

I stepped forward, accepting whatever fate may come to me. "You aren't taking me, and you aren't taking my dragon away from this cottage." I now stood next to Jameson, holding my sword in plain view in front of me. I was ready to use it if need be. All three of them eyed the blade, then focused back on me without a budge.

"What? You gonna stab me again?" Judah tilted his head, a mocking smirk playing at his lips. The tension in the air was palpable.

"If you come close enough, I'll do more than just that." My voice held steady, but I felt Jameson stiffen next to me.

I didn't falter.

There were three of them, and three of us. I had a dragon, a sword, and a dagger at my hip. If we were strategic enough, we could drive them away and we could live past this.

Maybe.

"We'll see," Judah's eyes glinted with malice as he unsheathed a large dagger and lunged at me. I met his attack with my sword, the clash of metal ringing out as I forced myself out of the doorway and onto the stone path.

They backed away, allowing me into the open space, and I took an extra step forward, Zorath and Jameson on my tail.

"Valora," Jameson's tone was a mix of concern and warning, but I wouldn't back down. This would be their final warning from me, and then they would never come for us again.

Judah swung his blade once more, but I blocked him and thrusted my sword forward, narrowly missing him. Suddenly, Javie and Jovis unsheathed identical blades, and I found myself facing three armed men.

Shit.

"You didn't think we'd come unprepared this time, did you?" Javie sneered, sleazy smiles growing on his and Jovis's faces.

They anticipated this. They wanted a fight. Revenge.

Zorath appeared just on the side of me, growling uncontrollably. He wouldn't attack unless he knew it was necessary or unless ordered. I stood my ground and waited for their next move.

Judah stepped forward and I intercepted his blow once again, shoving him out of the way with my blade. Javie advanced next, but I dodged his attack, ending up closer to Jovis. He swung at me, but with my smaller frame and swift movements, I knocked the blade from his grasp, sending it flying into a tall section of grass. He ran off to search for it, leaving me with the other two.

Jameson stood to the side, his face a mix of awe and disbelief. It didn't seem like he'd ever seen a fight before. Not like this. He stood frozen to his spot, his eyes wide as the chaos unfolded before him.

Judah advanced once more, our blades clashing with a metallic ring as neither one of us could land a fatal attack. I cut the sleeve of his tunic as I pulled back, leaving a small gash in his arm. Blood seeped through the fabric, but he hardly flinched.

Javie was on the side of me, and I spun to dodge his attack again, slicing the bottom of his leg as he marched past. He stumbled, clutching his leg, his face hardly contorted in pain.

"Apologize!" Judah shouted at me, his voice filled with fury. Jovis hadn't approached with his blade yet, and Javie was still on a knee, caressing the wound I gave him.

"No." I spat, and charged at him once more. He defended himself, his eyes blazing with venom as he yelled at me again.

"Apologize!" His rage grew, but so did mine.

"No." He repeated himself over and over as we fought, and I stuck to my word, each refusal fueling my determination.

Javie got to his feet, and Jovis finally approached, his blade in hand. I snatched the dagger from my waist, and flung it straight at his chest, sending him stumbling backward as it landed. But he pulled it out within a matter of seconds, and flung it to the side.

"What the—"

My sword was knocked from my hand. That distraction may have cost me. Judah neared just as Zorath leapt to my side and growled, his eyes locked on the advancing men.

Jameson ran for the sword, but the three of them were growing so close now, that it probably wouldn't make a difference.

He may watch me die here.

"Apologize," Judah said in a firm, but less harsh tone than earlier. He knew he had the advantage now.

I glanced between the three of them and shook my head. My blood boiled. Rage seeped from my gaze as I shared eye contact with each of them. I could feel every muscle in my body tensing at the thought of beating these men—of finally ending them.

I looked at Zorath. I had never seen him so angry. His eyes met mine for a split second, and they were fierce, burning with intensity that matched the storm brewing within me. A low, menacing growl rumbled from his throat as he stood protectively by my side. Though he'd only grown to a couple feet tall, his wings were flared, making his appearance even larger and more intimidating. His face showed no mercy.

Neither did mine.

"Apologize," Judah said again, his voice seeping with venom as he readied his blade.

I didn't respond. Instead, I grounded myself to the earth below my boots, my gaze unwavering as I stared at all three of them, raw power coursing through my veins. And I saw red.

"Apologi—" Judah began, but I cut him off.

"No."

Before anyone else could move, both of my palms were raised in front of me facing all three of them. A blast of green light shot from my hands in a fiery rage.

CHAPTER SEVENTEEN

A FLASH OF FIRE. Green fire. More than Zorath or I had ever produced single-handedly.

Once my dragon saw what I was doing, he followed suit. Fire blasted from his mouth, junctioning with the wide path of my flame.

It only took a few seconds for us to stop. Because I heard it . . . the screaming.

The screams of men burning alive.

Judah, Javie, and Jovis rolled and tumbled on the grass, trying to put out the flames eating away at their flesh. But it was no use. Too much damage had been done already.

A few minutes later, their cries grew quieter. They'd be dead any moment, if they weren't already.

Then the silence followed. The silence was the worst part.

I stood frozen in place staring at the crisp corpses before me. At what I had just done. They were just alive, and now they weren't.

Jameson cautiously eased his way toward me, like I was a bug he was debating on squashing, unsure if I was a threat to him or not. He rested a hand gently on my shoulder and I flinched at the touch.

"Sorry," he said, his gaze fluttering between me and the bodies.

"I—" I stumbled over my words. "I didn't know I could do that. I'd seen a spark erupt from my palms once before, but it was nothing like that. That was . . ." I drifted off into nothingness.

"I never would have guessed you were capable of that." There wasn't an ounce of quivering in his voice, unlike mine. "But if you could learn to master those flames, learn to wield them as you wished, you'd have one badass power, m'lady. I mean, Valora." He chuckled once.

I looked at his face, into his eyes. "You don't think less of me? For . . . for what I did?"

"No. They seemed like people that needed to be taken out. They were toxic to this world. They were destroying you."

I smiled faintly as I stared ahead of me, frankly uncomfortable now with the entire situation that just unfolded before us. I killed people, and Jameson didn't seem to have a care in the world. But he was right. This happened for a reason. They needed to be rid of.

"I'm sorry about the yard."

"This place has magic embedded into the earth. The grass is the least of my concerns. The cottage will take care of it as it sees fit. Let's get you inside." He placed his arm around my shoulders and led me back inside the cottage. I sat gently on the bed, where Jameson took his place next to me. Zorath wedged his snout under my hand, resting his chin on my leg. "I knew they were bad people, and they had what was coming to them, Valora. I just didn't know that you'd *char* them like that."

I finally looked at him again, truly understanding now that they *did* get what was coming to them. "Those men did unspeakable things to me. They did deserve it. They deserved to die." I shifted my focus back to the wall in front of me.

Jameson must have understood all the wild thoughts that were running through my head. He wrapped an arm around my shoulders and rested his other hand on my knee, pulling me to him. "Take all the time you need to get through this. Just know that you've done the world a good thing, because they were bad people."

"I just didn't mean to be so . . . so *violent*," I retorted, the thought of burning people alive haunting me.

He didn't respond.

However, my mind continued to wander. I knew I'd wanted those guys dead, especially Judah. But I didn't see it happening the way it did. They'd kidnapped me. Twice. Then raped me. I thought my stabbing attempt would drive them away. Instead, it seemed to have provoked them more. I thought after I'd done it, then he would go die on his own and I wouldn't have had to *watch* them die.

Deep down, I *was* glad I was the one that decided their fate, but I was afraid it would haunt me the rest of my life.

When my brain ventured back to reality again, the sunlight was disappearing. I must have been in a daze for a while. I hadn't noticed Jameson leave the room or noticed when Zorath had moved from under my hand, and was now on the bed behind me, keeping me propped up with his body.

I stood to find Jameson, my dragon perking up with me and following.

"Hey, there she is," Jameson's voice broke the silence of the cottage as I entered the main room. He was squatting next to the fireplace. "I took the liberty of heating the leftover fish for dinner. I hope you don't mind it twice in one day."

A grin took over my lips. "Not at all."

We settled in a nook of the cottage, surrounded by piles of books and using them to prop ourselves up comfortably.

Dinner was practically inhaled, assuming because my body was drained from the power I'd released today. Jameson led most of our conversation, allowing me to focus on eating my food. Most of what he talked about involved our experiences at the forge, and described some funny stories of my father that I wasn't present for. I laughed. I hadn't done that much recently.

He reiterated how much my parents missed me, and my smile faded. I missed them too.

"They'll be glad to know that you're safe whenever you decide to go back home."

"They won't have to worry for too much longer. I think I'm about done here," I responded as my head faced the empty plate of food on my lap.

"Are you sure?"

I made eye contact with him. "Yes. I've seen and done enough here for one trip. I don't think I can be alone here another day after what I did out there."

Jameson's eyes softened into mine. "I understand." The corners of his mouth twitched up slightly as he rested an arm around my back. "You don't have to be alone, though." He stroked the hair away from my face with his free hand. "I hope you know how beautiful you are."

It was something I'd heard many times over, but never believed for myself. Not really. I'd never heard it in this context from someone my age. Someone *attractive* that was my age.

"I'm glad you think I am."

"You are," he reassured, and my cheeks heated. I focused my gaze back down to a random book in front of me. He lifted my chin back up to face him. He brushed another fallen stray hair from my temple, his thumb grazing the skin on my cheek.

We were close. So close. I knew he could hear the quiver in my breath, see the tremble in my lip. I tried to look away again to hide the nervous buildup of energy, but I couldn't. His hand cupped my chin with purpose, forcing my gaze to lock onto his. His eyes, a beautiful deep brown, seemed to hold me captive. The arm he kept behind me rested on my shoulder, and his other hand slowly found its way to my knee, fingers tracing hypnotic patterns against the fabric of my pants. A shiver flew up my spine.

With a slow inhale, I attempted to steady my breath, but the anxiety and anticipation was overwhelming. His presence enveloped me. His eyes never wavered from mine. As I exhaled, he pulled me toward him, our bodies inching closer. Closer.

Until his lips eased onto mine, a little heavy at first, but then I felt them soften. His lips were tender, warm, ready. I'd never been kissed before, but this was a moment that I'd been waiting for for a long while.

He pulled away and stood, gesturing me upward. His hand grasped my own as he led me toward the bedroom. Jameson's hand then wrapped around my waist, guiding me down as we sat side-by-side at the foot of the bed.

He pulled me to him with purpose, closing the gap between us. His other hand cradled my jaw as his lips once again met mine, this time with a more driving force. He kissed me heavily, and I kissed him back, our bodies drawing nearer with each passing second.

Jameson's hand drifted lower, fingers gliding down the entirety of my tunic until he reached its hem at the bottom. His fingers played with the fabric, teasingly tugging on it. I pulled away ever so slightly to look at him, my breath trembling.

I'd never been so nervous.

He grasped the bottom of my tunic with both hands and lifted it straight over my head in a practiced motion, leaving me in only a bra. He repeated the movement with his own shirt, unveiling a lean figure that I never would have imagined existing underneath his clothes. His skin seemed to glow in the dim light, each contour of his body proof of the strength he used for his work.

He advanced toward my boots, untying and sliding them off with precision. I went to help him with my pants as he reached for the buttons, but he slid them off within a second. Each movement was deliberate, and his touch sent waves of electricity through me.

He cupped my jaw with both of his hands, standing over me while I stayed seated at the edge of the bed. He kissed me hard, as if he'd been waiting for me to give myself to him this whole time—waiting for *me*. My hands fumbled around the top of his pants until he pulled away slightly.

"It's a little hard to do with shaky hands. I don't know why I'm shaking so much," I admitted, feeling a warmth spread through me as he stared down at me. He slid his pants down with a swift motion, revealing his excitement through his undergarments, then met my eyes again. "I'm sorry I couldn't—"

"Shhh . . ." he whispered as he moved in.

My breathing grew heavier, my chest visibly rising and falling with each labored breath. His body pushed my back onto the comforter as he positioned himself over me from the foot of the bed, lips crashing against mine with a ravenous hunger I hadn't yet felt from him. His hands tangled in my hair as he kissed me deeply, forcing his tongue into my mouth as they entwined in a dance of desire.

Jameson's body closed the space between us, his weight hovering just above me. Every inch of him grinded against the innards of my thighs, the friction of my underwear rubbing against my sensitive spot.

Our haggard breaths mingled as he pulled away slightly, continuing a trail of kisses down my neck . . . then down to my collarbone.

He moaned as his hands found purchase on my breasts, feeling their way down my body until his fingers slid toward the seam of my underwear.

But he grabbed his cock from his undergarment and grinded it with a heavy motion against the apex of my thighs, thin fabric the only thing between us.

He moaned again, and I let out a low sound with him.

He leaned over me again, burying kisses into my neck, biting at the skin, and then landing back onto my lips.

He grinded harder against me, and I bucked my hips slightly for him. His finger traced the ring of my nipple and chill bumps coated my skin. He moaned into my mouth.

His hand drifted lower. And lower. Until his fingers slid where his cock met fabric and he began to move the inseam to the side to allow access.

Then a wave washed over me. My heart pounded in my throat, but not in the same way it was a moment ago. No.

His weight pressed hard on top of my body. The thought of being held down and being driven into . . .

Jameson's lips lingered on me as he released growls of pleasure, his length ready to take entrance as his fingers played with the fabric holding him back.

I wasn't ready.

I wasn't ready to be touched.

"Jameson," I whispered, putting a hand on his chest in an attempt to ease him up.

His voice stayed low as he continued. "You're gonna feel so good, Valora."

No. I wasn't ready.

"Jameson," I pulled back, my eyes meeting his with a mix of emotions as he gazed down at me. I hesitated, the air flowing through my lungs still an uneven mess, and I whispered, "I'm sorry. I can't do this right now." He released a labored breath, but didn't respond. I gulped. "With everything that happened today, I'm not in the right place. I thought I was, but I'm not. I'm sorry."

My voice trembled with vulnerability, my body tense with the weight of today's events. I thought I was ready to give myself to him. After all, I'd been attracted to him since I began working with him. But I couldn't right now. Not this soon. I couldn't force it.

I sat upright and scooted toward the headboard. My arms wrapped themselves around me, cradling me, a silent plea for understanding embedded in my eyes.

Jameson paused as he pulled his undergarments over himself, concern drawn on his face. He wandered to the other side of the bed and sat beside me, and patted me lightly on the shoulder. "Okay." It was the only thing he said before he laid down next to me, tucking himself in under the covers.

The room fell into a heavy silence as I laid down facing away from him. A singular tear escaped my eye and followed gravity down my face. The air was thick with unspoken emotions as we drifted off.

There was no sign of him. Not next to me in the bed. Not rustling around in the next room. The empty sheets beside me were cold.

Zorath had made himself a cozy spot to sleep on the floor at some point in the middle of the night.

I stretched and yawned, trying to wake up from the long day that preceded me.

"Jameson?" I called out. Maybe he was outside, or just being quiet in the next room. But there was no response.

I hauled myself out of bed, noting the aches and pains that took over my muscles as I did so.

"Sword fighting will do that to you. And exerting your power." Well, at least I knew Zorath was awake now.

"Jameson?" I called out a little louder, but there was still no reply.

There was no sign of him. He was gone.

But the dagger that I'd used in the fight yesterday—my father's dagger—had been placed on the nightstand. Good thing he retrieved it, because I'd almost forgotten about it. And I would hate to face my father knowing that I'd lost it.

Thunder boomed in the distance, and that was my cue to get moving.

My mind a fog, I dragged my body around the cottage picking up my belongings. The backpack of supplies that my parents lended me was packed up in no time. There were only so many things I could fit in there, anyway.

I put back any books that I'd taken off the shelves myself.

I knew I couldn't be here any longer. Not right now. While this place had offered me a home in a time of need, and provided me with information and entertainment, it had drained me physically and mentally. I was ready to go home.

I just couldn't find my sword. I sheathed my father's dagger at my hip, so at least I still had one weapon on me, but there was no sign of the other one anywhere. I thought we'd left it by the door with blood dripping down the blade onto the floor. But there was no trace of it. Not a drop.

Zorath was ready to go as soon as I was. We stepped toward the front door. I opened it slowly with a creak, then paused. Zorath continued outside, but I turned around, admiring the inner beauty of this place one more time, feeling the magic hum along my skin.

Though I didn't learn everything I wanted to on this trip, I'd learned more about myself. And the bond that existed with dragons. *My* dragon. But now I knew what I was capable of: I could defend myself if need be.

One day, perhaps I could learn to wield my power whenever I wished, just like Jameson said.

For now, I'd savor the time I had here and the memories I made and what I accomplished. I'd done this on my own, with Zorath by my side, of course. I had a feeling I'd be back someday.

I stepped out the front door, to the clean green grass that left no trace of yesterday's happenings. Dark clouds rolled in in the distance.

I needed to get home.

We ventured back toward the kingdom of Solaria the same way we left it.

CHAPTER EIGHTEEN

BEFORE I EVEN MADE it through the threshold of my home, my parents' arms were wrapped around me.

"We've missed you dearly, Val," my mother sobbed into the crevice of my neck.

My father embraced me tightly, a little less worry in his eyes than in my mother's. Though, he'd seem to have more faith in me from the start. "Let's head inside so you can tell us all about your week."

And tell them, I did. Once we'd settled down at the kitchen table, I told them about all the books I'd read, whether they'd been helpful or not. I told them how intrigued I was by the books about spells, incantations, and histories. I explained the details of my bond to Zorath, and that his breed was a Nocthale, the rarest of all dragon breeds, and went on about all the other extinct breeds.

"And," I continued, "I have powers. I suppose it's the same as Zorath's." They gasped, their eyes shifting to my mouth. "I don't breathe fire," I chuckled. "Flames spark from my hands. The times that it happened was when I was frustrated or angry." They gasped louder.

"But that's not the half of it," I assured. "Some men showed up. I have no idea how they got there, but they gave me a bad feeling, especially since no one else was supposed to be at that cottage." My father had to suspect that these were the men I'd talked about at the shop, but he didn't interrupt. "I threatened them and scared them off with my fire."

I couldn't dare tell them what I'd done. Ever. They'd for sure see me differently. But they seemed to believe it, and I felt the tension lift from my shoulders.

I didn't tell them that Jameson showed up. That may raise even more questions. I'd rather avoid it all together.

Sobbing commenced from my mother at her seat. My eyebrow raised. "Why are you crying?"

"I knew deep down that you could handle yourself, sweetie. It's just hard to admit, as a mother," she sniffled.

I nodded and smiled.

They were *proud* of me. I'd accomplished something on my own, with the accompaniment of Zorath. We were a good team.

"Oh yeah," I jumped up, reaching for the dagger at my right hip. Rather skillfully, I flipped it in my hand and pointed the pommel toward my father.

He took it from me, the golden cross-guard glistening in the sunlight as though being called to him. "Valora, I've been thinking about it ever since you left. I'd like for you to keep it."

"I can't do that. This has always been your lucky charm."

"But you can. It served you well on your solo adventure, whether you needed it or not. May it bring you luck in your coming years as it has done me. I'm passing it on to you, my daughter." He flipped the blade in his hand and handed it out to me the same I'd done him.

I hesitated, but he went on.

"How about you accept the gift, and you keep working in the forge as payment for it?"

My lips curled upward as I laughed. "Deal."

It was only my father and I at the shop. Jameson hadn't shown up for work, and he hadn't given me or my father a reason why.

I'd argued with my brain all morning in search of a reason. He and I never made a name for what we were, or what we were going to be—*maybe* going to be. We weren't a couple. We'd never discussed anything extending beyond our friendship, other than admitting that we were attracted to the other person. So, he was in no way obligated to tell me why he wasn't at work.

It still stung, though.

I'd rejected him. I thought I'd wanted more than friendship from him all this time, and he'd believed the same. But he had to have known that after everything that's happened, it just wasn't the right time for me. Maybe in the future. I liked him. I really did, and even my mother teased me about it because it was written on my face at every mention of his name.

My brain raced with questions, wondering what I'd done wrong to drive him away. Did it piss him off that I'd turned him down? Enough for him to stop coming to work?

Should I have sucked it up and continued through with it, even though the reality of what I'd just done at the time was haunting me? Maybe so . .
.

His absence put a damper on our daily progress, but we managed, even in the torrential downpour that began early that morning.

It was nice to have trout for lunch without having to catch it myself. My mother had packed it for all three of us, if you included Zorath in the mix.

He was far too large to carry on my shoulders now, so it's a good thing that we could speak to each other mentally so I could keep tabs on his location and what he was doing. I didn't want him venturing too far off and ending up in the wrong hands.

There could be other "Judahs" out there.

"You know," I began as my father and I took our quick lunch break, "I missed this job while I was gone. Even though it involves getting drenched in sweat and grime, it's worth it with your company."

He draped his free arm across my shoulders and gave me a friendly shake. "I'm glad you're back." He planted a kiss on the top of my head.

Everything I'd said was true. But this job also gave me something else: it usually kept my mind occupied from intrusive thoughts.

Usually.

However, the past two days, my thoughts would return back to the bodies. The stench of burnt flesh. The sounds of people burning alive until they were scorched into the earth.

I still had no idea what happened to them that morning. Jameson had mentioned the cottage would "take care of it" . . . whatever that meant. While I didn't doubt the cottage's magical abilities, it didn't seem possible to make the evidence that they were ever there just *disappear*. But, I didn't know enough about magic to be certain.

I shook away the thoughts as they started to drown me, and was simply thankful that they'd come to me in the daytime and not during the night during another nightmare.

I wiped the sweat and the hard day's work from my forehead before I stepped into our home, an aroma filling my nostrils that certainly couldn't be coming from *our* kitchen.

The grin on my father's face told me I was wrong.

"Good evening!" My mother exclaimed as I crossed the threshold. She was setting the table with dinnerware, and a feast laid before her. "Dinner is served," she playfully bowed, and my father went to greet her with a kiss.

Butter, bacon, eggs, toast, and a small, but various assortment of jams and jellies were spread amongst the table.

"This looks . . ."

"Incredible."

"Incredible," I agreed with Zorath as he passed me, heading straight for his seat at the table like a little human. "Wow."

I set down my own bag and drifted toward the fresh aromas of bacon grease and toasted bread.

At that very moment, it was the most delectable meal I'd ever had, and it reminded me how thankful I was for this amazing family of mine.

Vertigo took hold of me the next morning as my eyes opened to a strike of lightning flashing through the window. A headache followed soon after and I could hardly find my bearings to stand.

A nightmare had provoked it. I knew that's what it was. But it wasn't as visually memorable as the other ones I'd had. This one was more of a *feeling,* like at one moment I'd been standing in one spot and then moving the next, never settling in one space for too long. It felt as though I'd been dragged through a black hole and I couldn't escape the sucking force that was taking me away.

It was only a bad dream. But now it made sense why my temples were throbbing and why I held the covers over my face to keep the dawn's rising light and a surprise flash of lightning from my eyes.

After the sweat on my skin dried and the pressure in my chest and head eased enough, I made my way to the bath. Every minute that passed gave me more relief from the pain and throbbing pulse beneath my skin.

After a relaxing soak, I was cleaned up and I dressed in my usual attire of work pants and off-white shirt. I swept my hair back into a slick ponytail, but after examining the wet strands that fell down my back, still dripping with water, I braided that chunk and tied it off instead. It was raining today—there was no need for loose hair.

My new dagger on my nightstand caught my eye as I laced my boots, and I tucked the sheathed blade into a comfortable spot of my boot. I didn't always need a blade on my hip, anyway. Too flashy.

"Have you heard if Jameson will be at work today?" I asked my father as I took a hefty bite of eggs.

Disappointment took over his expression and he shook his head.

"Maybe he doesn't like to come to work when it's storming?" I said, trying to lighten the mood, though it was a stupid excuse if it were true. He continued eating without another word about it.

"I wonder where he is," a young, sleepy voice chimed into my head.

I found that thread that connected us in my mind. *"I'm not sure, but I'd be just as upset as my father if I had a good apprentice that ditched me the way he did."*

"Do you think something happened to him?" Zorath asked.

"I'm sure if something had happened on his way home from the cottage, we would have seen a clue. He knew the way there and back."

A knock on the door interrupted our internal conversation. No one chewed or swallowed, especially me and Zorath.

We never had visitors. We were the quiet family on the street that never caused problems.

At least I knew that the only ones that had ever sought me out were no longer alive, and they wouldn't be at the door seeking me. That was a relief in itself. But who could this be?

Another knock sounded, and my father finally stood to answer it.

When he swung open the door, two men of the Eclipse Guard forced their way in.

CHAPTER NINETEEN

Instinct surged through me and I stood from my seat. My mother followed suit, her movements slower and more hesitant. She gave a wobbly curtsy and spoke with a strained smile, "To what do we owe the pleasure, good men?"

The room felt smaller as the guards took another step forward, the morning drizzle dripping onto our floor. Their movements were almost mechanical, and they moved with a practiced grace despite the thud their boots gave against the floorboards. My father stood tall before them—as tall as he could, at least, in comparison to their height.

They towered over him, but they didn't pay him any mind. Their eyes swept over him, over my mother, and landed on me, then Zorath.

They stood easily a head taller than my father, almost two taller than me. An imposing sight. Their armor, though tarnished, still gleamed with menacing sheen. In the center of their chest plates rested a silver star, almost resembling a snowflake during a cold winter. A crest ran from the brow of their helmets to the very top.

"We are here to escort your daughter and her *pet* to the king," the guard closest to me announced, his voice carrying a depth that made the walls feel smaller; it made *me* feel smaller.

Zorath chuffed in my head. *"Pet."*

A thick silence fell. I took a step backward, my breath catching in my throat.

"You aren't taking my daughter to your king," my father broke the silence, his breath low but unwavering.

"He is your king too, and you will obey his command." The guard practically growled the words. His cold tone sent a shiver straight through me, but with a look back at my father, I saw him standing firm. Unshaken.

"She has a job to go to. She helps to provide for this family. What do you need her for?"

"That is the king's business with her."

My father's jaw tightened. "Does King Altair even *know* my daughter?" The question hung in the air. He turned to look at my mother, who stood just a few paces back, her face pale and tense.

"That is the king's business," the guard repeated. The other one stayed silent.

My mother inched closer to my father, her fingers gently brushing his arm in a plea to stay calm.

But then I saw it—the flicker of something darker in my father's eyes. Rage. A rage that had never fully burned out after all these years of hardship and poverty.

"The king," he scoffed. "The man who had stolen the throne through bloodshed. Deceit. You want me to give my daughter up to him? The one who left his new, conquered kingdom in the dust after destroying it?" His voice trembled with bitterness.

"Sweetie," my mother grabbed his arm.

"No, Reyla. Don't you wonder why they want our daughter? After everything Altair has done to this kingdom? Or should I say after everything he *hasn't* done for us?" A venomous glare at the guards standing in front of him. "Why would we want anything to do with him? I don't want my dau—"

The air was shattered with a sharp *crack* as the back of the silent guard's gauntlet collided with my father's cheek. The force was enough to send him stumbling to the ground.

A strangled gasp escaped from my mother as she rushed down to his level. "Theos!" She cried as she knelt over him, her hands trembling. The room pulsed with the chaos that had erupted.

But I stood frozen, my heart pounding in my chest. I couldn't move. I could hardly breathe. Everything seemed to blur as I watched my mother cradle my father's head as he came to, groaning as he tried to stand back up.

I hadn't realized that Zorath leapt in front of me, his wings unfurled like a shield, until I heard his voice exclaim in my head.

"Master! Run!"

But it was too late. The guards were at either side of me, and I had no chance to defend myself before their arms were interlocked under my shoulders and my feet were no longer connected to the ground. Their grip was an iron force, the cold metal of their armor sending a pang down my spine as it grazed my skin.

I was theirs as they effortlessly carried me toward the door.

"I can burn them!"

"No. Don't risk my parent's safety or the house," I responded, turning back to see Zorath standing taller than ever on the kitchen table, his eyes burning with fury.

He followed us out the door, watching me struggle to break free of the guard's grip, but it was no use.

They let my feet to the ground on the dusty road, but their grasp on my arms held firm. Their fingers were a set of jaws in my flesh as they led me toward the castle. Zorath stumbled out the door, but in a single and fluid motion, another knight appeared with a cage, surrounding him with iron bars. His wings rattled helplessly against the bars and the screech of pure terror that expelled from him crushed my soul. My heart twisted violently knowing that I couldn't do anything to help him.

And then, I saw my parents, and my heart shattered further. They were frantically running for me. My father's face was a pure mask of rage and fear, his cheek already bruised and bloodied, and I could see from here the swelling beginning to develop under his eye. His movements were frantic as he reached out, as though he could pull me back by sheer will. My mother's breath hitched in a sob as she reached for me, but it was no use. We were ahead by too many paces.

The realization of what was happening hit me like a physical blow to the chest. I wasn't just being taken away. No. I was being ripped away from my family.

A fresh wave of guards appeared from the alleyways and blocked my parents' pathway to me. They shouted my name in raw desperation.

I wanted to scream back, to tell them I saw them, and that I was still here and fighting just as they were fighting for me. But the words caught in my throat. The sharp thuds of fists against armor rang in my ears. He was trying . . . I knew they were trying to get to me.

The world around me seemed to blur into a haze of motion when the thud of metal striking flesh pierced the air. My father's voice, the one that had been shouting my name so fiercely, fell silent. Every nerve in my body screamed.

My mother's voice broke through the silence. A raw, guttural cry of anguish, not directed at me, but toward the guards. She screamed, but the words were lost to me as the distance between us stretched farther, the rain plummeting harder onto my skin.

A break between guards allowed me to see the cause of her cries. My father laid on the ground, his face pressed against the mud. One of the guards stood over him, his boot kicking forward with a sickening precision that made me want to hurl.

My mother rushed forward, but she was quickly subdued by another guard, her arms flailing helplessly as she now screamed my father's name. All I could do was watch until I was dragged too far away from the chaos to see them.

"Why are you taking me?" I forced out the words despite the long series of breaths I had taken to calm myself down. The uncertainty of what would happen next gnawed at my stomach, twisting it into knots I wasn't sure would undo.

Zorath's commotion against the bars of his cage had finally settled down, though there was a heavy silence between us and the guards.

"I'd get you out of there if I could," I assured him.

"I know."

"Why are you taking me to the king?" Still no response from either of the guards beside me. They continued to drag me forward. We were nearly halfway through the city now. The castle loomed on the horizon, its stone walls sucking the blue life out of the sky.

I turned my head to the other guard, the quiet one from earlier, and asked him the same question. Silence. Were they blatantly ignoring me? He'd hardly spoken since entering our home, and I think that unnerved me more than words could. His eyes stayed locked straight ahead, not a flicker of emotion in them.

I have to know.

"Why does the king want me?"

"Quiet, girl. Do you always talk this much?" The first guard spat and broke the tension like a crack of thunder. I didn't dare argue back.

I had to be in trouble for something. There was no other explanation. From the guards' harsh treatment of me, the brutality toward my father, the way they shoved and manhandled me: it didn't make sense unless something far worse was coming for me.

Were dragons exiled since going extinct? Was I not allowed to leave beyond the city walls and go into the Nova Forest? It didn't make sense.

Then it hit me. The bodies. Somehow, someway, they must have found out about the three men I killed.

"They would have no way of knowing," Zorath said.

"You can't be sure of that."

"There was no one else there to find them."

"But if the king knows what I did, then this all makes sense. The guards aren't just taking me in for an interrogation or a friendly visit . . . I'm a criminal."

A heavy silence down the bond.

I would have to pay for what I did.

The streets blurred around me as we marched through the remainder of the city, my mind reeling. The weight of stares from every corner pressed down on me. Eyes followed me from the windows above, from the shadows of doorways. I could feel the judgement, the whispers of those who watched. I was nothing more than scum beneath their boots, nothing more than a criminal being carted off to meet her fate.

The path sloped upward now, the silhouette of the castle growing larger with every step. The street wound around the castle like a snake, its towering walls cutting off all sight of the horizon now. I had never been this deep into the city, never ventured beyond the familiar west side of the kingdom. The fish market, the shop, my home—it was all there. It felt safe. But this was a place not meant for me. I was a girl with a dragon here, with a secret I would have to admit to, and face the consequences of my actions.

The gates grew closer, and with them, the dread in my chest only deepened. Whatever awaited me behind those walls, I knew would be something we couldn't escape.

CHAPTER TWENTY

THE AIR WITHIN THE castle walls was thick with a strange, heavy silence, as though the stone itself had absorbed the suffering of countless souls since the war. Our footsteps echoed loudly, and the scent of dust and decay mingled with the cold air.

The guards finally allowed my feet fully on the ground, but kept a firm grip around my arms as if I had somewhere I could escape to right now. The sound of my shaking breath was all I could focus on— as well as the water falling into my eyes, my soaked clothes, and the drops falling from me onto the floors.

The hallways stretched before us like endless corridors of stone, lit only by the flickering light of torches mounted to the walls. Their flames danced in the still air, casting long distorted shadows that seemed to follow me, whispering as they reached for me.

Zorath's excitement grew behind me at the sight of the flames. His wings flapped in his cage and it made the guards carrying him stumble.

"Settle down," I spat at him, and he obeyed.

"Be quiet, girl," a guard ordered. I was in the heart of a castle that betrays its people, so I had no choice but to listen.

We passed through from hall to hall, every inch a reminder of the war. Even under the torchlight, dust, dirt, and clutter could be seen strewn in the most random places, as if the king had thought it too much work to take care of the territory *he* conquered.

But it would make sense. Mystique was a kingdom high in the mountains, so high that it was said the clouds drifted *below* you. People described it as an ominous sight. Maybe that's why King Altair accepted Solaria the way it was. It reminded him of his own home. Oppressive and neglected. Dark and dingy.

At least, that's how I saw it.

Suits of armor stood sentinel in every other alcove, their hollow eyes fixed on nothing. The other spots were taken up by a variety of aged antiques: a ring, a goblet, a necklace, and other trinkets that had only collected dust during its time here.

It all felt like a mausoleum for a kingdom long dead.

Two guards ahead stood on either side of a set of massive wooden doors adorned with intricate engravings. Their faces were unreadable, their expressions carved from stone. They swung open the doors with a swift motion, allowing us to enter a chamber that seemed to suck all the light from the air.

I was in a vast, grand hall that stretched high into the shadows of the ceiling, with arches that disappeared into the darkness above. The stones our feet stood upon seemed to have been equally as ignored as the people of this city. They were chipped, jagged, and some were even missing completely from its space. It would be a wonder if people didn't often snap their bones walking on this floor.

Around me were the stares of groupings of people, all donned in fancier clothes than I've ever worn.

There, at the far end, was the throne, sat upon a raised dais and perched in front of a towering window.

I could feel his presence even before I saw him. It was as though the throne itself had a pulse, and that pulse reverberated in my chest. The king was there, watching me, waiting for me.

We inched closer toward the throne. Closer.

And then, I could see him faintly in the dim light.

King Altair.

He sat upon his throne, his posture straight and commanding. His face was obscured by the lack of light shining in behind him, yet I could still feel the intensity of his gaze. A stream of white hair fell to just above his shoulders and a groomed white beard framed his jaw.

Next to him stood a young man that couldn't have been much older than me.

"Bring her forward," a voice ordered, its tone like thunder, and thunder sounded at the same time as I was eased forward with more force from the guards than I would have liked.

My body was stiff with fear, my mind a whirlwind of thoughts and questions. The king didn't move. He watched me approach, while his fingers rested on the armrests of the throne.

The bottom of the dais was in front of me, and there was nowhere else to go now. One of the guards shoved me forward another step, sending me stumbling and almost smashing my face on the steps. I held my ground and peered up.

"Valora Emberlyn," the king's voice echoed through the hall. I gulped, almost positive he could hear it. He only raised his hand and gestured to some guards out of my line of vision.

Footsteps approached, and Zorath's cage was placed next to me. His eyes scanned my face.

"Don't put up a fight," I ordered him. *"Too many guards. Too many people around."* Zorath nodded in understanding.

"Is this your dragon?" King Altair asked, gesturing to the cage beside me. I looked up at him and nodded my head. My vision blurred at the thought of losing Zorath, but I had to accept my mistake. He was with me that day, and we killed them together.

I blinked the moisture from my eyes. "Yes. It is." Despair gripped at my throat.

The king sat in silence.

The pounding of my heart settled in my throat. I could feel it in my temples.

It was self defense. It was self defense.

"They did bad things to you," Zorath said. *"Make sure they know that,*

Master."

"Valora, I've travelled a long way from Mystique to meet with you. Take a look around. You see these people? This room? You and your dragon are here for a reason."

I glanced around even though I'd already surveyed the room when we walked in. There wasn't much worth looking at. But this would be the first and the last time I'd be in this room, seeing these people, this castle, and seeing Zorath.

I'm going to die. They are here to watch us die.

Tears began to fill my eyes again.

The king cleared his throat. "We received a letter from the Capital. King Polaris has personally requested you to visit him in Velorum across the Vast Sea."

THE WORDS HUNG IN the air like a fog that refused to lift. My chest tightened at the mention of Velorum and the mention of King Polaris. I'd heard rumors of his kingdom across the water—the magic, the mysteries that lie there. Did I ever think I'd go there? Never.

I swallowed hard. "Why . . . why would he want me?"

King Altair didn't answer immediately. His fingers lightly drummed on the throne, his gaze still unreadable.

"Do not presume to understand the matters of the Crown, Valora Emberlyn. But King Polaris believes you are of some *use* to him, if you will. Therefore, you will go."

The word "use", stung. It felt like I was being spoken to like a mere object. Something to be utilized and discarded when no longer needed. The thought of travelling across the Vast Sea, when I had never stepped foot into a castle before today, seemed as daunting as it did incomprehensible.

Zorath was becoming unsettled, rocking in his cage and rustling his wings.

"We have no choice," I told him. *"We are both prisoners here."*

"We can fight them. Destroy them. Be free."

"We won't be free if we kill more people. Something is waiting for us across the sea, and we have no choice but to face it. Now settle down."

He grew quieter, and sat still in his cage.

The king finally leaned forward slightly, and his profile came into better view. "You both are bound by a much greater force now. The Capital. The Crown. There are no longer any simple choices for you. You do not walk freely."

Meaning that I wasn't going back home . . .

My heart twisted in my chest as I realized just how precarious our situation truly was.

King Altair rose from his throne, situating the sword at his hip that looked to never be used, his eyes never leaving me. The man next to him stepped forward to line himself up beside him.

"Valora. Do *not* fail Polaris. He has his reasons for summoning you, whatever they may be. But do not fail *me*. Doing so will be failing your kingdom. You will represent Solaria with pride."

I nodded, gulping hard. *As if he cared about this kingdom, anyway . . .*

Altair began to make his leave. "You leave at dawn. My son will show you to your quarters." Within moments, King Altair had left the throne room accompanied by his guards, and the young man next to him approached me.

His dirty blonde hair reflected the flashes of lightning just right, despite the dusty air that surrounded us.

"I'm Heath, and I will be escorting you to your chambers for the night." He nodded in half a bow, as if I was so far below him that I didn't deserve a proper greeting.

He motioned to the guards, who didn't latch onto me this time. Instead, they rested their hands on my arms to lead me forward, and then let me go. We marched through the corridor, a line of men separating me and Zorath's cage behind me. It was eerily quiet as we walked to my sleeping quarters.

"So, are you Mystique's prince, or Solaria's prince?" I blurted.

Heath walked next to me, and turned his head to face me. His sky-blue eyes met mine. "My father rules over both kingdoms, but he is growing older. I am of age to rule my own kingdom. When he feels the time is right, I will rule over Solaria and he will rule over Mystique. As of now, I am Prince Regent here when my father resides in Mystique." His voice was a lullaby of high etiquette, and I could tell in his demeanor he was almost ready to be a king.

But what kind of king would he be? Would he follow in his father's footsteps, destroying cities and neglecting them, or would he rule his own way? It was too soon to tell.

The door to my room was opened, and the guards stepped back to allow me in. The sight was almost as disappointing as the throne room. Less holes in the floor, no doubt, but it reeked of dirt and decay.

It was one room, with a cubby that hosted a toilet. No bathtub. The sheets looked like they had been changed into whatever sheets they could find, dirty or not.

At least it was only for one night.

"If there is anything you need, let us know." Heath offered as a set of men brought Zorath's cage into the room and set him near the window. Heath's hospitality was kind, at least.

I nodded, and stared out the window that overlooked the castle grounds. Zorath perched himself in a manner where he could see out the window too.

"Can we unlock his cage?" I asked before they could shut the door.

Heath shook his head. "Father's orders. I'm sorry." And then he was gone.

They just couldn't trust him. They couldn't trust him not to burn the place down. I get it, I guess.

Even through the rain, the view from the window overlooked the horizon, where I could see the edge of the Vast Sea, the ocean's waves toppling over one another in clashes of blue and white, and the city that sprawled out beneath me. My parents were down there somewhere. I wished they knew that I was okay . . . for now. I wished I could see them from here, and that they could see me and know that I was alive, at least.

I rested on the bed, silence heavy in the room as I thought over this day that had lasted an eternity.

I remembered the dagger that I had sheathed in my boot, that was thankfully hidden well from everyone I'd been in contact with today.

It was the only piece of home that I would have with me. It was the only thing I'd have that reminded me of my parents while on this voyage across the ocean.

They didn't even know what was happening to me.

All of the thoughts and emotions consumed me, and I buried my face in my hands and wept.

The next morning took long enough to arrive.

The previous day, I'd waited in my room all afternoon until a servant finally made an appearance to bring me something to eat. Lunch, dinner, I wasn't quite sure. She'd brought a bowl of stew and what looked like part of a carcass for Zorath to snack on, then she ran out gagging at the smell of it.

Granted, the stew was a larger portion than what I was used to at home, but I'd expected a little more from a royal court.

I hardly slept at all. Throughout the night, my aching body could not find a comfortable place to rest. Every position made my muscles crawl beneath my skin. Fighting back against those guards all morning had drained every ounce of me, mind and body, and the soreness would not ease enough for me to rest.

Dawn's first light had finally rose, painting the sky bright in its wake. No new clothes had been given to me for today, so I stayed dressed in the pants and shirt from yesterday and left my hair in the braided ponytail since I hadn't gotten a chance to bathe yet. I made sure to keep the dagger in my boot concealed.

Soon enough, the guards were knocking at my door, giving me little time to answer before they made their way in. Then, Zorath and I were being escorted once again.

The air at the harbor was cool, crisp, and carried the scent of saltwater.

The castle, which had once seemed like a towering fortress before I entered it, now felt futile and insignificant.

The ship was waiting at the dock, a crew scrambling about in an organized fashion readying it for the journey. It was a tall, black vessel with sails that seemed to absorb the sunlight rather than reflect it. The Vespera.

I'd heard the name being thrown around in whispers throughout the afternoon by servants that roamed the halls, as I had nothing else to do but listen out of my locked door for any interesting or useful information. There was something unnerving about the boat, its dark, sleek hull cutting through the waves, and the sails that harbored the sigil of the Velorum: two dragon wings unfurled, a star in the center instead of a body.

I wasn't sure if I feared the ship itself, or the journey that lay ahead with it.

Zorath never said anything to me, but he seemed to feel it as well. His head was low, his eyes flickering with tension as the guards walked him up the ramp ahead of me. His wings laid tucked against his sides, almost as though he were trying to make himself smaller. I couldn't blame him. My own heart felt heavy in my chest at the unknown of what was to come.

"Good morning, Lady Valora," Heath greeted me when I stepped aboard. "This is Captain Rurik. He sails for the Crown, and is trusted by King Polaris to bring you safely to Velorum."

The captain of the ship, an aged man with an eyepatch and scars tracing the left side of his face, greeted me with little more than a grunt.

"We leave now," Captain Rurik said in a voice thick with an accent I'd never heard before. "Settle in. You'll find your quarters below deck."

I nodded, but the urge to ask Rurik, Heath, anyone more questions burned at the back of my throat. I kept my silence.

By the time I found my way to the bunker I'd been assigned, I could hear Rurik from the top deck call out, "All hands on deck!" The Vespera shuddered under my feet as the anchor was pulled up.

At least this sleeping arrangement was slightly better than what the castle had to offer. This one harbored much less dust, at least. A hammock was hung up in the middle of the small room, and hosted a private bathroom stall that I could hardly move around in, but at least it was there. Across the hall was a private room with a tub.

Within no time at all, the Vespera was setting sail. The waves slapped against the sides of the boat with an almost unnatural force. The ship groaned, and the wind howled as if the sea itself was alive.

I made my way to the top deck, nothing but the vast expanse of water stretching before us.

Behind us, Solaria was drifting farther and farther away. My home. My parents. Everything I had ever known grew smaller in the distance.

I didn't know if I'd ever be back.

Zorath pranced up next to me as I leaned against the side of the ship. They'd released him from his cage only a minute earlier, once they realized that we were far enough away from the kingdom where he couldn't go back and destroy it—not without flying a great distance.

Even though he had yet to fly. Clearly they didn't know that. Or they merely didn't have enough sense to ask.

Night fell quickly as though the day had simply slipped into the sea. I had spent my day drifting between the privacy of my cabin and roaming the top deck observing the crew and the scenery. Thankfully, I'd been given lunch and dinner, both some sort of salted meat and cheese served with bread.

I sat down and nestled my back against a corner of the top deck, Zorath nuzzling in just beside me. I laid my head back and let it rest against the wooden surface behind me. The stars overhead were unlike any I'd ever seen: sharper, brighter, their patterns unfamiliar. I'd always paid attention to them when I'd sit by the shoreline to ease my mind, but I'd never seen so many unfamiliar patterns. I didn't know this many stars existed.

I could get used to this view.

Once my eyes grew heavy, I stood to lead me and Zorath below deck for bed.

But I stopped as Captain Rurik seemed to appear out of nowhere, and stood in the darkness before us.

"Captain Rurik? What's going on?" He stood motionless staring at the expanse beyond the ship.

His eye locked onto mine, and narrowed, but he didn't speak at first. Instead, he pointed out into the nothingness.

"There's something out there," he said, his voice a low grunt.

I followed his line of sight, squinting into the night. The sea was dark, the waves rolling gently . . . No. Those weren't waves.

"What's out there?" I asked, my voice a whisper.

Rurik didn't answer right away. He turned his gaze toward the ship's mast, watching the rigging as if expecting something. "Not sure. I've seen it before, though, usually when we're closer to the Capital. Comes and goes on this voyage. Like a watcher of the night."

I frowned. "A watcher? Like a *spy?*"

"Aye," he replied. "Something is alive out there." His tone was more cautious now. "Something that waits and watches us. Patrols us. It's not the sea itself. It's more than that. I don't usually stick around long enough to find out, but it's never harmed me or my ship or my crew."

"So, you're afraid of it." A curious statement more than a question.

He flicked his gaze to me. "A captain isn't afraid of what lurks beyond his ship. If it's something worth fighting, I fight. If not, I acknowledge its presence and go on. I sail for the High King and if this is their means of keeping tabs on me, then so be it."

Before I could ask him more, Zorath growled low in his throat, a sound of warning. His head was raised, nostrils flared as though he could scent something that we couldn't yet see.

"What is it?"

"Movement. I hear it."

And then, I started to feel it. A change in the air. The pressure seemed to rise, and the ship rocked more violently as if something beneath the waves stirred.

Then slowly, from the side railings, from every surrounding direction, a dark shadowy fog weaved onto the deck. Slowly, as though searching every inch of the floorboards.

Until a figure formed in front of us. A shadowed, tall, human-like figure stood on the deck just a few paces ahead of us. It had no face. It had no eyes or mouth. But it seemed to stare at us. Stare at *me.*

I felt it.

Zorath roared when he felt it, his wings unfurling to their full span and a green glow resting in the back of his throat, ready to strike if need be.

Though I didn't know how I'd attack a shadow, I palmed the dagger from my boot and readied my other hand to prepare a rage of fire to unleash from my fingertips. Heat rose on my skin.

But the shadow hardly moved, and neither did Rurik.

If this was a threat, he would be preparing. But he told me he never worried about it.

"You've spent your time lookin' around. I'm bringin' her to ya. Get off my ship now." He ordered it in a calm, yet firm voice.

The shadow figure didn't argue. It seemed to shift its non-existent gaze between Captain Rurik and me, studying me, until it dissipated and retreated back into the waves where it came from.

Zorath and I put out our internal fires and heaved a sigh of relief.

I turned to the dragon. He was trembling. His wings shuddered with residual energy.

"We're alright, buddy," I said as I knelt to comfort him.

"I know, Master. I just wanted to protect you."

I grinned widely. "You were doing great." I didn't seem to need protecting in that moment, but I was still thankful for my companion.

Captain Rurik grunted, grabbing my attention to stand and face him.

"Whatever that thing was," I pointed to the darkness that surrounded us, "I felt it *looking* at me."

"It happens sometimes, not quite like that, but . . . Usually it simply travels the ship, searching for the gods-know-what, and it disappears where it came from. I don't question it anymore." He turned to where the stairs to

the Captain's quarters began. "Just don't burn my ship if it appears again."
And then he vanished into the black.

CHAPTER TWENTY-TWO

THE DAYS BLURRED TOGETHER in a monotonous cycle of creaking wood, gusting winds, and the constant sway of the ship on the water. No one spoke of the shadow creature again. And it never came back.

The morning after it appeared, I awoke to a change of clothes below my hammock: black pants, a white top with long, frilly sleeves, and a black lace-up top to cover it. After making my first appearance on deck for the day, Rurik told me that not only would it keep me warmer at night, but it would protect me from the sun on these long days. I didn't argue.

He'd been right. For the first couple of days on the Vespera, I was on the top deck with Zorath practicing his flying. He grew more and more by the day, and so did his wings. He'd venture to the front of the ship, leap as high in the air as he could jump, and soar until he landed at the back of the ship where I stood. He'd flap his wings as best as he could, usually ending up on the deck with a *thud* by the end of it.

After a few days, he was much better, and could hold himself up quite well with a steady breeze.

But Zorath was growing restless, more than I'd ever seen him before. The uneasy flick in his tail and his growling in the night told me he was unsettled. Every time I woke up from an uneasy sleep, I'd find him staring out over the water through the porthole, as if it were a portal to take us out of here and into a better world.

But we both knew there was nowhere to go.

On the twenty-second day on the Vespera, I felt a shift in the tide, the hull leaning a different direction it had before. I rushed to the deck..

Captain Rurik stood with his usual stoney expression, his hands gripping the side rail as he gazed out into the water.

"What's going on? I felt something change." I asked him. I'd gained more trust in him over the weeks, and he grew to trust me, too. I'd asked him about his eye and about the scars on his face, and though he was hesitant to tell me, he went on about a monster he fought in the depths of the sea that took down his ship. He invited us most nights to have dinner with him and his crew where we talked about absolutely nothing for most of the night.

He knew that neither me or Zorath was a monster, or his enemy, even if he did work for Velorum. The trust built quickly between us.

"The tides change," he said simply. "That's a sign we are getting closer now. Very close."

I swallowed, my eyes scanning the horizon. There was nothing. I dreaded the answer that I already knew, but I had to ask him anyway. "Close to . . . ?"

"Velorum. The Capital. The Fortress of Magic and Mystery, as they call it. It's waiting."

The ship made its final approach to the shore. It happened out of nowhere: one moment there was nothing but sea and sky ahead of us, and the next, a mass of land could be seen on the horizon.

Velorum. It was inching closer and closer to me. My heart raced at the thought of stepping foot onto this land. It was a place I never thought I'd come to. I'd been dragged from my home to come here, and I had no idea what was in store for me.

It was the enemy of my father—a place he'd never trusted. I had no idea what to expect.

And then, it all came into view. It wasn't like any shore I'd ever seen.

Nothing like the one I used to walk on in Solaria. The beaches were dark, not sand, but something that appeared like black glass that caught the light in strange, colorful patterns. Cliffs stood behind the beach, and next to that, venturing further back than the eye could see, was a dense forest.

Above it all, towering so far in the distance it could hardly be seen, stood a great citadel. I could see its spires reaching toward the sky, and they were made of some material that caught the light that seemed to shift and pulse as if the structure itself were alive.

Zorath's eyes were wide, and I could feel his uncertainty as we set anchor on the shore.

Rurik stepped near us as the crew lowered the ramp. "This is the Obsidian Shore. It's where I've been told to bring ya."

I gulped, looking at Zorath. *"Are you ready?"*

"If you are, then yes."

We stepped off the boat and ventured down the ramp until my boots crunched on the glass-like surface. A strange tingle ran up my legs and into my veins.

I turned to face Captain Rurik, who was at the top of the ramp still, but not coming down.

"Aren't you coming?" I asked.

He shook his head. "My orders were to get ya here safely. There will be other means of transport for ya to the castle. My crew will take stock before I must journey to my next stop." He waved a hand goodbye before he turned his attention back to the crew. "Take care!" He called out as he disappeared behind the rail.

I returned the wave, then turned back to Zorath. I placed a hand on his neck, his spines scratching my skin. We were on our own now with no idea of what's to come.

Only a few steps forward, toward the forest and toward the kingdom, and I was stopped in my tracks.

A figure.

A horse stood on the edge of the treeline. I eased forward more, intrigued by the creature standing in front of a carriage. Its coat was a pure, deep black, as if it had been kissed by darkness. Its mane flowed in the breeze like liquid night. As we inched closer, I realized there was something even more remarkable than this creature's elegance—a third eye in the center of its head. It glowed with an ethereal, auburn hue. I could feel the weight of this singular gaze growing heavier as I approached.

The carriage behind it was a magnificent piece, seemed to be made of a material I couldn't quite place, like a polished crystal or marble. Neither of those were in abundance in Solaria.

I noticed the curving lines embedded into the carriage that twisted into elegant spirals, and how it was adorned with vines that seemed to bloom and wither as the light danced across them. The wheels were a smooth, translucent stone.

"This thing is nicer than my house."

"Well, we aren't home anymore."

Indeed, Solaria and Velorum were vastly different so far. It was a scary feeling not knowing what I'd see next.

Zorath nudged open the door to the carriage, but there was no one inside.

"Did this horse come to us by itself?" I asked aloud, checking the front of the carriage again to be sure a rider was not present. No one. Only the gaze of that horse's eye.

"Velorum is known to be a wondrous place. There is no way of knowing." Zorath said with a huff as though he's seen more of the world than I have.

Every step toward the carriage seemed to make the world around me more vivid, more alive. Colors seemed brighter here, the air seemed crisper, and there was an undeniable hum in the air that I couldn't quite place, like a power tugging at my soul and speaking through me.

As I stepped into the carriage, the third eye of the horse followed my every movement. Zorath wasn't far behind me.

The interior glowed softly. The seats were cushioned in a way that seemed to mold perfectly to my body, as if *made* for me.

The door closed behind us with a soft sound as Zorath settled on the cushion opposite me. Then the horse began to pull.

I glanced one more time at the Vespera. The people there that I had spent the last few weeks with. It may be my last time seeing them or the ship, so I took it all in for a moment, then faced the window beside me as we entered the forest leading to the castle.

CHAPTER TWENTY-THREE

Solaria's forest couldn't compare to what was before me.

I thought the Nova Forest was the grandest expanse of greenery I'd ever see, but never would I have imagined the beauty that this forest held. It stretched endlessly before us, the trees impossibly tall, their trucks wrapped in vines that shimmered with the sun. The leaves overhead were mixes of emerald and gold that flowed as if they were alive with the wind.

The ground beneath us felt soft, like moss, yet gave way to roots that twisted and danced beneath the earth.

"Between you and me," I said to Zorath hardly more than a whisper, "I wouldn't be surprised if this carriage wasn't on the ground at all and it was floating us there."

"Then what's the horse doing?"

"Good point," I chuckled. "Maybe he is floating too."

"I doubt it."

Well, at least he's straight to the point.

Though the path winded through the forest, guiding us deeper into the heart of it, the carriage never faltered. Zorath's head stayed close to mine as we peeked out the window, his eyes wide, taking everything in. His tail began to flick gently against the carriage wall, a subtle sign of unease, but even he seemed entranced by the beauty of this place.

Time seemed to lose its meaning as we ventured deeper into the woods. It was quiet, except for the occasional rustle of leaves or the distant call of an unseen creature.

Then, there was something there. And my breath halted.

At first, it was only a shadow at the edge of my vision, but the farther forward we moved, it became a clear sight. A figure standing still among the trees.

A dire wolf.

I'd only ever heard about them in stories, but this one was absolutely breathtaking. Its coat was as dark as night, nearly blending into the shadows of the forest, but its eyes were a piercing amber. It was a color, a sight, that I'd never forget.

Most would be afraid. I was entranced.

It watched from a distance. Zorath tensed beside me, but didn't say or do anything. Neither did the wolf. It simply *watched*.

The wolf's eyes locked with mine, and for a split second, I felt something unique in that gaze, something wise and knowing. As though the wolf had seen countless travelers pass through these woods, had watched the land for ages.

It raised its snout slightly, as though simply acknowledging my existence.

Then, with a quick shift of its massive form, it turned and disappeared into the trees.

Zorath finally let out a low growl, but I placed a hand on his neck.

"It wasn't a threat to us. The horse probably would have freaked out if it had been."

Zorath didn't respond, but I could feel anxiousness lingering in him. There was something about Velorum that felt different than anything I'd ever experienced before.

I leaned back against the cushioned seat of the carriage, staring out into the endless stretch of trees. And yet, despite the tension in the air, despite all the unknowns, there was something comforting about this place. It was as if Velorum, for all its mystery and magic, was guiding us somewhere important.

Somewhere I was supposed to be.

Before we knew it, we'd left the majesty of the forest. We'd turned on a new path, one made of cobblestone, and yet the carriage never wobbled. I would have believed we were gliding on ice if someone told me.

Solaria's city never really had cobblestone streets, except for maybe the roads leading around the castle. The rest was mainly made up of dirt and dusty paths.

Zorath had grown quiet, his eyes resting steadily on me now, sensing that something was about to change. We were nearing our destination. As we passed onto a more open road, I could see it in the distance. The castle.

It sat high on a hill, towering above the rest of the city below it, its golden spires catching the sunlight with a glimmer as though it were imbued with its own radiant light. Its walls were a smooth and seamless material that shimmered light gold. A soft, almost translucent gold that glowed with an inner warmth, like the castle itself breathed.

My pulse quickened at the sight.

As we neared the base of the city, the carriage slowed. The door opened on its own, and the mysterious horse in front lowered its head, its third eye never leaving us.

Before I could properly exit, a figure appeared: some sort of attendant or servant, draped in delicate robes that looked like the very moon, and a hood that hid most of their face. They moved with a fluidity that I couldn't quite describe, as if the fabric of their clothes were part of them, woven into them.

The figure nodded to me. "Your arrival has been anticipated, Lady Valora." His voice was calm and clear, but with an undertone of something deeper. Wisdom, maybe? I wasn't sure.

I nodded, my throat dry as I stepped out and took in my surroundings. The attendant gestured for me to follow, so I did. Everything in this place felt alive, as though the very earth and sky were attuned to some greater energy. The hairs on my arms rose at the thought.

"Before you meet the High King and his court," he began, shifting his head to take a look at my outfit, "we need to get you changed into less of a

. . . pirate look."

I took no offense.

We moved toward a beautiful stone structure near the base of the city and entered. It was a small chamber from the outside, but inside was something extraordinary.

The space was large on the inside, softly lit by something not made of fire, but by *light*—small balls of light that floated overhead. The walls were made of a pale stone, and in front of me was a gown. It was simple, yet the material seemed to glow. The dress was a soft, tan color, its fabric rather sheer, but modest in its cut.

I stepped closer, my fingers tracing the edges of the dress. The fabric felt like the touch of moonlight, soft and light and vibrant. A few more attendants stepped out with a silent grace and helped me change from the outfit I wore on the ship.

When I stood fully dressed, my reflection in a nearby mirror startled me. The girl staring back was unfamiliar to me, foreign. It took them almost no time to change my dark, tangled hair to pin straight, accessorizing the look with braids throughout. The gown clung just enough to show the shape of my figure, but in a way that felt rather graceful as it hung at my ankles.

I ran my fingers along the delicate fabric of the dress, feeling a deeper connection to this place, a sudden understanding that Velorum's magic didn't just have an effect on the landscape—it was altering me, too. From a normal girl who lived in poverty in another kingdom, to one that was called to royalty and magic.

"Lady Valora," the attendant interrupted my train of thought. "It's time to go."

With a final glance in the mirror, I followed them out of the room.

The path that led to the castle was nothing but a dream. The castle's golden walls towered above me higher than I could fathom, its spires twisting like vines into the sky. The entire city seemed to curve around the base of the palace, putting the castle on a pedestal. The buildings that we passed were crafted from a similar material as the castle, just not as potent in sheen. Even the ground we walked on was a golden-lit stone street.

As we travelled closer, I could feel the weight of the city's gaze upon us. Every person who passed seemed to look up in quiet curiosity, yet no one spoke.

Up the hill stood a large wall with a high archway in the center. Guards perched atop the battlements, armed and ready. But we were led seamlessly through the wall without an extra glimpse from the guards.

The entrance to the castle. A massive door of gold swung open with a gentle ease, revealing a long stretch of hall. Unlike the hallways in Solaria's kingdom, these walls did not seem to cave in on me, making me feel small and meek. No. These walls were open and inviting, lit by similar lights I had seen in that chamber I dressed in.

We continued forward until we made a sharp turn to the left, an identical door to the entrance we came through standing in our path. The doors opened for us, finally revealing the inner sanctum of the kingdom. Inside, the air was thick with the scent of incense, and the space was bathed in a welcoming, warm glow. The ceiling seemed to stretch upward endlessly, with intricate carvings and patterns etched into it. A large, golden chandelier hung from the center of the room.

At the back of the hall stood a raised dais, where a throne sat, and upon it, was King Polaris. His presence was felt long before I could even see his figure.

As I crossed the threshold, I paused.

The energy of the castle pressed down on me, wrapping around me as though testing me, judging my very being.

I slowly began to cross the room, a knight stepping forward from beside the throne before I could make it far.

"You stand before the High King of Luminara. King Polaris III, Master of Magic, and the last dragon rider of the realm."

The people gathered around the room bowed at his titles as I passed.

A moment later, a booming voice echoed through the hall. "Valora Emberlyn. You have arrived at last."

CHAPTER TWENTY-FOUR

We were led across the room toward the throne. Closer. And closer.

The journey across the expanse of space seemed to take ages. King Polaris sat on his throne, more relaxed than King Altair had been. His hands were grazing his lap nonchalantly, his elbows propped on the arms of his seat. He was dressed in an intricate golden outfit, full of stunning patterns and accented with blue stitching. A dark brown cloak sat over his shoulders, and the crown atop his head perfectly matched the gold of his clothes, though its center stone was black. Yet somehow, it all worked for him.

His blue eyes pierced through me as I approached, and I gulped.

No words had been spoken, but I was in the presence of royalty. I had to do *something,* no matter how much me or my family despised him and Altair. This was *the* High King of Luminara. So, I bowed slightly, unsure of the proper etiquette. He waved his hand as if to dismiss it.

"Do not kneel to me," he said. "You are no servant here. You're our *very* special guest." His words were calm, but beneath the surface there was a ripple of power, a force I couldn't ignore.

I remained standing as tall as I could, my heart pounding in my chest. "Yes, Your Majesty." I mustered up. Zorath chirped next to me by way of greeting. At least he wasn't locked up in a cage here.

A smile crept onto the King's lips. "Do you know why you're here?"

A billion questions raced in my mind. I had had them all planned out on the journey here: everything I would ask and say when the time came. The images of burning bodies flashed in my mind, and I shook it away, hoping that that wasn't the reason I came all the way here. To be punished. To face death in the ultimate way.

They wouldn't have gotten me dressed up just to die, would they? Surely not.

I simply shook my head.

"You are here because you were *born* to be here."

The weight of his words hung in the air, and my mind desperately tried to grasp it.

"There's a prophecy," he continued. "It has been passed down through generations of my ancestors. A prophecy that speaks of one born of a dragon egg. One who is the ultimate decider of the fate of the realm. One who has both blood of dragon and human within them."

The air seemed to have been sucked from the room. I remembered reading about that prophecy in the cottage. It was the one Jameson showed to me. Maybe it really *was* true, and I'd doubted him that day.

King Polaris leaned forward slightly, his sapphire eyes narrowing as he studied me. "You, Valora, *are* The Girl of the Prophecy. The dragonblood is within *you*. We all know it, and we've been waiting for you."

The truth was suffocating. The room seemed to spin around me.

"I sense your confusion. Allow me to further explain. When you were born, after the war in your kingdom, after the dragons had died out, the land quaked. It was said that when you hatched, the balance of Velorum would be irrevocably changed. Your coming was foretold to bring either the salvation or the undoing of Luminara."

I looked down at Zorath beside me, who stood there silently. He said nothing to me. But I shook my head at his words as I tried to process them.

"What does that mean for me? Why would I *want* to be the undoing of this kingdom? What would I be saving it from? It doesn't make any sense." I admitted, unable to wrap my head around it.

"There are some who would seek to exploit the prophecy for their own gain. Some would choose to use you as a weapon, while others would wait to claim your power for their own benefit."

A chill ran all the way down my spine. My very existence and my bond with Zorath could be the focal point of a war.

"But you are here under my protection, and know you are not alone. You are our guest, Valora. More will be explained in due time, but you and your dragon's presence has been long awaited, and together, we can keep this realm safe. But let's not worry about that right now. Enjoy yourself. There is a celebration for your arrival. Velorum welcomes you."

CHAPTER TWENTY-FIVE

THE KING'S WORDS ECHOED in my mind as the attendants led me from the Throne Room and deeper into the heart of Velorum's magnificent palace. Despite the weight of this prophecy hanging over me, the hallways were alive with the hum of magic, vibrant with energy. The atmosphere itself was intoxicating.

"I don't know if I could get used to this," I mentally whispered to Zorath. *"It is very majestic here, yet welcoming."*

I could agree with that. Despite the unwanted journey here, I had never seen such majesty in one place. Every corner offered something new to see. Something new to *feel*.

We approached a grand set of double doors and my heartbeat quickened. When they opened before us, I was met with a sight so stunning, it nearly took my breath away.

The Throne Room had been massive. But this room was so extraordinarily vast, I wasn't sure if I'd cross the entire expanse before the end of the night.

Before me was a sea of people, all draped in lavish robes, adorned with jewels that glinted like stars. The atmosphere was electric, a mix of quiet reverence and barely contained excitement. They watched me and Zorath with curious eyes that felt like a thousand needles pricking my skin.

This was a celebration for my arrival, the king had said. Were they glad to see me? Or were they weary?

There were nobles, guards, scholars, and anyone else of importance you could think of, gathered in a space so expansive it seemed to stretch on forever. Columns of gold lined the room. Straight ahead on the far wall was another raised dais, where several high-ranking officials sat in a semi-circle, some with regal poise, others more casual.

I felt so small, so insignificant here. How could the fate of this world rely on *me?* I'm not from here. I'm nowhere near as important as the people gathered in this room. My word means nothing here.

The attendants ushered me forward, guiding me through the sea of faces. Their whispers followed us like a soft wind. Every step felt heavier than the last. I was acutely aware of the way I looked in my delicate gown, with my hair straightened and braided, yet I did not belong. And they knew it.

I nodded in greeting to some people in passing, hoping for their acceptance, yet had no clue as to what to say to them.

The attendants introduced me to a few friendlier faces as we travelled past.

It took ages of being followed by eyes and being spoken about, but we finally neared the base of the dais.

Then, I was met with a sight that left me absolutely breathless I could have crumbled to my knees.

At the top of the dais was a man unlike any I had ever seen. He stood with an air of quiet confidence, broad-shouldered, dressed in deep black that seemed to absorb the light around him, making him stand out in a sea of gold and glam. His face was striking—sharp, but beautifully so, with high cheekbones and a strong jawline contorting to the shape of his short beard. His dark curls fell to either side of his ears, swooshing slightly with every movement of his head. I drank in every detail of him.

His gaze shifted from the people he was speaking with to *me,* and the world seemed to still. My lungs ceased to work. My body jolted as a tingle shivered through my veins. His eyes . . . *those eyes* . . . were dark, nearly black, and they seemed to look straight through me. Straight into me. And they somehow lit up the room all the same.

For a heartbeat, everything around me seemed to fade, leaving just him and me in that moment.

But before I could move again, a soft voice interrupted the silence.

"Knox, there you are."

I turned my head to the left to see a woman approaching behind me, my heart sinking at the sight. She was beautiful, with curly, fire-red hair that burned like embers, and blue doe eyes that seemed to peer deep into souls. She wore a gown of the deepest amethyst, and her presence was commanding. Elegant. Poised. Yet undeniably powerful.

Was she a princess? A queen? She was surely someone of importance in this court.

She placed a delicate hand on the man's arm, and he immediately flicked his gaze toward her. The woman's eyes briefly met mine before turning back to the man beside her.

She led him down the steps. Toward me.

"Knox, you arrived a little late and weren't in the Throne Room earlier to see her arrive. This is Lady Valora," she said, her voice smooth and graceful. "The Girl of the Prophecy."

Knox turned back to me, as if not surprised by my introduction. He bowed slightly, a formal gesture, but his eye contact never broke with mine.

"Lady Valora," he said softly, his voice deep and rich. "It is . . . an honor to meet you."

I wanted to speak, but my throat was dry as sand as I stared in awe at this man before me.

"Pull yourself together." Zorath intruded.

Shit, he was right. I forgot Zorath was right behind me, watching, and listening to my thoughts.

"It is nice to meet you all." I mustered up a curtsey despite the tremble in my legs.

The woman, still gripping his sleeve, smiled faintly and glanced between the two of us. "Knox, do not leave me standing here alone tonight. We mustn't keep the others waiting, after all."

He responded with a slight nod, though I saw the briefest flicker of tension in his shoulders as she squeezed his arm. He took a sip of the dark liquid in his hands, which I only just noticed, giving me one last glance before turning back with her.

As she turned to lead him away, I couldn't help but feel an overwhelming mix of confusion. And *longing*.

But as they met up with the other nobles on the dais, I was left with a heavy silence. The same silence I felt initially walking into this room. The feeling of being an outsider, of being watched by everyone, returned in full force. My breath quickened and I had to steady myself against the overwhelming pressure of the eyes upon me.

But at the top of the dais, accompanied by his guards, King Polaris made his way up to meet the others.

It was a rather overwhelming introduction to the city and its people. After meeting Knox and the woman with him, I was ushered through the hall and introduced to even more faces. Everyone had sharp eyes and subtle smiles, like they were hiding their emotions beneath their polished exteriors.

Maybe I was just overthinking it.

But I noticed some courtiers would glance at me, their eyes flicking quickly to the dragon at my side. His presence here in Velorum was an undeniable power as the last dragon of Luminara, but it was also a visible threat to anyone who would seek to use me for the wrong reasons.

I passed various conversations about me. Would I be able to save this realm or will I be the harbinger of its fall? They called me "Prophecy Girl," "Dragon Girl," and "Lady of Dragons".

The comments sent a chill down my spine. The weight of the prophecy pressed down on me like a chain glued to my neck. There was hardly room to breathe, not in this place.

The only solution I had was to show them a friendly smile, as if I was delighted to be in their presence. I introduced them to the dragon at my side, and continued on.

But somehow, I met eyes again with Knox, whose eyes were already fixed on me from across the room. Though he spoke with another member of the court, I seemed to be the one his gaze lingered on.

The day gave way to evening, and the Grand Hall was transformed in a blink. More balls of soft light burned in every corner and crevice. The air became filled with the sound of soft conversations and the clicking of goblets as if the mood of the evening was beginning to lighten.

I had been swept from one formal gathering to another, introducing myself and Zorath and being bombarded with questions I simply didn't know the answer to. Hours upon hours had been spent socializing.

Zorath watched over me all day until he had been escorted away to a private sanctuary where he would be spending his time here, and I found myself wandering the hallways of the castle, trying to clear my head.

But without warning, my head felt clear. Not by my own doing—but because *he* stood in front of me. He was perched against an open window, his back to the double doors of the hall as he gazed out at the sprawling city below.

I hesitated before approaching him. He didn't turn immediately to me, but I could sense his awareness. I stopped a few feet behind him, unsure of what to say. If I'd even be able to say anything.

But I was finally able to break the silence. "Knox, is it?" A dumb question. *Such* a dumb question. I knew his name from the moment that woman spoke it.

He turned his head toward me. "Lady Valora, are you roaming the hallways to get away from us already? We aren't *that* bad, are we?" It seemed like a quip, but his tone was quiet, and there was an edge to it that made my pulse quicken.

I took a step closer, and his dark eyes followed me. I finally saw his face up close, and there was something in his gaze that made my breath catch. "I needed to get away from the crowds," I said softly, glancing back toward the party behind me, where laughter and conversation bubbled through the halls.

"Don't worry, Lady Valora," he said quietly, swirling the drink in his hand. "I don't blame you. I like to keep to myself most of the time here."

"It's quite overwhelming," I admitted, rocking on my heels. "Also, you can just call me Valora. I'm no Lady. I've never been a part of that life."

Knox nodded, his eyes never breaking away. A smile tugged at one corner of his lips. "Very well, Valora. I know it can be overwhelming. I, myself, have to get away sometimes, like right now. There will be a lot for you to learn about the people here. Some aren't all they seem to be . . ." he trailed off, shaking his head as if he refused to say more.

I felt a pull to his presence, the same feeling I'd been drawn to when I first saw him. But there was an invisible wall between us that I couldn't get through.

I held my voice barely above a whisper. "Is there anything you can tell me? About the prophecy? About the King? Any advice at all?"

He stiffened slightly, his expression hardening for a moment before sighing and running a hand through his dark curls. "I'll tell you this," he took a gulp of the amber drink in his hand, and lowered his voice. "Everyone has a different story about the prophecy. About what they think it all means. Some say you'll be the savior of Velorum. Others think you'll bring it to ruin. Others say you're merely a weapon of war."

"A savior from what, exactly? Why would I want to bring the Capital of the realm to ruin?"

"No one knows, but it's said when the time comes, that's when your decision will matter. And you will know then. That's what the foretellings that have been passed down have always said." He took another swig of his drink. "The magic in this land is slowly receding, Valora. Dying out. Between you and me, the King believes you may be here to restore it, and that it would save the realm, thus fulfilling the prophecy. But there's no way of truly knowing until it happens. I think there's more to it."

I took a cautious step forward until I stood directly beside him. "What do you mean?"

His eyes darkened, and he took a quick scan down the hall before continuing. "Yes, you're the girl of the prophecy, but nobody—not even the

King—knows what you're truly capable of. Some think they can control you, or use your powers to their own advantage, but that power within you, the dragonblood, as they call it, is something these people have never seen. A magic so ancient that the King may not even know how to handle it."

My brow quivered upward. "If Velorum is known for its magic, then how would he not know?"

Knox waited a breath before responding. "This is the birthplace of Illumae, where magic is channeled by dragons, and the ones who bond to them. The King, and the entire Polaris lineage, were blessed by the gods and the stars with their own gifts, and have bonded dragons for centuries before they died out. But you're not a Polaris, and I think you're more powerful than you lead on because of it. Especially with the *last* dragon by your side."

There was a long pause between us, the silence stretching thick with unspoken truths. I had so many questions, but I noticed the tension in his shoulders and his face as he spoke, and something told me that if I pushed too hard on this subject, I would drive him away. I could see this man becoming a friend in the future. A confidant. Plus, I didn't know how much more information regarding the court my brain could handle for one day.

But I couldn't help but ask one more question. "Who was the woman that escorted you away earlier?" Maybe this subject would relieve some tension in this conversation.

He chuckled, taking another sip from his drink. "That's Scarlet Astralyn. She's my betrothed."

Betrothed. Scarlet was a fitting name for someone like her. There was a fire in her, inside and out.

"She's from Astria. Her parents, and the rest of the Astralyns, have ruled over their kingdom for generations. She was sent to eventually be my bride." He paused as though thinking of his next words carefully. "Though, a date has yet to be made."

His eyes burned into mine, and I could almost make out flecks of fire burning in them, like Scarlet was watching behind those beautiful, dark orbs.

"Well, congratulations, and I hope to see more of you in the future." I spun on my heels to exit the conversation, then glanced back quickly. "Of both of you, of course."

He released a laugh, not like the pathetic one he'd let out earlier, but a genuine laugh. "Nice to officially meet you, Valora."

He was supposed to be wed to someone else . . .

So, I made a vow to myself to not allow mere physical attraction to this stranger affect my relationships here, or his relationship with his bride-to-be. If anything, there was a friendly connection there that could be pursued if he wished. I felt it.

I caught his gaze one last time over my shoulder, and for a fleeting moment, I thought I saw something soften in his eyes, a flicker of emotion—care.

But I was gone before I could think too much about it.

CHAPTER TWENTY-SIX

I'D BEEN LED BY the attendants to my room. Down a hall, up two flights of stairs, and down another hallway. It amazed me how massive this castle was, and I was certain there would come a time that I'd get lost in these hallways.

Finally, they unlocked a bronze door at the end of the hall, and I couldn't help but take a long, awestruck breath as I stepped in. The door closed softly behind me, and I was left standing in the middle of a chamber so opulent, it almost felt surreal. The walls were draped in silks of deep, rich colors. Every corner seemed to glow with warmth and light.

I made my way around the room, starting at the bed on the left wall that was made of dark wood and carved with detailed patterns of vines and dragons, allowing my fingertips to brush the soft comforter that lay atop it. Straight ahead from the foot of the bed, I found access to a private bathing chamber with a deep tub and a vanity. But in the far corner of the room stood a grand mirror with a golden frame that reflected the warm flicker of the candles and balls of light in their sconces that lined the walls. My own reflection could not do the piece justice.

The space felt like it was made for royalty, and here I was, a girl from the poorest kingdom in the realm, yet I was Velorum's prized guest.

Soft footsteps approached outside, and with a gentle knock on the door, two ladies entered the room. One was an older woman, with dark skin and silver hair pulled into a tight bun, while the other was a young woman who couldn't have been much older than me. They both bowed their heads and the older lady began to run the bathwater in the bathing chamber.

The young woman spoke gently, "Lady Valora, welcome to Velorum. We are here to prepare you for cleansing. If you require anything else, please don't hesitate to ask."

I nodded, though my throat tightened at the thought of being pampered, and being called a *Lady*. Then I remembered the voyage I was on to get here. I hadn't had a proper bath in weeks. Normally, I would have probably shooed them away and tended to myself, but they seemed at ease, and carried on as though this was simply their duty.

I sank into the tub, letting the warm water and fragrant oils satisfy my senses. It eased the tension in my muscles that I didn't know I had. But after the journey across the Vast Sea, and all the information I had to take in today, the tension clung to my skin like a layer of dust.

The servants worked in silence, scrubbing away the grit and grime of my travels until I felt like a new woman.

By the time they were done, I felt both refreshed and slightly vulnerable. They helped dry me, and left a gown out for me to change into for bed.

I couldn't deny that there was actually something comforting about all the attention—some of the attention—and I began to think I could get used to it.

But as I laid in bed, I couldn't help but cry.

The next day flew by like dust in the wind. I was taken on a thorough tour of the kingdom's grounds by some attendants that I didn't meet yesterday.

I was shown the gardens, the library, the armory, and then they led me to Zorath's sanctuary. The entrance was at the base of a hillside behind the castle, where the path sloped down into the earth into the caverns below. A passerby or foreigner would never even know that it's there.

I couldn't believe my eyes when I saw it. I had expected something more like a glorified horse stable built for him.

It was as though I'd stepped into the dwellings of a cave that had been turned into a hidden, ancient city by magic. Old pillars and archways stood throughout. The pathway was lined with vibrant plants and fruits, filling the air with an assortment of fresh aromas. Cliffs had been made in the cave with mossy tops that could overlook the waterfall flowing into the pond.

And there sat Zorath, bathing under the light beaming in from a carved hole in the top of the caverns. Once he saw me, he ran for me.

"Master!" He nudged me by way of greeting.

"Are you having a good time here?" I asked. *"Be honest,"* I added mentally.

"Yes, this place is wonderful. I wish you could stay here with me."

"Me too, buddy." But that wasn't entirely true, because my room was also grander than anything I've had the pleasure of staying in.

The attendants told me that just behind the sanctuary was a field where animals such as sheep and cattle and goats roamed freely for him to hunt. So, he had plenty of food and enrichment. He could hone his wild instincts here. I'd forgotten that Velorum used to home dragons and they knew what to do. They knew how to care for them.

It was a weight lifted off my shoulders knowing that Zorath had found comfort here. It was one less thing I'd have to worry about.

It was early evening before we finished our tour for the day, and I was escorted back to my room to get ready for dinner. They informed me I'd be having dinner with the King.

I changed out of the fine clothes they had chosen for me to wear while walking about the castle, a lovely, flowy gown that hung off of me just enough to keep me comfortable all day, and then took another bath.

My two room assistants drew my bath, and freshened me up. They scrubbed my scalp thoroughly, and once I was squeaky-clean, they helped dress me into an even finer gown.

It was a golden, long sleeve gown that flowed past my ankles and cinched my waist tightly. I felt like royalty for once in my life, a feeling that I never imagined I'd have the pleasure of having.

Erika, the younger woman with golden locks that matched the exterior of the castle, worked on my makeup, while the older lady, Jules, bedazzled my hair.

By the time they were done and showed me what I looked like, I hardly recognized myself. In the mirror was a girl adorned with eyeliner and rosy cheeks, with hair braided into a crown across the top of her head.

Now I looked the part.

My nerves started to fray as I walked down the staircase and through the long corridors of the castle, knowing I'd be speaking face to face with the King tonight. My knees nearly buckled at the thought.

As I entered the formal dining hall, I was immediately struck by its grandeur. The long table, made of dark, polished wood, was laden with gold plates, goblets, and elegant crystal decanters. The high ceiling above was embellished with celestial patterns, constellations, and dragons: all the things Velorum was known for. The air was filled with the mingling scent of roasted meats and spices.

This place was absolutely magnificent.

King Polaris sat at the head of the table, his presence commanding and stoic as always. On either side of him were several other notable figures, including a woman whose beauty immediately drew my attention. She sat on his left, her posture regal and perfect, her hair a striking gold. I assumed she was the Queen, though she was silent, her sharp gaze scanned the room with disinterest.

I took my place at an empty seat, still acutely aware of how out of place I felt.

But when I looked up, my gaze landed on Knox. He was seated across from me, next to the Queen, his eyes already focused on mine, and for a brief moment, the buzz of conversation around us seemed to fade. His eyes, dark and intense, held me there, until I had to glance away, feeling the heat creep up my neck.

I couldn't let his appearance interfere with my time here. I remembered the vow to myself. At least I *only* had to see him at dinner.

"Lady Valora," a voice boomed, cutting through the low hum of the court. "I trust you've had a chance to settle in?"

I nodded, raising a polite smile to my face. "Yes, Your Majesty. The accommodations are beyond what I expected."

King Polaris chuckled softly, his piercing blue eyes gleaming with a hint of amusement. "Velorum has always prided itself on hospitality. But I suppose, with everything changing as the girl of the prophecy, you'll need much more than fine accommodations to feel at home here."

My throat tightened, but I kept my expression neutral, my fingers gripping the edge of my empty goblet. A servant behind me noted my hand placement and approached me with a pitcher of dark liquid. I declined with a hand gesture.

"It's just fine for me, thanks," I added. I don't think he realized that I did not grow up with such accommodations, mostly thanks to him and King Altair's neglect to our kingdom. This castle must be where all the money went, rather than to Solaria to help rebuild . . .

"Perhaps Knox can continue to show you around and make you feel more comfortable here." He gestured to the man sitting across from me.

Knox choked on his drink.

I raised an eyebrow. Well, there went my thought of only seeing him at dinnertime.

"Son, you know the kingdom's grounds better than anyone. When you're not training or on your patrols, you'll be our guest's personal protector and her guide during her stay. We don't want anyone toying with her or her dragon. Not on my watch, and certainly not on yours now." His crystal blue eyes narrowed on Knox. "It's an order."

"Yes, Father."

I looked up to find Knox watching me intently, his eyes soft but his face unreadable. Next to him sat Scarlet, her posture stiff, her beauty almost cold. Her curly, amber locks were pulled up as she wore a red-lipped grin. The burnt orange dress she had on almost matched her hair. She caught my eye for a moment, her lips curling into a polite but distant smile, and then turned her attention behind me.

"Ah, there you are, Thorin," she stood from her seat to greet the person approaching behind me, but Knox did not move. Instead, he turned his attention to a random spot on the table and sipped his drink. I turned to take a glance.

A man, with hair the same red as Scarlet, hugged her. Once the embrace was complete, he made his way into the empty seat to my left, then turned to me.

He was a dashingly handsome man, muscular and fit. His eyes were bright blue, and the stubble on his face matched the fire in his hair.

"Lady Valora, this is my brother, Thorin."

"Well, hello to *you*." His eyes widened as he took me in. "It's nice to meet you, Lady Valora. I have heard many things." He reached for my hand, giving it a subtle peck, and released it. I kept silent, but returned a soft smile. "My apologies for the late arrival. The hunt returned a little late this evening."

"The hunt?" I asked.

"Every few weeks, a group of men will go out for a few days and hunt." His eyes softened into mine. "I could take you sometime if you'd like."

I smiled politely, and nodded, not knowing if there was a more appropriate thing to say or not, and returned to the plate in front of me. I could feel Scarlet and Knox's stare between me and Thorin, but I didn't dare look up with everyone watching me.

Then we began to feast. I'd never seen a spread like this in my life. Roasted chicken and ham, fresh vegetables, fruits, and breads lined the table. I didn't even know where to start.

"This kingdom was founded so long ago, Lady Valora," the Queen's voice rang out like the sun, pulling my attention toward her. "The prophecy has been written for ages, said to have been written in the stars. We've kept it close for many years. And now, you're here at just the perfect time, since the stars will be aligning soon."

A murmur rippled across the table, but my puzzled expression allowed

King Polaris to elaborate.

"A ball in honor of the stars. Not just a celebration, no. It is a pivotal moment in Velorum. Their alignment only occurs once every century, and it's celebrated on that one night every century. With it, our Master Astrologists are able to predict the forthcoming years.

"It is also the event that Velorum looks forward to in terms of its magic. During The Ceremony, Illumae will be given back to the kingdom, by the stars *and* by its people. It's an important piece in the preservation of our magic now that dragons are no longer here to channel it across the land."

The words sent a wave of tension through the room.

I glanced across from me once more, where Knox now seemed distracted from the conversation, his fingers tapping the surface of his glass. His gaze was distant, his mind elsewhere, like he didn't want to be here.

So many questions ran through my head, but I swallowed hard and shoved them back. I needed to focus more on the present, and take it one day at a time, even though all of this information was settling on my shoulders like an iron crown.

CHAPTER TWENTY-SEVEN

Dinner came to a close and the dining hall began to empty. Only the echo of the courtiers' footsteps were left behind. I stood there a moment, lost in thought.

I'd listened carefully to the various conversations around the table, but I didn't partake in them. Not much, anyway. Not until I knew my place here and knew who I could wholly trust.

The pressure to figure out my role was suffocating. To take me away from my home, the only thing I'd ever known, and be shoved into a whole new world I didn't know I was destined to be part of . . . It was driving me up the wall.

And Thorin. He was a mystery man. Very chattery and bubbly, he seemed to love all the attention on him. He was a rather beautiful man to behold, a type I hadn't seen before in a place like Solaria. After stealing glances at the powerful biceps poking through the sleeves of his tunic at dinner, I couldn't help but to want to know more about him.

Just as I reached the door to leave the dining hall, a voice stopped me.

"Valora."

Knox.

I turned to face him. He stood next to a side table full of liquors and meads, pouring a fresh drink from the decanter.

"I'm to escort you wherever you're going tonight. I presume your room?"

I stayed silent.

"My father's orders. I—we want you to feel safe and welcomed here."

I nodded and gestured toward the door. He followed.

But I didn't lead the way. Knox cautiously led me away from the main hall, down a series of softly lit corridors that grew brighter as we passed each ball of light. The air here was cool and quiet. We moved in silence for a few moments, our footsteps the only sound.

When we reached a small, private balcony overlooking a vast expanse of gardens, he stopped, leaning against the stone railing and looking out at the moonlit sky. The city stretched out to our right, a sea of lights as far as the eye could see.

I approached beside him and leaned against the rail. "It's beautiful here."

"Yeah, the gardens are quite lovely."

"No, really," I said. "Everything here is beautiful. The gardens. The lights. The golden pillars on every corner. Everything."

He turned to look at me. "You're right." The lights of the city reflected off of his loose black shirt.

My breath halted again. *Damn.* He was art. "I'm not really sure what to make of all this," I confessed, stepping an inch closer to him.

"Make of what?"

"Until recently, I didn't know there *was* a prophecy, and now I feel somehow bound to it all because of my blood. The whole *realm* is bound to my dragonblood, apparently. But I don't even know what I'm supposed to do here. I don't know what the King wants *from* me. It's all overwhelming. To hear whispers about me around every corner . . . the things people may want to do with me . . ."

"I'm sure you'll here from the King soon. But no one can control you, Valora." His words were firm, but there was an underlying tension in his voice. "Not the King. Not the court. Not anyone. Remember that."

"I thought the King was supposed to be the most powerful man here. I don't see why he can't just tell me what he wants. What he expects from me."

He was silent for a long moment, his jaw tense.

"My father is a powerful man, yes. He has many abilities, more than anyone in his lineage was ever born with. He will eventually discuss plans with you, but there's a lot on his plate, too. He's also a cunning, greedy man . . ."

"You're not starting off on a good foot here." I raised my eyebrows. He let out a single chuckle and took a sip from his glass.

"He honors his throne, and I respect him for that. But this kingdom is tangled up in old rules, prophecies, and traditions, and it overtakes him. He's relying on the prophecy falling his way all while relying on this ball to go in his favor, too. There's a lot at stake. This *ball* is not just a celebration. The fate of this particular kingdom is also to be decided."

He paused for a moment for me to process. I nodded for him to continue.

"This ball is called the Syzygy, but everyone refers to it as The Ceremony of the Stars. It's when the celestial bodies align in a perfect pattern, and it only occurs once a century. They say it's a sign of a new era. Sometimes, a potential shift in power." He hesitated, taking a swig of his drink before locking eyes with me again. "For Velorum, the stars' alignment is a powerful omen. My father has told me that historically, the crown could be passed on. And, if that's how the Astrologists predict it, then it may be my time."

"So, you're next in line for the crown?" I asked softly, a sudden understanding dawning on me. The pressure of being the next one to rule was weighing on him. On being *the* heir to the throne. Prince Knox Polaris to *King* Knox Polaris . . .

"I don't want it," he said, his jaw clenched. "And I'm afraid that my father won't be happy to give up his crown in all honesty, even to me, though he says otherwise. I think his underlying goal is to stay High King until his death, and he's worried about this ceremony. Typically, the heir to the throne takes over after the death of the King, you know. Well, this damned ceremony is the only exception, where if a new era is to come, the stars themselves choose for it to happen, and it happens quickly. It's something that our great ancestors have been partaking in for centuries."

He breathed out hard. "I have other responsibilities here. Expectations. I didn't ask for this. I hope the stars pick my bastard brother over me, but I know they won't."

"Your brother?"

"My brother *does* want the crown, far more than I do." Knox brushed a fleck of dust from his black shirt sleeve. "Everyone has their expectations of me—my father, my mother, Scarlet. I just can't help but feel like my future is being decided for me."

So much information whirled in my brain at once.

"Is it realistic that *you* could give up your claim to the throne if you don't want it?" It was an honest question, coming from someone not educated in royal court and traditions.

"Ha. Normally, you could, though it's rare that a Polaris doesn't want the crown. The only exception is if you're chosen on the day of The Ceremony, it's believed that the ancestors and the gods are the ones that choose you. To decline would be a burden to the kingdom. The kingdom could be cursed, or the King could be cursed. It's a bad omen to even consider."

The stress could practically bleed from his eyes. He wasn't just a prince. He was a man trapped by his own fate, burdened by a crown he didn't want. It made me feel a pang of empathy for him, despite being the son of a man I've deemed an enemy all my life. I took half a step closer.

"I didn't ask for this either, you know," I said, my gaze softening as I met his eyes. "But, here we are."

Knox's lips twitched as though he wanted to smile, but the tension there still remained. "I can't show it," he said quietly. "That I don't want the crown. Not here. Not with her." He glanced behind him, where his betrothed was likely still in the castle somewhere, unaware of the conversation that was unfolding.

But I understood what he was saying. Scarlet was part of his political obligation. She was a symbol of his duty, of what was expected of him.

"What of Thorin? Who is he?"

"*Thorin,*" he said mockingly. "If I'm crowned, he is to become the General of the Starfire Vanguard, which was the position that *I've* always wanted. He doesn't necessarily want the position, but he will accept it, and I don't want the crown. Thorin and I don't always get along, and I *don't* want him as General if I become the king. I lose on both ends." Knox wipes his face down with his palm, sighing heavily.

"Then, you not only would have to rule a kingdom, but someone you don't like will be appointed to lead your army? Yeah, that's logical." I nudged him lightly with my elbow and he smiled, but quickly wiped it away. Why was he so closed off from emotion?

"I'm sorry that I brought you here instead of your room. I didn't want to go back to my normalcy . . ." He stopped himself from continuing as he lowered his head. "I saw you as someone unbiased that I could talk to about this. There's no one else I can confide in without being chastised for how I feel."

"We are in the same boat here, or a similar one at least. We don't have much of a choice. Not right now. I wouldn't judge you for how you feel, Knox."

The corners of his lips finally curled upward and his eyes glimmered.

"Do you have any more advice for me?"

He pondered for a moment before speaking. "Stay true to yourself here. It's easy to get lost in the politics. Don't let anyone make you do something that you don't want to do. Stand up for yourself. Don't let anyone walk over you."

I nodded, and thanked him, but I didn't know what else to say. He stared at me for a long moment, his dark eyes searching mine as though trying to say more.

"I should go," he said, his voice strained. "I'm sure we will talk again soon. Do you need help finding your room?"

"I'll manage. Thank you." I watched him as he turned away, stuffing his free hand in his pocket.

"Goodnight, Valora." And then he was gone.

I didn't cry that night.

CHAPTER TWENTY-EIGHT

"Lady Valora, will you take a walk with me?" King Polaris's voice echoed through the hallway I'd been exploring on my own. Knox had some errands to run for his father regarding preparations for The Ceremony, which left me to wander on my own time.

I turned to face him as he approached, two guards flanking him. Taking a walk with the High King? My father's greatest enemy, a man he resents to his core. Still, it was the only way. I was a guest here with no real power over anything or anyone. I nodded, and followed his path.

He led us down another hall, one I had yet to venture down. The walls were lined with old portraits of past rulers, I assumed all of the Polaris lineage. Next to each portrait was a picture of the dragon they'd bonded.

I recognized the dragon breeds based on the descriptions I'd read of them in my books. The Amberclaw, a red beast of energy. The Stormscale, a swirl of whites and blues that could blend into the sky. The Diamondtail, as black as night itself.

"This was my great-grandfather and his dragon, Akka. He was the greatest storm manipulator the realm had ever seen." He pointed to an old man in a portrait and the Stormscale pictured beside him. "That dagger next to him, there, meant as much to him as his dragon did. Sadly, most of it was not recovered after his death, but what we found of it, was made new." I noted the sapphire embedded between the blade and the hilt, and in a way it reminded me of my own from my father, currently hidden in my boot. But I shook the memory away as quickly as possible, refusing to allow the image of my father being struck down in front of our home to affect me in front of King Polaris.

We continued down the hall as the King fed me information about his ancestors.

Then we reached his portrait and the Nocthale pictured beside him. A white blur of light was portrayed behind the dragon, allowing the variety of colors within his black scales to pop.

"This was my dragon, Lucia. He was fierce, and beautiful all the same," King Polaris lowered his head and his hair fell in front of his face. "I miss him dearly. A piece of me died when he passed on."

"How did he pass?"

King Polaris looked at me. "I did some things in my past that I'm not proud of. Greed took hold of me when I realized I'd bonded the rarest dragon in existence, and I'm not ashamed to admit it." He looked up at the picture of Lucia. "The cunning inside me is what killed him. And it's what seemed to ultimately kill the growth of magic in Velorum."

I gulped.

"Lady Valora, this realm has ties to magic thanks to this land and thanks to the dragons that have always channeled it through their matings and their bonds to us. Somehow, the magic died, and therefore, the dragons died with it. There wasn't enough to feed their bonds or feed the eggs for them to hatch. Lucia was the last hope, and idiotically, I sent him to his death by aiding Terrion Altair during his conquering. It cost us. It cost the realm its abundance of magic, and now every kingdom's Illumae is decreasing by the year."

"How does this all relate to me? What do you expect from me, Your Majesty?" My voice trembled with anticipation. I wanted so badly to ask why he did what he did . . . why he helped attack my kingdom when he was the High King who was supposed to aid his kingdoms and not let them suffer. Why did he never send supplies when he knew the destruction he'd caused in Solaria?

"You have bonded the last dragon, a Nocthale, at that. I need you, and whatever powers you and him may possess, to find a way to bring this kingdom its magic back. Replenish our sources. Don't make mistakes like I did. Because somewhere deep within me, there is a young boy that wishes he could start over and undo all the things he did." The High King tilted his head back and inhaled deeply.

It was hard for me to breathe now. "How do I replenish it?"

The King shook his head. "I've been wondering the same thing, but I wanted to let you get settled in here before springing this on you. You have access to a new form of magic, something ancient. You are a mystery. We're relying on you to find a way to access our Illumae."

"I've only ever wielded some fire," I glanced down at my feet, now shaking my head back and forth. "I'm not even sure how to *channel* my own magic, really."

He placed a hand on my shoulder, and I looked back up into his piercing blue eyes as they narrowed on me. "Give it some thought. We need you, Lady Valora. Do anything and everything you must, no matter the cost. If you're able to save the Illumae permanently, you may fulfill the prophecy, and save the realm."

With a swift motion to his guards, he left the hallway.

Days had passed since my conversation with King Polaris that still whirled inside my brain. Even more days had passed since Knox and I stood on that balcony and he confided in me. Their words each weighed heavily on me the more time passed.

I'd try to make my way to the kingdom's expansive library when I could to get a headstart on gathering information for the King, but it was no use. The archives were far too large to explore on my own, and I wasn't quite confident enough to know how to ask the archive workers for help.

But I'd venture with Knox every day, and he would show me a new part of Velorum I had yet to explore.

The Capital was unlike any place I'd ever seen. The streets of the city were alive with people, bustling with trade, chatter, and movement. The market squares, with their colorful tents and street vendors, contrasted sharply with the castle behind me.

"Many people in Velorum have *basic* magic capabilities," Knox had pointed to a man at a shop levitating a small tray to the workstation in front of him while his hands were occupied. "Some have more than others depending on their bloodline. You'll see."

"Even ordinary people have magic?" I asked.

"Yes. This kingdom had been blessed for centuries with Illumae, which is the essence of everything we have and are. Over time, certain bloodlines have begun to run deep with magic. Some others are not so fortunate."

"Huh. I never saw anything like that in Solaria."

His face went blank and he continued leading me through the city. "So," he began, "tell me more about your family and your life."

"You want to know more about me?" I asked.

"You came from a kingdom I am not familiar with. No one knows much about you. If I'm to spend time with you, protect you, then I'd like to learn about the person I'm with."

I hesitated to bring back the memories, but then I answered. "My father is a blacksmith, one of the best I've ever known. My mother didn't make as much money as us as a seamstress. I used to work in a fish market selling oysters and fish. I'd have to roam the dirty streets of the city and sell to whoever called me over." I glanced at him, and found his eyebrows raised at me. "What?"

"I just never imagined *you* would have to work like that."

"It was a debilitating job that I hated every second of," I said. "But then I started to work with my father at his shop and things got better. I liked that more."

"So, there's no magic there?" He asked, as if I were speaking a foreign language.

"Nope."

"Interesting," his gaze travelled back ahead of us. "I heard there used to be."

That's what the King had told me a few days ago. Magic had existed in every kingdom in Luminara, yet disappeared in Solaria. If the Illumae didn't replenish permanently, every other kingdom may end up in the same state as my own.

"It was before I was born. Their castle is nothing like this one. It's old and dirty and not kept up with. The streets are lined with dirt and dust, so no matter where you go, you'll end up covered in it. There wasn't enough food to go around. So yeah, it's a little different than this place."

Knox looked at me with an expression something like pity. "Well, now you're here. And there are many things to see and do here without having to walk through dirt and dust."

He was right. Though the castle was a fortress of gold, Velorum's true beauty lay in its natural wonders. I found myself wandering through the sprawling gardens, the ones Knox and I had looked over that one night, while their trees and bushes lay heavy with fruits and flowers that bled the hum of magic. Every so often, I would pause, breathe in, and feel the slightest tingle as if the kingdom were whispering to me.

While wandering those gardens a few days later, I found Knox leaning against an apple tree. No drink in hand.

"Valora," he greeted me, a hint of urgency in his voice. "I had an idea, and I'd like to show you something."

He looked different. His face was slightly drawn, as though he'd been awake for hours.

"Something?" I questioned.

He smiled, his teeth gleaming in the light of the afternoon sun. He glanced around wearily. "It's a secret. Something I think will make you feel a little more comfortable here."

I didn't hesitate. Perhaps it was the way he'd just smiled at me and pulled me in, or maybe simply my own curiosity. It was *not* because of his good looks. I told myself that. Whatever it was, I found myself nodding, intrigued that he wanted to make this place feel like home. For me. "Lead the way, sir."

He smiled faintly, and without another word, he led me through the gardens and to a hidden doorway exiting at the back. The path ahead was narrow and winding. Thick trees passed us by until we reached a wooden door set into the side of a hill.

"This, Valora, is the entrance to Velorum's secret. A sacred place. The dragon hatchery."

I blinked, almost not believing my ears. "What?"

"A dragon hatchery. Before the war, dragons were already starting to die out. Fewer were hatching, and fewer were staying alive and not bonding. So we bred the dragons we did have in hopes to repopulate. After the war, dragons ceased to exist. But the eggs we made have been here since then, yet they haven't hatched."

His words stilled me. They tried to repopulate the dragon community for its magic, and failed. But here I was, born of a dragon egg while bonded to the last dragon. The irony wasn't lost on me.

Knox gestured for me to enter, and as I stepped inside the dimly lit chamber, I was overwhelmed by the sight. The walls of the hatchery were lined with stone cradles, each one gently rocking, almost as if alive. Underneath sat a kindling flame to warm the cradles. Inside, nestled in beds of moss, were eggs. There were at least half a dozen of them. I stepped closer, and they began to glow softly with an ethereal light.

"To be truthful, I've never seen them glow this much," Knox added.

"Maybe they are getting close to hatching?" I suggested.

"Maybe they just like you." He snickered lightly.

I looked at him, and he looked back at me with a soft gaze, his eyes scanning my face before swiftly looking away. I turned my attention back to the eggs, gently brushing my fingers along the scales. The dormant magic and life inside hummed against my skin. I felt the souls that existed within that shell.

"Dragons would usually hatch when they were around an abundance of Illumae once mature. It usually came from the parents channeling their magic into their eggs, but since that isn't exactly possible anymore, we've been trying to figure it out since." He shook his head. "No luck, yet."

My fingers drifted around the scales of each egg. "I really hope they're able to hatch one day."

"Me too," he breathed. "I hope I was able to help you feel more relaxed. I was up nearly all night trying to figure out how to make you more comfortable here. I'm sure it's hard to be in a foreign place. Especially without your dragon next to you now."

He was right. I'd still try to visit Zorath every day, and I'd reach out to him through our mental bond to check on him, but I missed having him next to me with every step I took.

But Knox had spent his night thinking of how to help me. My chest tightened at the thought of him caring about how I felt here.

"It is hard, but this definitely helped me," I smiled down at the eggs, then looked back at him. "Thank you, Knox."

"You're welcome. Would you like to head back?"

I contemplated. "I think I'll stay here a while. If you trust me alone here, of course."

That remark made his eyebrows raise. "Of course. Let me know if there's anything you need." He turned on his heels, and left me to myself and the eggs.

CHAPTER TWENTY-NINE

The sun was so close to its horizon, yet there was a light that still casted an amber glow over Velorum. The evening shadows followed me through the city.

I'd visited Zorath earlier this morning and spent a few hours with him. I told him how pleasant the kingdom was becoming, despite being a scary change at first. I also told him what my duty was, according to the King's words. We'd bounce ideas off one another, but he told me he had no idea how to feed Illumae back into the realm or replenish what was lost.

Then, he decided to let me know that he could hear every lustful thought I had when I was with Knox. *And* the thoughts I had when I sat next to Thorin at dinner and he kissed my hand every time he saw me. That's when I politely and firmly told him to stay out of my head.

But at least he was thriving in his sanctuary.

I'd been trying so hard, and usually succeeding, to keep those thoughts out of my mind, since Knox was off limits to anyone but Scarlet, and Thorin was a high-ranking member of a court. Not that I had a chance with either one of them anyway.

But Thorin, however, was a lovely sight at dinnertime, and distracted me just enough from Knox. We'd chat here and there about our day—how he'd been working with the Vanguard and the current General on new training techniques, and how I'm still finding my way around. He was nice, charming. And *available*—not that I necessarily needed a relationship anytime soon. But, it was nice to know that such a powerfully built man could be an option . . .

I'd been wandering the city for hours since visiting Zorath, my feet carrying me through a labyrinth of winding streets, passing colorful markets full of magic and grand buildings that stood tall in my wake. My mind was still clouded with thoughts, but the city was alive with activity.

Then, in the midst of my wanderings, someone called my name. I whirled around as the voice rang out and my heart skipped a beat.

Knox stood on a corner of the street between two buildings, his shoulder pressed against the wall and his arms folded across his chest, allowing the muscles underneath his clothes to bulge. A slight smile tugged at his lips.

"Knox," I greeted him as I approached. He pushed himself off of the wall.

"Valora. Lovely to see you. Sorry for leaving you alone to wander today. I was on border patrol and we had a shipment at the dock today." He eased closer to greet me. "Would you like to see something? Something that means a lot to me?" He asked, his tone gentle, but inviting.

My curiosity peaked. Something that was special to Knox . . . why would I not want to see it? "I suppose," I responded coolly.

"Follow me." He started toward a narrow path between two buildings. I fell in step beside him, my feet light on the cobblestone as we moved into a quieter part of the city.

The buildings soon began to thin out, and the chatter of the cityfolk grew farther away. We stepped through a wrought-iron gate, its intricate design of swirls a work of art. Behind it, a large open space stretched out.

A vast training arena, bordered by stone walls that held rows and rows of seats for an audience. My gaze drifted over the racks of weapons scattered along the edge of the arena: swords, spears, daggers, shields, and bows.

"This is . . ." I breathed, my voice trailing off as I took in the sight before me. It was a place of raw energy and history. I could vividly picture fierce knights training here and honing their skills over the centuries.

"*My* sanctuary," Knox said softly, his voice taking on a deeper tone. "A place where I feel like myself. Where I don't have to worry about my betrothed, or my duties. I can forget who I am supposed to be and just . . .

be."

I looked him up and down, my curiosity deepening. There was something about his words that made me believe he kept a lot more cooped up inside than he led on.

Knox moved toward the center of the ring, his boots crunching on the gravel as he picked up a sword. "I'll get this lucky every so often. This place is usually flooded with knights and squires. But Thorin has them practicing in the Colosseum today, so it's all ours."

Ours. A chill ran across my skin.

I stood against the inner wall, my eyes following his every movement as he swung his blade in fluid, practiced arcs. The control. The strength. Each motion was precise and powerful, a dance of skill that I could hardly take my gaze from.

The way his body moved, the way that black tunic was buttoned down just enough to reveal his chest. It was mesmerizing. He moved with such grace and confidence. Knox wasn't just a prince. In this moment, he was something else entirely. Someone fierce and free, as though he was born for this.

He finished his movements, breathing slightly heavier now, and turned back to me, a light smirk on his face. Short locks fell down his forehead, tainted with sweat.

"Impressed?" he asked, his tone teasing, but not entirely joking.

I blinked, shaking myself out of my intruding thoughts. "You're incredible. I mean . . . your movements. They are incredible." A faint smile tugged at my lips, my cheeks heating. "I've never seen anyone move like that with a sword. They normally just swing. You'd make a great General."

Knox chuckled, sheathing the sword in its original spot before heading for the weapons on the wall. "Thank you. Fighting isn't all about strength," he said, his voice softening. "It's about understanding yourself, your movements, your purpose." He paused for a moment, then glanced over at me with a knowing look. "I think you'd be better than you think." He motioned to the weapons. "Go ahead. Pick something."

I paused at the rows of swords before me, and past memories flooded me. I wasn't sure I was ready to wield one again. Not yet, at least. Not after what happened the last time I used one. My hands clenched at my sides at the thought of what I'd done to those three men.

Instead, my gaze flicked over to a set of bow and arrows propped against the far wall. My heart raced. "I'll try the bow," I said, surprising myself with the certainty in my voice.

Knox raised an eyebrow, clearly intrigued. He waltzed over and handed it to me, gesturing to the target at the opposite end of the ring. "Let's see what you've got."

I took the bow in my hands, feeling its weight settle in my fingers. It was much lighter than a sword, but I had to be more precise with it. Stepping forward toward the targets, I nocked an arrow and pulled back the string, testing the tension. A sense of power flooded through me. The air around me seemed to still, the world shrinking to just the target ahead.

With a deep breath in, I let the arrow fly.

The moment the string released, the arrow cut through the air with a sharp *whoosh*, striking the target dead center with a satisfying thud.

I blinked in surprise, my heart racing with adrenaline.

"Master? Are you alright? I felt your power."

"Yes, Zorath, I'm alright. I'm practicing with weapons. I didn't use my power."

"It wasn't the same as your usual power, but I felt something there. Between us. Continue."

Knox's eyes were wide as he looked at the target, then back at me.

"You're a natural," he said, his voice full of awe.

I couldn't help but smile. The feeling of the bow in my hands, the power behind the shot. It felt exhilarating. "I'm not sure I'm a *natural*, but thank you."

"Try it again."

I was drawn by the confidence in his voice. So, I nocked another arrow and drew back.

"Here," Knox interrupted, stepping up behind me. "Just make sure you don't hurt your back. The drawback and these repetitive motions on your muscles can easily strain them." He placed one hand around my core, feeling the tension of the little abdominal muscles I had, and then made sure my shoulders and elbows were in proper alignment with the bow. I sucked in at his touch, and straightened up.

"I can feel your heartbeat from here. Slow it down," Zorath intruded my mind.

"Shut up."

I shot again, and this time, the arrow went straight through the previous one, shredding the wood along the way.

Knox let out a low and drawn-out whistle. "Mother of Tyche, you've got perfect accuracy, Valora."

He knows the Old Powers, the same gods that I pray to.

"I guess Luck could have blessed me just this one time." I shrugged.

"I've trained many people, using various different weapons. I have never seen anyone pick it up so quickly."

I turned to him, feeling a warmth spread through my face at his praise. "Then maybe it's just in my blood," I said with a wink. "Like it is for you."

Knox smiled at me with that charming smile that made my head spin. "Maybe, but I think it's all you. I'm proud to say that I never doubted your potential."

The air seemed to shift slightly, the distance between us narrowing as we shared an unspoken understanding.

He scratched the back of his neck. "If you want, I can train you more often. It never hurts to be able to defend yourself, right?"

I thought it over for a heartbeat. "That sounds efficient. I have a blade with me that I'd like to know how to properly throw in case of emergency."

"You have it with you right now?"

I nodded my head. "Yes, but I keep it well hidden. It was my father's lucky charm. I need it with me wherever I go."

He stood a little taller. "May I see it?"

I unsheathed the blade from my boot that I hid under my dress and handed it to him pommel side out. His eyes widened slightly, his mouth agape.

"It's a gorgeous blade."

I smiled, remembering how talented my father was, and tried not to tear up at the thought. "Thank you."

We stood there for a while, going over some movements, all while talking and laughing between forms.

Knox showed me how to properly toss a dagger. I'd sheathed my father's back into my boot because there were plenty here for me to practice with. No need in ruining his blade. But eventually, the sunlight grew dimmer, and the tranquility of the afternoon gave way to the realities that awaited us in the castle.

"We should probably get going," I suggested, pointing to my dress and the boots underneath. "I don't think *this* will be appropriate for me to wear to dinner."

"You're right," he put the knives and bows we had used back where they belonged. "It wouldn't be appropriate. I'll walk you back."

I chuckled as we made our leave. "I'll see you at dinner?"

"I'll see you at dinner."

But I grabbed his arm and stopped him. "Thank you for showing me this place today. I feel closer to this place now. Closer to you, and I feel like I have a friend here now. So, thank you."

He smiled warmly, looking down into my eyes. "Anytime. Friend."

CHAPTER THIRTY

"So, Lady Valora, I heard you and Knox have been doing a lot of sightseeing around the kingdom," Scarlet aimed her tone right at me.

I shifted the food around on my plate, swallowing the bite I had just taken. "Uh . . . Yes. He's been showing me around." I glanced over at Knox, and then at the King and Queen. "I've thoroughly enjoyed seeing your kingdom, Your Majesty. It's beautiful."

They both nodded politely.

"I showed her the training arena today," Knox interjected, his eyes landing on me, though a duller expression made up his features than the one I'd been present with all day today.

Scarlet gazed over him. "You've taken her to your favorite place?"

"Well, Scarlet, you've never wanted to go. Meanwhile, she actually wants to train with me," he snapped, taking a sip of his liquor. "And Valora is actually really good with a bow."

"Son," the Queen stepped in, "that's no way to acknowledge our guest. This is *Lady* Valora, and she should be respected as such. She's part of us now."

Knox only lifted his eyebrows and took another swig.

"A bow, huh?" Another voice chimed in behind me, and fire-red hair sat down next to me. I could feel the weight of his gaze pressing through my temple until I turned and finally found Thorin's striking blue eyes. "That reminds me. Lady Valora, we are going on another hunt at the end of the week. It would be an honor for you to join us. I'd like to see what you've got up your sleeve." He reached under the table for my hand, and raised it to his mouth to press a light kiss to the back of it. I couldn't help but blush.

Knox downed his drink, not taking his eyes off of the future General.

"That sounds like a great idea," Scarlet agreed. "Maybe you two will be able to bond on this hunt, then all four of us could hang out together when you return." She wrapped an arm around Knox and winked at me and Thorin.

I knew what she was suggesting, but I tried not to play on it. Thorin was a good-looking man, no doubt, but I didn't want to start making moves right now. If something happened naturally between us, that would eventually be alright and I would welcome it. But I didn't need to expect it.

Because what I needed was someone strong, and there was not a doubt that Thorin was that. I needed someone who would support me and understand my inner fire—and the flame that resides within me—and not judge me because of it. Instead, he would accept it, and accept me for me, wholeheartedly.

"I look forward to going." It was the only thing I could think to say.

The King swallowed his bite and cleared his throat. "Knox, you and Scarlet will help your mother with these precarious plannings for The Ceremony while they're gone."

Knox waved over the servant to pour him another drink, and he knocked most of it back in a single gulp, but he didn't say a word.

A smile tugged at Thorin's lips. "Good. I'll be in contact with you later, m'lady."

Every morning after that consisted of training with Knox. We practiced swordplay with wooden swords, archery, and he even taught me some hand movements if I was ever without a weapon in a fight.

I loved learning what he loved to teach. It was what he was good at. And the practice may help me on this hunt, though I had no idea what I was looking forward to.

At the end of the week, I awoke to a knock at my door. Sleepily, I hobbled to open it, hardly any light streaming from the window to guide my way.

I found Thorin waiting at my door, a satchel in his hands and a wide grin on his face. Suddenly, I was acutely aware of how little clothing I was wearing, and how sheer my nightgown was.

"Here ya go," he said, handing me the bag. "There's a pair of clothes for you to change into for travelling today. Extra clothes for the week as well." He looked me over. "I'll also have a bow, an extra tent, and extra supplies for you at the horses. Just head out the North Door." He turned to leave.

"Horses?"

He stopped and belly laughed. "Horses. You didn't think we'd be *walking* the entire way, did you?"

I shook my head, and he left with a wink.

I donned the clothes he'd given me: brown leather pants, a sleeveless black shirt, and black boots. The leather was surprisingly comfortable, and the black shirt fit snug around my waist and breasts once I laced up the back to my preferred fitting, but it was made of a material soft enough that allowed room to breathe. A large black coat was stuffed into the bag as well.

It wasn't quite what I was used to, but I'm sure I'd grow accustomed to it. Maybe it was just Velorum's style of clothes, or Astria's.

Jules pulled my hair into a singular tight braid down the back of my head in hopes it would stay put during my travels. I thanked her for taking the time to take care of me and converse with me when there was no one else to talk to. She was a sweet lady with many experiences in this kingdom throughout her life. I had nothing but respect for her.

"Zorath," I called out through the bond, finding that faintly gleaming thread that connected us. *"I'm going away on a hunt for a few days, so I may be far away from our bond's reach. I'll be back."*

"Yes, Master. Stay safe."

I ventured down the two flights of stairs, down the hall, and out the North Door. There, waiting, was Thorin.

He stood around a group of men—some guards, and some were squires there to assist on the hunt. There were at least a dozen horses total and two carriages for pulling supplies.

"There you are." Thorin approached me, taking my hand in his and kissing the top as he usually did. He wore brown trousers, a tan long-sleeve shirt, and a black vest on top, yet it failed to hide the strong muscles that laid underneath. "It's an honor to take *the* Lady Valora on a hunting trip."

"I'm flattered, really," I chuckled, not understanding why everyone deemed me as so special. Part of me was just looking forward to getting to know Thorin better. And this trip was mainly about hunting, exploring the Capital, and getting some true fresh air like I used to do back home on the beach.

Home. I shook the memory away before it could swallow me up.

He led me over to my horse, a white beast of magnificence. Her mane glistened in the light of the rising sun and her tail flicked in eagerness for the journey. I rested a hand on her soft coat.

"Are you ready?" Thorin asked me, eyeing me up and down.

"Yes." It wasn't me who said it. A different voice approached from behind me, and the hairs on my neck rose. I turned around as Knox signaled to a guard, "Bring me my horse, please, sir."

"You're not coming on this trip." Thorin stood straight.

"I am now." He stopped and looked at me, his eyes softening. "I want to."

"Don't you have duties in the castle with my sister and your mother?"

"I found my way around them. My father designated me to protect Valora, and I will do just that."

Thorin's bright eyes darkened. "Ah, you dirty dog. You got out of doing chores?" Thorin laughed. "I can keep her safe on my own."

"Actually," I interrupted their feud, "I can probably take care of myself either way." I playfully shrugged.

"I know you can," Knox's voice was velvet, but Thorin stayed rigid.

"But you don't hunt," Thorin growled.

"Not usually, but my job is to look after her, and I will do just that."

A black stallion was led over for Knox that reminded me of the one that brought me and Zorath here. It was just missing that third eye in the center of its head. He left to load up his horse.

I gulped. Two handsome men: the Prince, and the future General of the Starfire Vanguard. Both of them seemingly territorial over me, and they'd both be here, despising each other the whole trip. I couldn't back out now. The only option I had was to see how this played out.

"Need help?" Knox gestured toward the saddle while Thorin finished adjusting my reins.

"Sure." I said, our eyes meeting. The brown in his were flaked with gold in the rising sunlight.

I could have figured it out on my own, but I'd never ridden a horse. It was better to not embarrass myself right now, considering I'm supposed to be an asset to the realm.

"Alright, left foot on that stirrup there." I obeyed. He pressed each hand against the sides of my waist, his grip reassuring. "Alright, grab onto the saddle. One, two, three." And he lifted. Within a second, I had swung my leg around the other side of the horse, and then his grip loosened, but his left hand stayed on my thigh. "Feel okay?"

The horse took some steps in its place as it adjusted itself to my weight. "Yes, Knox. Thank you." I couldn't help but smile as I looked at him and his name rolled off my tongue.

The feeling of this horse between my legs was foreign, and I hoped I'd get used to it by the end of the day.

"You're welcome, Valora," his teeth gleamed. "Hold on to the horn there if you need stability. Keep your grip on the reins, but your horse should just follow the path of the others . . . and I'll stay close the whole time."

By midday, we were halfway through the most beautiful woods I had ever seen. Trees seemed to rise almost as high as the clouds, layers and layers of leafy canopies above us. The sunlight, the warmth, the fresh earthy scent in the air was all perfect. The sound of birds chirping and fluttering away made the magic of the forest come alive.

Thorin led the group most of the way, followed by two guards, then me and Knox, then the rest of the entourage.

The horse felt unstable underneath me for a while, but I grew used to the feeling fairly quickly. I began to move my hips with the sway of her back with each step she took until it felt natural.

Knox stuck to his word and stayed close by. It was quite obvious I'd never ridden before, but I kept myself calm and composed. Not only for the horse's sake, but for myself.

"Let's stop here for the day and see how this spot is." Thorin lifted his right hand into a fist, and we slowed to a halt. There was a clearing just ahead of us, and the sound of rushing water nearby came into hearing now that the hooves had stopped.

He dismounted, but I soon realized I was too small to simply jump down from this elegant mare. I'd never done it before. I waited while everyone else began to lead their horses to a nearby tree to tie to. I followed them. Thorin led the carriages by and positioned them on the edges of the clearing.

"Need a hand?" Knox hopped down from his horse and approached.

"Yes, please. I'd rather not fall and break my neck."

"We wouldn't want that now, would we?"

I rested my weight in the stirrup, and swung my leg around behind me. Before his hands could fully reach me, my foot got caught, and I began to fall backwards.

But I didn't hit the ground. I landed back-first onto Knox, who had shielded me from the ground's blow. His arms wrapped around my core, holding me tight to break the impact.

My breath caught, and I thought my ankle broke when it twisted from the stirrup. But I felt no pain, and had full mobility of my foot.

Simultaneously, we stood, but his hands stayed firm on my waist.

"Are you okay?" Concern overtook his eyes.

"Yeah, are you?" He nodded. I brushed off any dirt that had littered my black shirt, careful not to brush his hands away in the process.

He studied me. His eyes trailed my face, down to the curves of my hips in the brown leather pants, then back up to where his hands sat. He removed them quickly.

Yet, not *too* quickly.

"Good catch, my prince," Thorin intruded, his focus between me and Knox. "We don't need anything happening to your guest. But remember, you're betrothed to my sister." He nodded to where Knox had just been holding my waist and shot him a venomous glare.

"She's *our* guest, you know. *You* invited her here. The least you could have done is checked on her to make sure she was okay to ride along." There was a tension in his voice. "And I don't need *reminding* of your sister."

Thorin looked back at me and bowed. "My apologies, Lady Valora. I didn't mean to offend."

"None taken. Besides a moment ago, I can typically take care of myself. Thank you for the help though."

Thorin turned back to his crew and cupped his hands around his mouth. "Let's set up camp here, boys, and we can fish for dinner! The hunt begins tomorrow!"

CHAPTER THIRTY-ONE

THE CAMP WAS SET up with a practiced precision, and within no time the clearing was sprawled out with tents. In the center, a large fire pit was set up, and men were dragging logs to lay around it. I stood around my horse, brushing her mane to keep myself occupied while I watched the men worked.

And then it hit me.

I was the only female in this camp. There were at least a dozen men around me. A wave of remembrance washed over me.

The way Judah, Javie, and Jovis gathered around me and pinned me down, leaving me helpless. There had been no one around at that moment to protect me. They'd violated me.

A sound broke my train of thought. No. A voice.

It wasn't speaking to me, but I could hear it from afar, through the trees to my left.

I followed it like a calling in the wind, like I was being pulled to it on a rope.

Through the treeline and down the hill I went until I heard another voice. The sound of rushing water grew louder, and so did the voices.

There they were. Knox and Thorin rested their packs on some large stones against the rocky shore of the riverbank. They were conversing while they prepared their fishing lines. Then, they noticed me.

"Lady Valora, have you been okay since falling?" Thorin's gaze shifted from me to Knox. An obvious stab at Knox, but he didn't budge. Knox only peered at me as I walked closer, stepping carefully over the uneven surface of rocks.

"I'm just fine, thank you. May I watch?" I nodded toward the lines in their hands.

They shared a look.

"Of course," Thorin grinned.

I found a boulder to sit upon while they tied their lines and baited them. They simultaneously reeled back their poles and released them into the river ahead.

Minutes went by without a catch.

"Let's move upstream a bit," Thorin suggested. So they did. It seemed to be one of the few things they've agreed upon. They drifted to the other side of where I sat.

A few more minutes passed, and finally Knox had a catch. A beautiful trout—one of my favorite meals from back home.

And then Thorin caught one, placing it in the basket behind them with the other fish.

One by one they reeled them in, until the basket was about half full.

"Man, it's getting a little warm out here," Thorin fanned his tunic. He set down his fishing pole, and pulled his shirt off over his head, making sure to flex his abs just right in the afternoon sun—right where I could see him.

He was fit. He had the body of someone that could lead and train an army. It was obvious that *he* trained for it. The thick, powerful muscles of his back flexed as he reached down to grab his fishing pole, and I gulped.

Knox looked at him, then turned to me. He caught me peering at Thorin with a raised brow, but not for long, because as soon as his eyes met mine, he set down his pole as well.

Then his shirt was off.

"It's definitely getting warmer," Knox agreed, nonchalantly glancing back at me. Yes, I was staring.

His lean abs glistened in the sunlight, and looking down, I followed the V-shape that drifted lower . . . lower . . .

"Valora?" Knox broke me from my dissociation.

I cleared my throat as if nothing had happened. "Yes?"

"Do you want to try?"

I just *know* he saw me looking. I know he did. But I had to play it off. I had to pretend that the two shirtless men in front of me weren't distracting me from moving any muscle in my body right now. I simply nodded.

I stood, trying to focus more on balancing myself across the stones rather than the muscled, bare skin that stood in front of me.

When I ended up between them, Thorin handed me his pole.

"Just swing back and throw it forward," he told me as he stood close to my back, his breath almost reaching my ear.

"I've fished before in a stream."

Thorin placed his hands on my elbows to get me into position to swing.

"She said she's done it before, Thorin. Let her go." Knox ordered. The future General backed off, but only an inch or so. I could still feel his breath behind my neck.

I drew back the pole, then I released the line, but it got caught behind me.

Fuck me. Now I look like an idiot.

However, neither of them laughed like I thought they should have. Instead, Thorin inched closer and reeled back the line. "Here you go," he whispered, wrapping his arms around me to be my guide this time. His hands gripped my forearms as he led the pole behind me, his face so close to mine as I shifted my head closer without thinking. "And then with a fluid swing . . ." He swung forward. "Release."

It landed in the river. I could feel the weight of Knox's stare between us.

I tried to hide the tingle that shivered through me as Thorin stayed against my back as I fished.

This could get me in deep trouble.

By the time we returned to camp, the sun was beginning to dip below the horizon, and the fire pit was already at a crackling fire. The guards and squires sat around the fire awaiting our return.

Knox and Thorin set the heavy basket of fish on the wooden table nearby, and several of the men began to work, descaling, gutting, and filleting to prepare dinner. They all laughed and chatted while they worked.

My energy was no longer aligned with socializing at this moment. Between Thorin's flirtation, and Knox's ever-present gaze that followed me everywhere, they had my mind distracted.

I leaned back against a nearby log, the warmth of the fire hitting my skin just right. As the fish began to cook on a slab over the flame, more men drifted over to settle in for the evening. It wasn't lost on me how much attention I was getting, whether from the lingering stares or by their subtle shifts in body language. I was not only a woman, but "The Girl of the Prophecy". I was becoming known here.

Knox and Thorin finally took their places by the fire, sitting on either side of me on the logs like personal guard dogs. But I didn't necessarily mind being watched over by them.

"Lady Valora, aren't you hot?" Thorin rested a hand on my shoulder.

"What do you mean?"

"You're really close to the fire. Aren't you burning up?"

I observed where everyone else was sitting, and I was indeed a good foot or two closer to the flame than they were. "It's not that hot," I retorted, repositioning myself atop the log between them. I'd forgotten than heat didn't affect me, and they didn't know that.

Everyone around me conversed with each other, even the two on either side of me. But I kept to myself for that moment, feeling the weight of so many men around me starting to crush my mind.

Dinner was served a few moments later, and I took my portion quietly. I tried to focus on the food, on the task of eating, but part of me was still distracted. It was nighttime and I was in a camp with nothing but men.

I knew the two next to me wouldn't let anything happen to me, but in the back of my mind, I wondered what would happen once I went to bed and they weren't there to defend me.

Thorin, ever the one to keep the mood light, eventually offered me a grin. "How's the fish?" He asked, taking a bite of his own. "You look like you might be planning to eat with your eyes instead of your mouth."

I rolled my eyes, smirking while taking a small bite. "It's fine, Thorin. You didn't need to *catch* me staring."

He laughed, leaning in close enough to my right ear that I could feel the heat radiating off his body. "Yeah, but you weren't exactly staring at the *fish*."

I stiffened. Shit. I sure was looking at him while lost in thought. I must have been looking at him too long, too distracted. He looked down at me, waiting, expectant, and for a moment, it felt like I was the only thing in his world. It was both flattering and unsettling in equal measure. Not a feeling I was used to.

"She's fine, Thorin. Leave her be."

I looked to my left to find Knox's gaze locked on the fire-haired man, his jaw tight. It was a warning, but it was subtle. It was the king within him that you wouldn't notice unless you're paying attention.

Thorin raised an eyebrow and gave a subtle nod. "Alright, alright," he said, backing off, though there was still a playful glint in his eyes.

For a fleeting second while glancing between them, I felt like I was caught between two forces I couldn't control. One territorial man and the other.

The fire started to die out, and the other men began to filter off to their tents. The air had cooled considerably, and the flickering light of the campfire was the only thing that kept the darkness at bay.

I stood to gather my things.

"Sir, we seem to have made a mistake," one of the men muttered as he approached Thorin. "We thought we had packed Lady Valora's extra tent, but it must have gotten left. My apologies, sir."

My eyes flicked to the tents around us, and the extra large one that sat closest to the fire.

Thorin, quick as ever, noticed my hesitation. "Well, Knox and I have a shared tent now that he decided to come along." He flicked a quick glare in Knox's direction. "Good thing we packed the largest one available. Valora, you're welcome to stay with us. We're gentlemen, we won't bite."

I wasn't quite sure how to respond to that. My heart was already racing with the thought of what it meant to sleep so close to him. To *both* of them.

Thorin was single. Attractive. Confident. Talented. But I wasn't blind to the fact that he was a natural flirt, and maybe he didn't know or understand me as well as he portrayed.

Knox had been there for me since I arrived. Mostly on his father's orders, but also because he was seeming to begin to care about me and consider me a friend. He shared the dragon hatchery with me, a secret and sacred place, and the training ring with me. He's offered to give me lessons. He's been honest with me. He never made me feel nervous or uncomfortable. But he was betrothed to another, his life mapped out for him. I couldn't fit into that, and there was no need to force my way in. And yet, there was a longing pull in his gaze tonight that I couldn't ignore.

"Can I go change into something more comfortable?" I asked, wanting a little privacy from this moment.

"Of course," Thorin said, "I'll go get the supplies ready for the morning." He walked off.

"Will you . . ." I turned to Knox. "Will you make sure no one comes in while I change?"

He nodded without hesitation and followed me to the entrance of the tent, where I stepped inside alone.

CHAPTER THIRTY-TWO

THE INSIDE OF THEIR tent was rather simple: cots were laid on the ground, while blankets and quilts were strewn across each cot. A few bags were stowed against the back wall. The faint scent of pine mixed with the smell of damp soil, and the dimming glow of the fire from outside casted soft shadows across the fabric of the tent. It dimmed further once the curtain was shut, and I lit a small lantern to give me light to change.

I started undoing the laces behind my top, and I kicked my boots off to the side. The laces were knotted—and shit—my bag was still outside. I'd set it down when I'd heard the news about my tent. Because I didn't know where I'd be able to sleep tonight, if anywhere at all.

I didn't want to, but I had to do it . . .

"Knox?"

"Yeah?" He asked, still outside the tent.

"I, uh, I left my bag outside."

His footsteps trailed off, and came back a moment later. He reached inside with only his hand, and handed me the bag, pure nighttime peeking in from behind his arm.

"Thank you," I said, taking it from his grasp.

"No problem," he went back to his post.

I sighed through my nose as the laces of my top still wouldn't loosen.

"Hey, Knox? I wouldn't normally do this, but I need help . . ." I winced at my own statement. *Asking for help to get undressed by someone that was to marry another? Bad idea. Bad idea.*

He stepped inside, still wary of who was outside of the tent. "What is it,

Valora?"

"I think the laces are knotted up." I pointed to the back of my shirt. Why they would make a top for travelling with laces, I have no idea.

He simply nodded, and I turned for him to have better access to my back. He began to undo the laces. Slowly. One by one. Until I was holding my shirt tight on my chest. His fingers lingered against my back, almost playing with the laces, as if he were making sure each one was loosened properly. Or simply taking his precious time.

"Thank you," I turned back around and reached for my bag.

"I'll face the door so you can change. I don't want to open the curtain where people can see in." He turned around, and I changed as quickly as I could without making anything awkward.

"I'm done," I announced, now dressed in a nightgown.

He faced me, and looked me up and down. His shoulders rose. "I think I'll get ready for bed, too."

I took that as a cue to lay down and try not to look at him, which was mind-blowingly difficult to do. I pushed the cots together, and settled near the middle of them on my back.

"I need to tell you something," he started. "I really don't like Thorin. I don't trust him."

"You've told me that you two don't get along, and it's obvious you have something against him. Why?" Out of the corner of my eye, I saw him kick off his boots and undo his utility belt.

"His motives are wrong." He rested his sword up against one of his bags.

"He seems nice to me."

"That's what I'm talking about. Remember when I told you that he doesn't *want* to be the General?" I nodded, though I was still trying not to peer over at him as he undid the first few buttons of his tunic. "He wants a wife. He wants to stay in Astria and be the heir. Be a king. But he needs a wife in order to be able to do so. That was part of the deal he made with his parents when Astria made their deal with us. If he could find a potential consort by the date of his promotion, then he wouldn't have to stay here."

And then his regular belt came off.

Oh gods, I shouldn't be in this position.

I stared at the ceiling of the tent. "So, you're saying that no matter how much he flirts with me, he doesn't actually want me? He wants to use me to get the job he wants?"

"He may want you, Valora, but not for the right reasons. Not for the reasons you expect." His pants stayed on as he turned to face me.

"And what exactly are the right reasons?"

A moment of silence. "I know I'm not the one to give advice on marriage, but I don't want you to fall for his ploy and make a mistake."

I sat up on my elbows. "I've never had *anyone* want me for the right reasons, Knox, so I don't know *what* to fall for." His face drooped, and he eased closer after those words. I laid back down. He settled down on my left, and threw a blanket over the top of us.

"I just wanted to warn you, Val. I don't want you getting hurt. I consider you a friend now." His eyes relaxed when I looked at him. "Friends should be honest with each other, right?"

"How would Scarlet feel if she knew about us laying here right now? You laying next to your *friend*?" I whispered, a tremble in my voice. How could he tell me to stay away from Thorin, when his own fiancé had no clue that he was lying next to me?

His eyes narrowed. "She'll be alright."

That was his truth. He had no feelings for her. No remorse in his eyes. No guilt.

"I'm here for *you*." It was all he said before Thorin barged in.

"You two look ready to hit the hay," he snorted a chuckle. He undressed quickly in the same manner Knox had done and laid down on my right. "Goodnight."

"Goodnight," Knox and I said simultaneously.

Hours had passed since we said goodnight. The fire outside had long burned out.

I hadn't drifted off to sleep. Not very well, at least. The temperature was dropping, and my body started to shake profusely. I tried to hide it so I didn't bother either of them while they slept, so I curled up on my right side.

"Are you awake?" Knox whispered so low I could hardly hear him—not over Thorin's light snoring. "I feel you shivering."

Damn, I was trying to be discreet. "Yes," I replied.

Knox turned on his side to face me, and his left hand reached out to touch my ribcage. "Come here."

Before I could second-guess myself, I wiggled closer, and he pulled me in the rest of the way, settling his right arm underneath my head.

"Fuck, Valora, you're freezing," he whispered into my ear, sending my heart into a palpitating mess. Knox hugged me tighter, wrapping the blanket around every inch of me and securing all the gaps.

This was the safest I'd felt since being here. He knew I needed to warm up before I could even do anything about it.

"Better?"

I nodded. "Thank you."

"It's good to know that you can't get hot, but you can get cold." He chuckled lightly under his breath.

"I never realized it either," I admitted. Somehow, his body heat was already starting to help.

His thumb gently brushed the skin of my arm under the blanket, reassuring me that he was still there, that he was with me.

Within moments, my shivering stopped, and I fell into a deep sleep.

"We should head north through the woods," Thorin suggested, his voice cutting through the stillness of the morning like a blade. His eyes were scanning the paths ahead of us as we gathered our belongings for the hunt.

In the first light of the morning, I couldn't ignore the way his muscles flexed with every step. And his *confidence*. He'd gotten up early to make sure all of our supplies were ready and that I'd have everything I needed.

Thorin led the way. Knox's presence was undeniable as he walked beside me, a little closer than normal, as though the space between us was too much.

I could feel the tension in his every movement, the way his jaw clenched every time Thorin spoke or stole a glance at me. When the future General saw me this morning and gave me a kiss on my hand, Knox's mood immediately declined.

His words from last night repeated in my head. Thorin didn't seem like the type to want to marry for the sake of a throne. No. He seemed like a good leader, yes, with the confidence of a king. But to me, he seemed like a genuine guy that found himself in Velorum just like I did.

The silence between him and Knox stretched on until it became almost unbearable. It seemed like hours had passed since we ventured into the woods to hunt. The trees were finally thinning out.

Then I felt something. A tingle flowing through my veins like my sixth sense had just kicked in. They were close.

"Psst." I signaled to Thorin and he stopped. I gestured to the bow with a flick of my fingers, and without a question, he handed it to me, along with the quiver of arrows.

I shouldered the quiver and moved ahead of everyone, leading the pack. I could feel the stares behind me, but I never felt their doubt. They followed me silently.

I lowered myself into a crouch, my feet silent on the dirt. The bow was firm in my hands, the wood cool against my palm. There was a tension in my body—a blend of excitement and focus that made my heart race. I exhaled slowly, allowing the stillness of the forest to fill my lungs.

The faint rustle of leaves ahead of me grabbed my attention, and I approached a small opening through the brush. There, four deer grazed in a small clearing just beyond the thicket.

I nocked the arrow and raised my bow. I drew back and then the world narrowed down to just the deer, the beat of my heart, and the sound of the wind shifting through the leaves. There was no Thorin. There was no Knox. No Velorum, Zorath, or High King in existence. There was only me.

I breathed in, and then released the arrow. It flew with a perfect arc, and in an instant, the buck that had been standing there, dropped without a sound.

I let out the breath, the adrenaline washing over me in a rush. I stood, a quiet smile tugging at the corners of my lips as I watched the others approach from behind me.

"Impressive," Thorin spoke first, his gaze lingering on me longer than necessary. "I didn't want to believe Knox when he said you had skill, but I didn't know you were *that* good."

I raised an eyebrow. Knox moved closer. "I told you, I never doubted you."

"Yeah, yeah, Knox. No need to brag." Thorin chuffed.

"What did you say?" Knox faced him.

Thorin's voice dropped to a lower, more threatening, level. "You need to be careful what you say. Don't pretend I didn't notice you holding her in the tent this morning, fast asleep. I'm not sure what you're up to, but you're with my sister."

"If you *must* know, Thorin," Knox took half a step forward, "she was freezing her ass off and couldn't sleep because of it. Or maybe it was because of your pathetic snoring?"

Thorin huffed.

Before he could get another word in, I gave the bow back to Thorin, and his hand reached out for it, his fingers brushing against mine and lingering as he took it from me.

Knox's eyes snapped to our hands. His shoulders stiffened, but they'd just had their quarrel. So, I gave him a warning look that told him not to provoke him.

"I'll go grab the deer," Thorin said, passing off the bow to a squire.

I watched as he slung the beast over his shoulders within a few seconds as if the weight was nothing to him. His arms, the way the muscles in his back flexed as he hoisted it up, I knew I wasn't imagining it. He was *always* doing something to try and impress me since day one. Or maybe that was just me watching an attractive man work. Damn, what was wrong with me?

"You seemed to have hit both lungs and the heart," Thorin told me as he approached. "Good job, Lady Valora."

My face flushed at the compliment.

Knox stood silent, but I could feel the way he seemed to hold his breath when I acknowledged Thorin's actions. I wanted to tell him so badly that I didn't care, but Knox should be the one that didn't care, right? Thorin was single, and so was I, and I should be able to look at anyone I wanted.

We eventually made it back to camp. I rested on a log while the other men worked to prepare the kill. I was proud of what I'd done today, but I tried to ignore the way my mind kept spinning.

Knox's presence tugged at me, the intensity of his gaze that never left me.

Thorin was always *there.* Thorin made me feel wanted, he did. But now, I wasn't sure if it was for the right reasons.

As the evening wore on, I came to the conclusion that neither of them were just competing for my attention. They were competing for my heart.

And in different ways, I wanted both of them.

CHAPTER THIRTY-THREE

THE FIRE CRACKLED, SENDING warm, flickering light across the camp as the hunters and squires laughed and drank. The scent of roasted meat filled the air. Lagers, ales, and meads were passed around, each drink raised in celebration of a successful outing today. The boisterous energy was infectious, and even I couldn't help but feel the pull of their camaraderie.

But there was still the underlying factor about being the only female here that I just couldn't let go. No matter how hard I tried.

"Hey, Valora," Knox sat down next to me. "We've had a successful day today, yet you're a little quiet this evening. Is everything alright?"

I hesitated on telling him how I felt—telling him what was bothering me—but I wasn't sure if he'd understand. "I'm alright, just a little anxious. Nothing I can't handle."

"Well, try a little sip of this. It should take the edge off." He offered me a goblet filled with what looked like his usual beverage.

I stumbled over my words for a moment. "I don't know."

"By all means, don't feel like you have to, but I promise it will relieve some tension in your mind. If you want that."

It's like he already knew deep down how out of place I felt. How uncomfortable I was around all these people that I didn't know and couldn't trust, no matter how much faith I had in Knox to protect me. And Thorin.

I took the goblet from him, and took a small sip.

I coughed and a shiver ran down my spine.

"Damn. That's strong." I chortled, handing him the drink back.

"Have you never had alcohol before?"

"My parents in Solaria could never afford it, so no."

"That's crazy," Thorin sat down on the opposite side of me, a goblet in his hand, "that you've never tried it, not that your parents couldn't afford it. It's great. Well, I clearly don't think so as much as Knox does but . . ." He nudged me with his elbow and belly laughed, chugging half of his drink in mere seconds.

"I've always been too poor to afford it, and *clearly* Knox enjoys it for his own reasons and *only* his reasons. No need to insult anyone." I retorted, snatching Knox's drink from his hand and taking one more sip. It wasn't much better the second time.

"My apologies, Lady Valora," Thorin said, immediately starting a conversation with a nearby squire.

When I turned back to Knox to hand him his drink, a smile played heavy on his face.

"What?" I asked.

He shrugged. "I like it when you're a little feisty."

Heat rose to my face, but it was a good thing the color could be hidden by the light of the fire. "It seems I sometimes have to be in order to get what I want. Besides, you told me to stand up for myself here, so why not stand up for you?"

A warm smile played on his lips. "That, you're right about. You're doing a great job." He let out a short breath through his nose. "I'm glad you're open minded to trying new things."

"Well," I started, "I don't see any reason to not try your fancy, *princely* drink. I might as well start off strong."

That merited a laugh from Knox, and I couldn't help but chuckle along with him.

Over the next couple of minutes, I'd steal a sip or two of Knox's drink to try and get used to it. Surprisingly, the more I drank, the better it tasted.

I watched as the others grew louder, their cheeks flushed and eyes bright with the effects of the alcohol. The clinking of mugs and the slapping of backs felt like distant echoes in my mind.

"The stars are gorgeous when you're away from the city," Knox breathed, looking at the sky above.

"You're right," I replied. "I've always loved the stars. The ocean. I used to go to the beach just to sit in the presence of something that was so much bigger than I'd ever understand. But when I was on that ship, travelling across the Vast Sea, I saw the stars for how they *really* were. And man, I'll never forget the way they scattered the sky as if they were trying to cover up the darkness one by one."

"They say that the bright ones are our ancestors and other powerful beings that watch over us. That's why The Ceremony of the Stars means so much to some. It's like their past, present, and future, all align in one night to decide the fate of their people and replenish the magic."

"I love the stars." It was the only response I had as I looked up at them, distracted by the way they twinkled as if they were winking at me. Blinking at me. *Looking* at me.

But then someone brought out a lute, and another grabbed a small duo of drums, and soon a lively tune filled the air. My foot tapped involuntarily. I hadn't heard much music in my years in Solaria, or if I had, it was nothing like this. This was a cheerful beat, a happy melody. And, tonight, with the firelight dancing in the shadows, I felt a flicker of that happiness, too.

Knox must have read my expression as I rocked to the melody. He stood swiftly, and offered his hand. "Will you dance with me under the stars, Valora?"

With no hesitation, I accepted his hand and rose from my seat. He led me into the clearing and held my hands. Our movements were careful at first, tentative. But as the music swelled, and his eyes gleamed at me in the darkness of the night, something inside me broke free. I loosened up, and then we were dancing.

He twirled me, pulled me in close, and led me into swirls of enchanting movements that I hadn't realized I was missing my whole life. I spun, and I spun, and I laughed—a sound I hadn't heard from my lips in a long while.

For a while it was as though the world melted away. The weight of everything was gone. It was just the music, the fire, and the joy of dancing with Knox under the array of stars.

When the music came to a halt, I landed firm against his chest, his arms steady around me. My laugh continued, and I attempted to catch my breath.

More music started, and I danced again for a moment. This time, on my own.

But after a few moments on my own, the air began to shift. The more the men drank, the more their eye contact fell upon me, their gestures more careless. Some began to stumble, their hands lingering too long on their fellow hunter's shoulders to stabilize themselves. The energy was changing.

My smile faltered. It wasn't the men's drunkenness that unnerved me . . . it was the memories that it stirred. I knew men could change when alcohol clouded their senses, but there were so many of them here tonight, and I was the only female.

Men had been my predators before. I had been their prey.

There was a sharp, familiar knot in my stomach as my mind spiraled back to a darker place. A place where I had been violated, and men had been the abusers. There was nothing I could do at that time. There was no one to save me.

I turned quickly, inhaling sharply at the thought. I needed air. Space. I needed to leave.

"I'm going for a walk," I said, talking to no one in particular, and before anyone could stop me, I slipped away into the trees.

I made it only a few paces away from the camp when a hand glided against mine. I whipped around, still too consumed by my thoughts that I hardly noticed who was before me. Before I could do or say anything, I found myself in tears collapsing into his chest.

His arms wrapped around me tightly, shushing me gently and rocking me back and forth. "Hey, it's okay." Knox's voice was gentle, his presence steady. "I'm here for *you*, remember? I'm not going anywhere."

His comforting words only made me sob harder, and my knees collapsed. He led me safely to the ground, never faltering his grip on me. Instead, he held me tighter, and rested his chin on the top of my head.

The roughness of his facial hair grazed across my scalp, and his fingertips brushed my sides as he tried to steady my breathing.

"I'm sorry . . . I'm—" I struggled between breaths. "I'm overwhelmed, to say the least. There's so many men. I feel . . . out of place."

He gazed down at me, an understanding in his eyes. His hands cupped my jaw, and his thumbs wiped the stream of tears from my cheeks. "Nothing is going to happen to you here. You have my word."

I believed him. There was a comfort in his words that settled in my chest.

"I'm not going anywhere," he repeated.

But the tears kept falling silently, and I wasn't ready to go back to camp yet. He knew it.

"Ask me something."

I looked up at Knox, who peered down into my blurry eyes. "What?"

"Ask me something. Anything. Whatever will get your mind off of the thing that's bothering you."

I looked up at the stars peeking between the tops of the trees. The clear night sky around them. I remembered the way they made me feel on that ship, and the way I felt only a moment ago dancing underneath them. "Does . . . does it ever rain here?"

Knox grinned lightly. "Oddly enough, no. The Illumae here is just abundant enough to provide water and life to everything here. Crops, forests, rivers, you name it. There's always a cloudless sky in Velorum."

I exhaled slowly as I stared skyward, the anxiety that had gripped me beginning to loosen its hold on me as I took in his words.

"Better?"

I nodded. "Better."

Knox offered me a reassuring smile. "Let's get you back to camp, Val. You're safe with me."

We eased back to camp, my mind becoming more at ease with every minute Knox was beside me. By the time we returned, many of the drunken men had returned back to their tents for the night.

"I sent the sloppy ones to bed," Thorin announced to us when we returned. "Knox, may I speak with Lady Valora for a moment?"

Knox gave me a questioning look, but I nodded to him, assuring him it was okay. He took my hand in his, and kissed it gently on the top. "Goodnight, Valora. I'll see you inside." His breath tickled my skin, and sent a chill down my spine.

Once he left, Thorin cleared his throat, drawing my attention to him. He watched me for a moment, a soft smile playing at the corners of his mouth. He took a step closer, a goblet of alcohol clutched in his hand, and lowered his voice just enough it almost felt like a secret shared between us.

"You know," he began, his gaze steady and warm, "most people will only see what's on the surface. The woman with a bow, the one who doesn't show her weakness. But they don't know you. I see more than that. I see the way you carry yourself, the way you move through the world. The world isn't ready for what you can do. And I'm not sure if you realize it, Lady Valora, but you've made a mark on me. Not just because of your skills, but because of who you are."

I locked eyes with him, and his voice softened further, the essence of liquor and mead laced on his tongue.

"Whatever it is that you're hiding deep inside, whatever pain you think makes you weak or unworthy . . . I don't believe it. To me, you're more than just a warrior. You're someone worth fighting *for*."

I could only stare in awe at his words. Maybe he *did* know me better than I thought.

Or maybe this was his way of making up for the earlier insult.

He leaned in closer, brushing a stray hair from my face and grasping my cheek. "Goodnight, m'lady. I don't think I'll be able to stop thinking about that shot you made today. You're something else."

His warmth closed in on me, and his breath was almost grazing my skin. Yet, for whatever reason, I didn't pull away.

He smiled, a slow, knowing grin. "Sleep well."

Before I could gather my thoughts, his lips pressed softly against mine—a kiss that lasted longer than expected.

As he pulled back, I just stood there, my thoughts a knot of emotions that I didn't know how to untangle. He didn't say another word. He simply turned and walked toward the tent.

For a long moment, I stood frozen, caught in the aftermath of that one fleeting kiss.

I steadied my breath, wondering if Knox knew that Thorin was planning to kiss me. Or even if *Thorin* knew he was going to kiss me. There was only one way to find out. I had to go to bed. But I waited for Thorin to get settled in before making my way there.

Scarlet would be thrilled. Thorin made a move, and I'd accepted his advance. But not anticipating it . . . that's what threw me off. And I really didn't know what to do in this moment, or what to think about it. Not until I made it into the tent with both of the men who deemed themselves as my protectors.

When I entered, both were already nestled in the blankets, and Thorin was already drifting off to sleep thanks to all the alcohol he'd indulged in. I released the nest of a braid that was my hair, letting the strands cascade down my back in soft waves.

While they weren't looking, I changed quickly into my night clothes in a corner of the tent, then settled in between them.

Thorin started to snore, but Knox's eyes were open as he laid facing me.

I hesitated to confide in him, not because I didn't trust him, but because I wasn't sure what that revelation might bring. Would it make him even more jealous if I told him about the kiss, solidify any feelings for me, or would he simply let me go to Thorin?

And then the thought of him letting me go was unbearable.

A single tear slipped down my face, and I quickly wiped it away.

"Valora," Knox whispered, careful not to wake the man on the other side of me. I faced my head to him, and his eyes read into me. "Turn around."

So I did. I faced away from him, and he began to hold me just as he did the first night. His hand drifted to brush my hair, running his fingers along my scalp with a tenderness that made my heart ache. It's as if he read my mind, sensing the turmoil within me. "Do you remember when we were dancing earlier?" I nodded. "Your smile and your laugh lit something inside of me that I haven't felt in a long time. Every moment with you feels like a beautiful dance, even when the music gets a little uncertain. Just remember, it's okay to take your time to find the rhythm that feels right for you."

His hands continued to run through my hair, his breath trailing softly against my neck, and I trembled at his touch.

"I can't hold it in any longer. You're beautiful . . ." he breathed. "But I say it for the *right* reasons. I don't want you to doubt that."

My breathing quivered, and the hairs on my arms stood up.

His lips pressed gently on my nape. Not a kiss—but a touch of affirmation. There was no doubt that he saw how I looked at him. He saw what I felt about him.

Then he grazed his lips against my skin again, this time a little farther toward my ear. And again, traveling ever so slowly down my neck. And then he stopped, just breathing in my skin. His breath trembled against it. He was soaking in every part of me. Every scent of me.

"Knox . . ." I breathed, knowing he should stop. Scarlet's brother was just a few feet away from us, though he was passed out cold. But if he were to wake up and see us like this *again* . . .

"Valora," he whispered back, sending a tingle through my body. "No need to overthink anymore. There should be no worries with me. Not with me."

His hand trailed down my arm, wrapping itself around my waist, and pulling me in. His rough fingertips clawed gently at my skin, assuring his want for me. I reached around, interlocking my fingers in his, keeping him close. A message of how I felt.

His other arm reached under my neck and wrapped around, grasping our hands that were already together and keeping them in. My head rested on his shoulder as he propped our heads on a pillow.

I turned my head slightly to face him, and he raised his a minute amount until our noses were just about touching, and we simply shared the same air.

The way he looked into my eyes, but didn't make another move . . . it was like he was seeing me for *me*. I wanted him so badly. I wanted his kiss, his touch, his body. Everything. But I shouldn't. It wouldn't be right. He was someone I considered a friend—my only true friend in this kingdom. Cheating on a partner, whether you loved them or not, was not something I believed in.

I slowly turned my head back, and he relaxed back where he was.

His breath trailed against the skin on my neck, his lips leaving gentle touches along my body.

I could have sworn I felt something harden behind my backside, but I left it alone.

"Goodnight, Valora," he breathed with one last touch of his lips on my skin. He didn't persist.

But it was the most satisfying sleep I'd had in a long time.

The journey back to Velorum had been quieter than usual. I wasn't sure if Knox found out about Thorin's advance on me, or if Thorin found out about the tension between me and Knox. Whatever it was, it was certainly different from the constant bickering I was used to hearing between them.

However, there was no doubt that the long days on this trip had worn everyone down, including me. The day after I slaughtered that buck, I had yet to find any game to kill, but another group of the hunt came back with two does that next evening.

We celebrated, and the dawn arrived early. I harvested another deer that morning, Knox killed a buck, and the others returned with two more deer that afternoon. Thorin went fishing on the last day, and brought back a large basket of trout that had to be carried in by two men.

By the time we were heading back, we had plenty of meat for the court's dinner tonight.

It was just after midday when Velorum's gates came into view, the golden spires of the castle gleaming in the afternoon sun. The familiar scent of stone and magic filled my lungs.

I called out to my dragon, letting him know that I was back in familiar territory. He purred in my head, and informed me of how excited he was to see me soon.

With the help of Knox, I dismounted my horse at the stables, brushing off the dirt I'd accumulated on the journey. I started to wander off.

"Where are you headed?" Knox's voice brought me to a halt. I spun around.

"Just going to explore a little longer before dinner." I smiled.

"Well, it was an honor to hunt with you, Valora." He winked, and left for the castle.

"He's right," Thorin's voice grabbed my attention behind me. "It was the best hunt I've held."

"You're just saying that," I cocked my head and giggled.

"You look like you were made for this place, Lady Valora."

I raised an eyebrow. "Made for this place? I don't belong here. I'm nowhere close to royalty. I'm not fit for a throne, and I have no place in the court. I'm not even a Lady." For a heartbeat, his expression faltered, his gaze flicking to the ground before returning to me. I remembered what Knox had told me, but I wanted to hear it for myself. "What brought you here? How did you make it in line to lead the largest army of the realm?"

His powerful forearms flexed as he shoved his hands in his pockets. "I've known for a while I'd end up here, and it took me a long time to like the thought of it."

I tilted my head. "What do you mean?"

Thorin's smile faded slightly. "You know, being appointed to lead the Starfire Vanguard wasn't exactly a choice of mine. It was . . . something that my family thought I'd be suited for. After all, when Knox was betrothed to my sister last year, they needed someone to take the place of the next Vanguard leader if there was to be a change of power. It was part of their Royal Alliance deal. They wanted someone who could lead an army, ensure the defense of Velorum, and handle all the weight that comes with that position, so they sent me over with Scarlet. I did the job at home, but this is much bigger. I've got a lot to learn, but I think I'm ready." He paused, his gaze drifting briefly. "Really what my family wanted was another one of their kin in the capital. They wanted to keep their power close. My sister would be Queen, and I would lead the army. Our younger brother would be heir to Astria's throne when the time came. That was their plan."

I listened, feeling the weight of his words. "That's not what you wanted?"

Thorin gave a short, humorless laugh. "Fuck, no. Well, not at first. I didn't get to choose, but now I'm growing into it, I suppose. I'm doing what's expected of me, and maybe I can become something. I've spent my life preparing for this. Training, learning, commanding. It's just become a job. An important one, no doubt."

I opened my mouth to respond, but he spoke again.

"Then, I met you," he said quietly. His voice softened, almost vulnerable. "And it felt like . . . everything else didn't matter as much. It felt like I was here for more than one reason."

Silence fell. He inched closer to me, and rested his palm on my cheek. I let him.

"And maybe, Lady Valora, if you let yourself grow into this place, you also can find another reason that makes you feel like you belong here."

With those words, he kissed me.

CHAPTER THIRTY-FOUR

The dining hall was a sea of laughter and chatter, the long tables brimming with food, the air thick with the smell of roasted meats and fresh bread. There was a festive atmosphere, a celebration of the successful hunt we'd returned from.

Erika and Jules drew me a nice, warm bath after I'd returned from visiting Zorath and then training a few hours by myself in the arena. They scrubbed off every last piece of dirt, forest, and sweat that I'd brought back with me. Then, they dressed me in a teal satin gown, adorned with white pearls that accented my curves. The sleeves draped over my arms. Jules did magnificent work to pull my hair back halfway into an assortment of twists and braids, and Erika dolled me up with light makeup that showed off my natural beauty without leaving me bare.

I stared in the mirror. "What do you know of the prince?" I asked, not thinking.

Jules chuckled while Erika continued working on the finishing touches.

"The prince has a lot of duties, my dear. He's held to a high standard by the King and Queen," Jules said as she finished my hair, her kind smile brightening the room.

"Is there anything you can tell me about him that I don't know? Or even of the King? He told me he made some mistakes in his past. What mistakes did he make?" I swallowed. "He's tasked me to do some things while I'm here, and I don't want to make the same ones he made."

Jules straightened. "I've worked for King Polaris most of my life, dear. I watched him grow up. When he found out he bonded a rare breed, and he found out that his power was stronger than the others, he became . . . different."

Jules glanced around as though someone else was listening in.

"I can't say much more. But ever since then, he'd gotten in trouble for doing things he shouldn't be doing. Delving in magic that shouldn't be messed with. All of that . . . *changed* him. After becoming king, dragons began to die, and nothing has been the same since."

Her words resonated with me, yet didn't give me a clear answer as to what to do or not do. I brushed it off, letting her honest words sit with me while I finished getting ready.

The seating arrangement at dinner was our usual.

I hadn't forgotten Thorin's kiss. How could I? It still lingered on my lips, soft but intense. I was startled by the first kiss, but the second had been a message—an invitation. He was interested, and I allowed the kiss to happen. Both times. Maybe if I considered his words, and opened myself up to the possibility of companionship with Thorin, everything would be different here. And it would be alright. I didn't want to think about the kiss and what it could possibly lead to in the near future, but I couldn't stop myself as I looked at the handsome future General that sat beside me, that watched over my every move while I was in his presence.

My heart ached in a way I didn't understand, especially as I watched Knox. He hadn't said anything to me all of dinner, but I could feel the simmering jealousy radiating off him.

It was hard not to. I could see it in the way his eyes snapped over to Thorin every now and then, his gaze sharp and cold, like he was trying to keep everything inside, but it was breaking through. A dam ready to burst. But Scarlet was next to him, and he usually kept tame in front of her. He *had* to. He had to hold steady.

The conversation moved around us. Something about the hunt, to the celebrations, to a lighthearted talk of sparring and dueling and training. I could barely focus on any of it. My mind kept drifting back to Jules's words, and the events of the past few days, from the way I felt about Knox, to the way Thorin looked at me, and how everything had shifted between us when he'd kissed me.

Then, without warning, Thorin spoke again, his voice casual, but the words sharp enough to send a ripple through the room.

"If the prince can wield a sword better than he can hide his feelings, I'm sure that as King, the kingdom would be safe for years to come."

The comment was light, even playful, and I wasn't even sure what had provoked it, but it felt like all the air had been sucked from the room. Knox's hand tightened around his goblet, his knuckles white. I knew what was coming before it even happened.

"Are you insulting me, Thorin?" Knox's voice was dangerously low, but it was enough to silence the table.

Thorin didn't flinch. He was so calm, his voice almost a whisper as he responded. "I'm simply stating the truth. If you can't take the heat, maybe you should step down from the fire. You should know what's right and wrong for you, but you can't seem to grasp that concept." Thorin's eyes flicked to me, so fast I hardly noticed, and then back to Knox.

And then I knew what this was about. He saw right through Knox's *supposed* hidden feelings for me.

"You don't have to insult your future King, you know," I retorted, trying to simmer down what I knew was about to happen.

"He is supposed to defend you, on his father's orders, yet, he's got his *own* issues he should be resolving. And here you are defending *him*?"

That was it. Knox stood, his chair scraping the floor as he rose to his full height, his face flushed with anger.

"Don't act like you're better than everyone, Thorin," Knox snapped, his voice ringing out across the hall. "You think just because I'm betrothed to your sister that you have the right to talk down to me? I'm not your brother, nor will I ever consider you as one."

Every set of eyes shifted to us, the silence now thick with anticipation. The King propped himself sideways in his chair watching this unfold. The Queen went pale as the moon. My heart thudded in my chest, and it rose to flush my cheeks.

Something about his fury tonight felt different, like they couldn't control themselves, and I couldn't keep pretending that this feud wasn't happening. It had been driving me up the wall for weeks now—the constant bickering and complaining between the two of them.

"Knox, that's enough." The words left my mouth before I could think. "This isn't the time for this."

He still stood, yet his attention creeped over to me ever so slowly.

"You listen to *me*," I said, my voice loud enough to cut the tension in the air. "I'm sick of you two treating each other like this." Knox stared at me with widened eyes. "You keep acting like he's the enemy when he's done nothing but be kind to me. To all of us. He took us on a hunting trip and I thought we all had a good time together and thought we grew our friendships." I kept my eyes locked with Knox, hoping he would remember the nights we stayed close together, where nothing else in the world seemed to matter. "We had a good time."

"Yeah," Thorin interrupted, "and that kiss was something else, wasn't it, Lady Valora?"

Heat filled my face as Scarlet squealed with joy and Knox's face lost all its color. I didn't agree with the statement, but I didn't deny it either. It did happen.

Knox sat back down next to Scarlet, and gulped down his glass of liquor. He didn't say another word.

Thorin's eyes met mine. "We're done here. Come on, m'lady. Let's get you away from this mess." By "mess," I knew he was referring to Knox.

My mind was too occupied in wondering how Knox felt to oblige as Thorin took my hand and led me out of the hall.

We didn't speak as we left dinner, the sound of the double doors closing behind us the only noise that followed us down the corridor.

When we reached my chambers, the door clicked shut softly behind us. I stood in the center of the room, not looking at Thorin immediately.

"Glad we are out of that disaster," he chortled.

"You're the one that started it," I turned around to face him now, his blue eyes sparkling under the moonlight. "You didn't have to tell everyone that you kissed me, you know."

"But we did. It's what they want. It's what *I* want. And I'll do it again."

He reached for me, finding my waist and pulling me closer. I tilted my head up to meet his eyes, unsure of what to do in this moment, or what would happen next.

He leaned in slowly and closed the distance between our mouths.

At first, it was a soft, tentative meeting of lips. But soon, the softness gave way to something deeper. His mouth moved against mine with hunger.

Thorin's hands slid from my waist to my back, pulling me even closer. His kiss deepened then, his tongue sweeping into my mouth with a quiet urgency, and I met him, my own tongue accepting it. Responding.

It's something I should want. I needed someone available that wanted me. Maybe I needed to keep an open mind, like Knox had mentioned that one night about the liquor, and give Thorin a chance. Maybe we could turn into something more, and I wouldn't have to worry about anyone else ever again.

His hands traced the curve of my back, and I gasped softly at his touch. He pulled me against him, and I could feel the hard planes of his body, the strength in him as he grasped at my dress.

"Gods, you're fucking hot," he muttered into my mouth. "You'd make a remarkable bride in Astria."

I pulled away slightly, Knox's words from the tent coming back to me. "What's that supposed to mean?"

"That you're so hot, anyone would bow to you if you were a queen." His lips pressed forward and met mine once more, but I pulled away again.

At least, I tried to.

"Don't resist," he mumbled, his grip growing stronger. But I shoved him back enough to look him in the eyes.

"You only want me as *your* bride so I can be *your* queen. So you don't have to stay in Velorum." There was a bite in my tone, but he needed to hear it.

He laughed, his grip still holding strong on my clothing. "You're a smart girl. I like that." He pressed his forehead into mine. "We'd be a strong couple in Astria. You with your powers. My lineage and my talents. We could be unstoppable. It's a great match."

"You have no true talents. You just got lucky to be born into a royal family," I rebutted, heat boiling underneath my skin. Perhaps he could see that fire ignite in my eyes—that simmering rage that was building up. "You're a shameless flirt that has no business ruling a kingdom."

With a swift movement, I found his hand clenching my throat, pulling me upward. I gasped for air as my toes tried desperately to find purchase on the floor.

"You will not speak to me in that way again," he seethed through his teeth, his eyes darkening to a color I hadn't seen before. "Don't insult me again. Or you'll see how strong I *really* am. Got it?"

Though his grip was too tight against my windpipe, I nodded as best as I could, anxiety taking hold of me.

"Good," he snapped, releasing me quickly, heading for the door. "I'll see you later, Lady Valora."

I hunched over, desperately trying to catch my breath. That was a side of Thorin that I never saw coming, and one I never wanted to see again.

In that moment, it finalized how I felt about Knox.

Knox sat across from me at breakfast, his usual ease and confidence replaced with a tautness in his posture. His gaze flickered toward me every so often, but he didn't meet my eyes directly. His jaw was tight, his fingers tapping absently on the edge of his goblet, though his attention was nowhere near the food or drink before him. His face was drained of color, dark circles surrounding his eyes, as though he had hardly slept.

I kept my gaze low, pretending to enjoy the delicate pastries and the rich fruit jam. The discomfort in Knox's posture was obvious. Every so often, I caught the faint twitch of his lips, as if he was struggling to keep his composure.

Thorin sat silently next to me, and I wanted nothing to do with him. But I pretended that nothing had happened last night, just as he did. He'd occasionally make small talk with the courtiers, and his proximity to me was simply enough to make Knox's frustration more visible.

But his mood wasn't the same toward Thorin in particular. There were no sharp words this morning, no biting comments. It was clear something had changed in him, holding back the feelings he's had toward Thorin for all this time, he was reconsidering.

I was still upset with him. His outburst in front of everyone, including his mother and father—*the* King and Queen—was uncalled for. Inappropriate. He had become defensive over a feeling he should've had control of.

I excused myself from breakfast once everyone finished and moved toward the back hall, and made it to an alcove before Knox was steady behind me. The hairs on my arms rose in his presence.

"Valora," his voice was low, but there was no mistaking the sincerity in it. "May we talk?"

I didn't resist as he stepped in front of me, putting me between him and the wall. His hand rested behind me against the stone. His eyes were searching, scanning my face.

"What is it, Knox?"

"You and Thorin," he said, his words laced with a quiet edge. "Last night . . . when you two left . . ." his voice drifted off as if the words were hard to say. He looked deep into me, and I looked up at him. Then his eyes lowered to my neck. "He didn't fucking *dare*."

His other hand reached up to gently cup my jaw, allowing him to examine the bruises there from Thorin's grip.

"I'm fine," I looked down again, though the more I tried to speak the worse my throat felt like it had been embedded with needles.

"He did this to you?" The pitch of his voice rose, echoing loudly down the hall.

I gulped, remembering the moment Thoring gripped my windpipe like he owned me.

"Valora. Did he do this to you?"

I simply nodded, lowering my gaze further. "You were right. He's not who I thought he was." He carefully lifted my chin back up to him.

"I'm sorry that I didn't protect you—that I wasn't there. I should have been there."

"You didn't need to be there. Not after how both of you acted in front of *everyone.*"

His eyes widened, then searched me over again. "There's no excuse. I had gotten angry with him too many times, especially over you, and it wasn't the time or place. Not in front of you. Not in front of them. I'm sorry, Valora, that I led you into that." Knox's gaze flicked to my mouth, and then back to my eyes. "You were right to tell me off in front of everyone. I deserved it. But the fact that Thorin did this to you . . ." He shook his head.

His words were genuine. I felt the pain in his heart. He leaned slightly closer toward me, toward the wall, his breath just inches from mine.

"It's my fault. I should have listened to you from the start." It's how I truly felt now. Now that my heart ached for him and only him. "What's going on with you?"

The question was direct, but it needed to be asked.

He pulled back an inch. "What do you mean?"

"You know that whole thing that Thorin said about your feelings . . . it was about me, right? He knows how you feel about *me.*" Knox's eyes opened a little wider. "It's obvious that you and I have something buried within us, some unspoken connection. When we're out and about, roaming the streets doing who-knows-what and training together, I feel so close to you. I feel like I can tell you anything and you'd never judge me, never belittle me for who I am. But when we get here, inside the castle, you completely shut it off and pretend you don't know me. I'm starting to get confused." I shook my head. "I don't want my feelings to be confused, Knox."

"Valora," his voice lowered in shame, "I can't let Scarlet see—"

"That's the thing. It's always about her, and she's not even the princess or queen yet. It's about how she feels ever since she's been here. And if the feelings you're hiding are true and just, would it *ever* be about me? Or do you keep me company because it's only what your father wanted?" It was a sharp jab, but it's the only thing I could think of to pry the truth out of him.

"Where is this coming from, Valora?" Concern grew in his eyes.

I sighed. "I know what I *don't* want, and I also know what I *do* want. But I can't keep feeling these emotions if you have to run back to her every night. Or if you have to abide by everything your father says you should do. You told me that first night I met you that no one can control me. Stop letting everyone control *you*. You are your own person, prince or not, and you need to express your feelings and your concerns," I lowered my gaze to the floor. "I can't be close to someone that distances himself so much from me. Especially if events like last night are bound to happen the next time Thorin, or *anyone,* pisses you off or makes a move on me."

"Valora, I'm sorry."

Water flooded under my eyelids, but I wouldn't let it fall. Not yet. "I can't let men keep ruining me. I won't. Thorin was the last straw. So, when you can choose what matters most to you, then we'll talk. Okay?"

He stayed silent for a moment, and nodded. "I won't let what happened to you last night happen again." His hand reached up to cup my cheek, his thumb gently brushing my skin. "*He* won't ever touch you again. It's a promise."

He released his touch and backed away, and before I knew it, he'd retreated down the hallway.

CHAPTER THIRTY-FIVE

Jules and Erika had once again spoiled me with braided hair, heavy makeup, and a dress that glowed like a diamond.

I could really get used to it—the pampering and the clothes that made me feel important here.

The atmosphere surrounding dinner was different than ever before—more electric as whispers floated around the room about The Ceremony of the Stars.

Scarlet was eyeing me with barely disguised disdain. Her sharp, calculating gaze met mine from across the table, and for a moment, I could have sworn I felt the coldness of her stare as if it were a physical weight.

She was beautiful—too beautiful. But there was something about her that made me uneasy. The way she clung to Knox's arm like she owned him, the way her eyes roamed over him whenever he spoke to someone else. It was indeed . . . possessive. It made me wonder if she, too, knew how Knox supposedly felt. Or if she heard about the words Thorin and I spat at each other last night. About how I rejected him.

Conversations bubbled around me, breaking my train of thought. King Polaris spoke now, his voice carrying across the whole table. "The Ceremony of the Stars will take place on the nineteenth of August, in just two days. But this time, it's especially significant. The stars are aligning in a way that hasn't been predicted before, and it is believed this truly will be a new era for Velorum, and for the realm as a whole. An abundance of Illumae is expected to be renewed."

A ripple ran through the table at the mention of a new era. I watched as Knox's jaw tightened slightly, his gaze flicking to the far wall where no one was. But his discomfort wasn't exactly what caught my attention. It was the way Scarlet's hand tightened on his arm at the words. The grip on him was unmistakable. She leaned into him, her words low, but just loud enough for me to hear, "And you'll be the one to lead this new era, won't you, dear?"

Knox's shoulders tensed, his gaze never fully meeting hers as he replied in a calm, controlled voice, "That's only for the stars to decide, Scarlet."

Then, a realization struck me like lightning.

The nineteenth of August.

"That's my twenty-second birthday," I said, almost absent mindedly. But once they were spoken, the room seemed to freeze.

I immediately regretted opening my mouth. I glanced up at King Polaris, hoping to somehow erase the attention I'd just drawn to myself, but it was too late. He was looking at me with something like surprise.

"Your birthday?" he repeated, his voice soft, almost reverent. "That . . . that is indeed a momentous day, Lady Valora."

"Yes," I said, my voice quieter now, but the heat still rose to my face. "I'll be twenty-two on the day of the ceremony. In two days."

It wasn't just The Ceremony now, it was the fact it was my birthday that began making people uneasy.

Knox's eyes were fixed on me now, and I could see the turmoil behind them. It was my birthday, but it also brought the pressure of what may be expected of him for the kingdom—a big day for both of us.

Scarlet, however, didn't seem to take kindly to the shift in focus. Her hand tightened once again on Knox's arm, her voice low but cold. "Well, the ceremony has always been a celebration, right?" Her words were nothing but sharp. "And now, we have a birthday to remember it. How convenient is that?" She squeezed Knox's arm.

His shoulders tightened again. His fingers flexed around his cup, yet he said nothing. He kept his eyes on the table ahead of him, trying to remain composed, but there was a clear, palpable discomfort in him now.

I met his gaze across the table. "Knox," I said softly, but loud enough to grab his attention. "You're not alone in this, you know."

The look he gave me was one I'd never seen from him before, like he'd seen a new world.

Scarlet's voice cut through the void. "Of course he won't be alone. He has me to support him. Right?" Her eyes never left Knox, as though daring him to contradict her.

Knox downed what was left in his glass. The weight of his silence was more telling than words could have been.

Everything was happening so soon.

King Polaris cleared his throat. "Lady Valora, that reminds me. Have you progressed any further on that matter you and I discussed?"

Shit. I'd pretty much forgotten about trying to find a way to replenish the Illumae. I'd been so busy with Knox. And Thorin. And training with Knox. *And* visiting Zorath. I'd been meaning to spend more time in the library, but my mind had been so occupied elsewhere.

I shook my head. The High King audibly sighed and sat back in his chair, his eyes narrowing to a darker blue. "That's too bad."

He stood shortly afterward when his meal was finished. "Council meeting. Pewter, please fetch the Master Astrologists and meet me in the Council Chamber." Pewter, a tall, bald man in robes, stood and left the room while King Polaris called a few more names that I didn't really know, but clearly were sitting at the table with us.

Chatter continued amongst the room as the High King and his party left for the evening. Knox stayed seated.

"You're the Prince. Wouldn't you need to go to these meetings?" I took the opportunity to whisper across the table while Scarlet laughed with the couple next to her.

He shrugged. "He hasn't had me in a meeting since before you arrived, and I'm not complaining. Apparently, it's not something he deemed necessary for me to know."

Scarlet glanced back over, as though she forbade us to speak.

I finished the deer steak in front of me, and silently made my way to my room.

CHAPTER THIRTY-SIX

I was drained by the time I returned to my room. The silence of the chamber welcomed me, a stark contrast to the murmuring of the court.

The soft, golden glow of the moonlight filtered through the curtains, long lines of light and shadows spanned across the room. I took a deep breath, trying to shake off all of the weight that followed me tonight.

I started to undress, removing the elegant silver gown I had worn to dinner, the complex lace catching in the candlelight. The gown fell to the floor, and Erika and Jules drew me a bath, laughing and chatting with me about nothing to ease the tension from the room. Once I felt cleansed from the night, I stood before the large, golden mirror in nothing but the deep blue nightgown that Erika and Jules gave me.

As I reached for a cloth to wipe the remaining makeup from my face, there came a knock at the door.

I froze.

My heart raced as I crossed the room. I knew who I *didn't* want to be standing at that door.

But standing in the dimly lit hallway was Knox. His onyx eyes met mine, wild and intense.

He wasn't dressed in elegance anymore. His black attire was slightly rumpled, his curly hair mussed. A nervous smile played on his lips.

"Knox?" I asked, unsure of what I was witnessing.

"I broke it off with Scarlet."

My heart nearly stopped. "You . . . you what?"

"I told Scarlet I didn't want to marry her. That she belonged in Astria and that she wouldn't be my queen." I was speechless.

Erika and Jules stepped out from behind me, and Knox stiffened. "We'll leave you two alone," Jules said on her way passed, patting my shoulder lightly. I caught a blushing glimpse from them as they took off giggling.

"You can trust them," I said as they disappeared down the hall. He didn't argue.

I gestured for him to come inside and shut the door behind him.

"Knox," I started. "Are you okay? That must have been difficult. How did she take it?"

"Not well, as you can imagine. Decor may or may not have gone flying." He pointed to the rip in his sleeve.

"I'm sorry," I said as I made my way over to the table by the window.

"No need to be sorry. I feel rather relieved." He lifted his closed fist to show me his reddened knuckles, almost bruising. "I took care of our other problem."

"You did *not,*" I said, my mouth agape.

"I did. He deserved it for what he did to you."

I turned back to face him, holding a glass and a decanter of liquor in my hands. "Would you like a drink?"

His smile grew to brighten the room. "You know me so well, Valora." I made him a drink and handed it off, pouring a small glass for myself.

"I had it brought here after our talk this morning. Just in case it was me that you chose," I blinked multiple times, trying to dry away the happiness swelling in my eyes.

"She never liked it when I drank. But to be honest, I only drank so much to drown her out."

"I'd need it too if I knew I had to be married to that," I said, giggling.

He laughed with me, then his features relaxed as they took me in. "You know, when I saw you that first day, so out of place in the Grand Hall, I was awestruck by your beauty."

Heat flooded to my cheeks. "You're just saying that."

"I'm not, though," he took his first sip of the drink I made for him. "I wanted to know more about you, but I knew how my father was. How *she* was. How controlling they both were. I knew it would be hard. And I just got lucky that I was able to spend time with you on my father's orders."

I grinned, taking my first sip, "I think so, too. You've been a great friend, Knox, and you've made this place enjoyable for me."

We shared a few more laughs, and shared looks into each other's eyes that I didn't quite know what to do with yet. Then, we settled on the edge of the bed and faced each other.

He gazed around my room, taking it all in. "This room is a little dull for you. I know something that may make it better."

My brows furrowed. "What's that?"

He looked at the ceiling above, lifted his hand, and snapped. In a blink, the ceiling shifted from gold, to an image of the night sky. Stars swirled around every inch, twinkling.

"How . . ."

"Like I told you a while back," he said, raising his hand and shrugging, "magic. Some have more, some have less abilities. I'm a Polaris. And though the Illumae is running low, I used what I have within me to create the stars for you. So you can go to bed every night staring at the beyond that fascinates you."

The thought took my breath away. The fact that he would even use up some of his magic just for me . . .

It reminded me of the upcoming event. "Can you tell me more about this Syzygy coming up? Like what to expect?"

His eyes drifted to the star-lit ceiling in thought. "Though the stars only align this way every century, we mark the day each year with a celebration. It is the largest gathering you'll ever see. Hundreds of people from all across the kingdom will be there. The reason being is so everyone can contribute back to Velorum."

I cocked my head. "How does that work?"

"In the Grand Hall, a fountain will appear. Strange, I know. But it's only available on this day every year, for this purpose. People gather around it, and everyone places a coin infused with a fraction of their Illumae into the fountain.

"By the end of the night, when the fountain claims as much magic as it needs for the year, it will glow brighter than the chandeliers above. It matches the stars' light. The stars will draw the magic up and feed it back into Velorum, and it's how the kingdom prospers. But less and less is being fed back into Velorum every year and we don't know why."

I found myself leaning into his words. "Do you contribute?"

Knox nodded slowly. "Every year."

"So," I started, my thoughts racing, "what about when the stars align?"

"It is said that when the stars align on this night, they tell the fate of the kingdom, of the people. That's why I'm so worried, and why my father is worried, too. The stars, the gods, the ancestors above, they could choose me as king. They could choose someone else, or choose for my father to continue his rule. They can call people together. Anything can happen, but it will all have meaning. That's why this celebration is so important, to know and preserve the future of Velorum."

I rested my hand on his. "If you are chosen, then know that it was simply your destiny. If you aren't, then the stars will have lifted a weight off of you. Either way, this celebration doesn't define you. Not who you *really* are."

He smiled softly. "Thank you, Valora. Your support is everything."

For a moment, neither of us spoke. "You mentioned at one point that you had a brother. Where is he?"

His smile seemed to fade. "He's an asshole that can drive me just as mad as my betrothed did." He trailed off, taking another sip. "The Polaris bloodline was born with gifts alongside their magic. He was sent out of Velorum on my father's orders, running an errand for him because of his power."

"What kind of power?" I inquired, but he shook his head.

"Can we not talk about him right now? He's a good-for-nothing liar that I wish wasn't a part of my life."

His words bit at me, but I knew his intention was not to offend me. I understood how it felt to be forced into a place, a life, that you didn't want to be in.

"What are your gifts then?"

He paused, as if wondering how to start, and sighed through his nose. "Do you remember seeing a black wolf on your way in here? On your first day?"

I nodded. "How could I forget?"

"Do you remember seeing a figure made of shadows on the Vespera?"

I hesitated. "Yes. I do." The image of that shadow still burned in my mind.

His eyes locked with mine. "I'm a shapeshifter, the wolf being my alternate form. My father gave me this—" he pointed to a pure black chain around his neck "—embedded with a fraction of his power, giving me shadow-wielding abilities."

I didn't know what to say.

"I use these for my usual duties about the kingdom, combining my powers however needed. I guard the borders. I can send shadows anywhere I please, and watch through them. I can roam the forests as a wolf, and I can see through that horse's third eye that brought you here."

I stayed silent, sensing he had more to say.

"I saw you on that ship, hands full of fire, ready to strike at me, and I was instantly mesmerized. There was so much power, so much fight in you. I wanted to know more about you as soon as possible. I didn't wait to send that horse and carriage out there for you. Once you were on your way, I just needed one more glimpse of you. I needed to see you one more time before you made it through the gates. Then when you arrived in that hall and I could see you in person, I didn't even know what to say to such a beautiful woman. I didn't want to stay away. And ever since then, I've been drawn to you."

I rested my hand on his, absorbing every word he'd shared. "I'm drawn to you, Knox. I have been for a while, but I hadn't allowed myself to accept it until now."

His eyes brightened. "You've asked me some things. Tell me something about you."

"What is this, a date?" I chuckled, and nudged his knee with my fist.

"Maybe it is," he said with a lift of his chin. "Does Valora Emberlyn have any other powers hiding in there?"

I thought back to everything I've experienced. Everything out of the ordinary. "Sometimes, I have these dreams, and they portray real life events. It's really hard to explain. Sometimes it will show me what will happen, sometimes it's only a feeling. I used to get them a lot before those guys—" I stopped, lowering my head, not knowing if I should continue.

"What guys, Valora? What did they do?" Concern overtook Knox's eyes as he lifted my chin to look at him.

I sighed heavily. "I was raped. In Solaria." His eyes widened, but he didn't speak. Only listened. "Two large men held me down, while another man forced himself on me. This was before my powers. Before Zorath hatched. I didn't have the strength that I do now." His hand held mine tight. "I'm okay now. They got what they deserved." I lowered my head in remembrance, indulging in a small sip of alcohol.

"Thank you for sharing that with me," his thumb brushed the top of my free hand. "I'm so sorry that happened. I could tell something was wrong on that hunting trip, but I never would have imagined that's what happened to you to make you feel unsafe."

"It's okay. I've learned healing isn't linear. It takes time. But it gets better." I grinned at him, and he realized what I meant. Everything would be okay now. I found him.

"No one can or will make you do anything ever again. Not while I'm around."

I believed him.

My limbs grew warmer and relaxed as the alcohol affected me more keenly and the conversations drifted elsewhere, accompanied by laughter. When Knox spoke to me, it felt as if he were saying more than just words.

His eyes read me.

"Valora . . ." It was more than just saying my name. It was more than just sound coming from his lips. His voice was soft, his gaze trailed over me in a way that made my heart race. His free hand reached up to cup my jaw, his thumb mindlessly trailing the skin on my cheek. "You occupy my every thought. I can't eat, sleep, or breathe without thinking of you."

I could feel the heat of his body as he inched closer, the pull undeniable. My pulse quickened as the temptation to close that gap became overwhelming. "Go on." I mumbled, my eyes drifting to his mouth.

He set both of our glasses down next to the bed, then both of his hands were cupping my face. "I never believed in fate, but then you came into my life . . . and now, all I can think is that I was always meant to find you. Like *we* were written in the stars." The feel of his fingertips brushing my skin made me breathless. *He* made me breathless. "You set something in me on fire, Valora. Something I thought was long gone." His body inched closer. Closer.

This is everything I've been wanting. Him.

Him.

His hand drifted to my knee, drawing patterns along my skin. "I will always protect you." His hand reached up to brush a strand of hair from my face, his fingers lingering.

As his words hung in the air, he closed the space between us and finally kissed me.

CHAPTER THIRTY-SEVEN

He's perfect. Everything's perfect.

The air seemed to crackle. His lips found mine in a slow, searching kiss. I let myself melt into him, as if all of my walls had crumbled at his touch. There was no urgency in the kiss like with Thorin. No desperation like with Jameson. There was no ulterior motive. It was quiet and tender. It was what I'd wanted for what felt like forever. Exactly what was missing in my life. Him.

He pulled back just enough to see my face. Neither of us retreated further. Instead, we sat a moment, gazing at one another, a tremble in our breaths.

"I didn't lock the door," I remembered, and my body twitched to get up.

"I've got it," Knox whispered, and he raised his hand toward the door and flicked his wrist. The locks clicked.

"That was unbelievably attractive," I breathed.

He laughed lightly. "Val, I told myself for so long that I wasn't allowed to want you. But I'm not sure that I can live in a world where you're not mine."

My breath shuddered. "Then make me yours."

He advanced once more. There was more intent with this kiss. The touch of his lips were tender, nurturing, *loving*. I lifted my hand to cup his jaw, keeping him close, feeling the roughness of his beard on my skin. There was an ease in being with him.

Knox's arms encircled me, pulling me in, as if he couldn't get me close enough. The warmth of his tongue seeped into me, and slowly, I let him in further. My mouth eased open, allowing room for his tongue to slip inside. It was a slow dance as they grazed each other, the room growing warmer with every touch.

His hand cradled the back of my head, and he leaned in, guiding me down until my back was on the bed. His fingers trailed my scalp, finding hair to run his fingers through. Slowly. Gently.

He pulled back one last time, concern in his eyes, asking permission to continue. I nodded. I didn't only want him. I had a rushing need for him. *Now.*

He pressed on.

His lips enveloped mine with a passion, his body inching closer with every kiss. Knox's hands explored every inch of my face, my jaw, my head, pulling me in, leaving me quaking at the feel of him. I kept my hands around his head, never wanting to let go of him. Never wanting this to stop.

His body hovered above me, the hardness of his groin slowly grinding into my pelvis. I jerked my hips closer as his tongue danced with mine, our breaths heavy with desire. He grinded harder.

The silken night clothes were slowly being lifted off of my body, his tongue pressing into mine with burning passion now. His hands trailed my naked body, breath trembling with every touch.

Knox's lips ventured from mine, and moved lower, kissing me ever so softly on the way down. My neck. Lower. Between my breasts. Lower. Down to my midsection.

His hand found its way to my left breast, his finger glazing over my peaked nipple as he playfully sucked at the skin around my navel, sending rushing heat down my core.

"Knox . . ." I breathed, and he moaned at the sound of his name.

"Say it again. Say my name," he murmured, the air hot against my aching skin.

"Knox . . ." I moaned, the struggle to contain my need for him almost unbearable. He growled, sending my body into a spiraling heat.

He sat up, and I immediately went for his shirt, removing it with a swift movement. I wanted to swim in those chiseled abs and the muscles surrounding his entire body. The way they flexed with every heave of his breath. A fighter's physique.

I nodded at his pants, noticing the protrusion waiting to be released. "Take them off."

His grin widened as far as it could go. "Yes ma'am."

He stood to remove his pants.

Holy Gods.

His generous length revealed itself, and he eased back on the bed, noting the way I gawked at him.

A predatory smile played on his lips. "Do you like what you see, Valora?" I nodded. I was unbelievably ready for him. All of him.

He backed up and lowered himself, his head looking up at me from between my legs. "But first, I want to take care of *you.*" His hand began again, venturing up my body to my breasts, his kisses landing on my inner thighs with a delicate touch that made me tremble.

Then Knox's fingers softly caressed my skin, drifting lower . . . and lower . . . and lower . . .

Until his thumb circled gently on a sensitive spot at the apex between my legs. My body quaked at his touch, chills running down my body, and I didn't want it to stop.

He pressed a little harder as he continued his circular motion, a moan escaping from my mouth. Knox's other fingers drifted lower to my entrance, and he looked at me through raised brows at the feel of me.

"You're so wet for me, Valora."

He slid a finger inside me, slowly, gently. His thumb kept its position on that sensitive spot. He pulled out, circled that spot with his thumb, and plunged again.

"Knox . . ." I breathed as I flung my head back onto the bed.

In an instant, he slid another finger in and his thumb departed that spot. But—

His tongue began to trace patterns against it. Oh. My. Gods. This man.

I bucked my hips as pleasure shot through every ounce of my body. The movement from his fingers continued slowly as he feasted on me, until he withdrew his hand completely and wrapped his arms around the underside of my legs, tugging me closer.

"Oh fuck," I cried as Knox buried his mouth into me as if it were my face from just a moment earlier. His tongue swished at the swollen spot and then drifted lower until it was tracing the circumference of my entrance. And then it plunged in. And out.

I moaned as he feasted on me, every touch of him mesmerising.

He crawled back on the bed, to my right side this time instead of on top of me.

"Knox . . ." I breathed, aching for him. I reached for his cock, and the feel of him made my breath tremble.

He groaned and his head tilted back. "Holy fuck, Valora." I stroked his length and felt every inch of it in my hand, memorizing every touch against my skin. He reached under my back with his left arm, and pulled me to him as he kept himself propped up.

He removed my hand from him, resting it against my chest, and drifted his fingers down my center.

"I told you, beautiful. I'm taking care of you."

I opened my legs for him further.

His fingers played where they started, touching every sensitive area I could possibly have on my body. The innards of my thighs and the top of my pelvic area. I trembled. I quaked. A finger went in. Then two. Then he was moving within me with such precision I nearly came undone. I called out his name as the pleasure brought me closer to a feeling I'd never felt before.

"Fuck, Knox, you're amazing," I cried out a little too loud. It took everything in me to not *scream* as tears of pleasure swelled inside me.

He knelt his head down to my ear and growled low, "Do you want this, Valora?"

"Yes," I whimpered.

"How badly do you want to come for me?"

"So badly." I could hardly form the words.

He plunged harder with his fingers. Faster. A finger circled my apex. "That's my girl."

With no warning, shadows covered the walls, little holes making space to form a light, mimicking the stars above. I was surrounded by stars. By the night sky. I couldn't help but smile as I called his name one more time.

"That's my girl," he repeated.

I crumbled. Every wall I could have possibly built inside me fell to the ground. I screamed. I cried. I yelled his name as I came on his hand. Knox moaned in my ear as I did.

He jumped back slightly, but didn't stop his movements until I was completely finished and numbed.

We stayed silent, catching our breath as we shared the same air. His gaze lingered on me as he waited for me to stop shaking. His fingertips grazed every inch of my body that he hadn't yet touched.

"Why did you jump?" I asked once I felt like I was back in my own body again.

He chuckled slightly. "You, uh . . . flames burst from your hands a little bit." When he saw the worried look on my face, he continued. "It wasn't much. Just enough to startle me."

I laughed through a breath. Gods, I was tired. But I wanted him. I reached for his cock again and began stroking, hoping he would come play inside me this time.

Knox reached up to cup my cheek. "Valora Emberlyn. My fire. You're exhausted, and you've had a bit to drink tonight. I'm not going to take advantage of you."

"But—"

"But, beautiful, there's always your birthday," he grinned, and I couldn't help but reciprocate the expression. "And I will continue to take care of you until then, and every day afterward."

"Deal," I breathed.

He was right. I was exhausted. Maybe I'd had a little more alcohol than I thought, as the room was spinning slightly. Whatever magic Knox had just done on me drained my energy completely that I could crash anywhere.

He settled down beside me, kissing my back and stroking my arm with his fingers as I backed into his embrace and he leaned closer to my ear.

"You're mine. And I'm yours."

CHAPTER THIRTY-EIGHT

"Valora, you must have slept well last night," Scarlet eyed me from across the breakfast table. "You seem to be in an awfully good mood."

A smile had been glued to my face all morning. It must have been painfully obvious that something happened last night, and maybe she thought it had been with Thorin since he hadn't shown up for breakfast yet. But neither had Knox.

We were almost late for breakfast because Knox decided first thing this morning he wanted to please me again. We couldn't keep our hands off each other, even through sleep. Lusting after him was the best feeling I'd ever felt. And now that he reciprocated it, it made it that much better.

"I was very tired yesterday, so I did sleep well. Thank you for asking." I tried to be as polite as possible with the King and Queen present. Knox had just broken up with Scarlet last night, and I didn't want to make it obvious to anyone that he came straight to me afterward.

"Good morning, everyone." Knox waltzed into the dining hall, a hefty grin on his face. He sat in the empty chair on my left, the one Thorin usually occupied.

Shit.

The icy stares from his parents could burn through the room. I could have sworn Scarlet's hair turned more vibrant as her face tightened up and turned pale as a ghost. They knew. They had to know now.

We began to eat rather than discuss it. Good. Let's avoid this topic as long as possible.

"Knox, aren't you going to have a drink, like usual?" Scarlet asked, a bite in her tone.

"No need today, thanks. I'm feeling rather good without one."

Her eyes flared.

Well, there goes being discreet about it.

Then, Thorin came in, noticed Knox sitting in his place, and then marched to the seat across from me.

Scarlet turned white as death. The left side of Thorin's face was swollen, bruised. His eye was almost shut, a red cut noticable on his cheekbone.

She looked between the three of us—me, Thorin, and Knox—noting Knox's red knuckles and knew one thing for sure.

Thorin and I were out of the question, and Knox was the reason behind it.

We continued to eat, mostly silently.

"Is everyone excited for the ball tomorrow?" The Queen squealed, eyeing Knox.

The majority nodded.

"Oh, Father," Knox started between bites, "I need to talk to you after breakfast. About The Ceremony. And some other important matters." His knee grazed mine. Oh, gods, I hope he wouldn't come clean about us this soon. But then again, I wanted to scream it from the rooftops that he was mine.

"I need to talk to *you*, as well," the King replied to his son, his words sharp. And that was all.

The rest of breakfast carried on with some chatter about the preparations for tomorrow here and there.

"How big do you think he'll be?" Knox asked as he stepped into the dragon sanctuary and sat down next to me on a rock.

I was in the middle of petting Zorath on my lap and talking to him about what happened last night.

"Yeah, I heard everything." Zorath admitted.

"Thanks for reminding me to shut off our bond." I rolled my eyes. *"I'd been a little busy, you know."*

"Don't worry, I did it for us once I understood what was happening."

"I'm not sure," I replied to Knox. "He's been growing pretty rapidly, but I wish he'd grow faster."

"It's not like I can make *myself do it."*

I shushed him in my mind.

Knox's eyes were fixated on me, pure desire burned in them. "I think it would be really badass to ride a dragon. Well, my father used to be a rider, and I'd always wished there'd been a dragon for me to bond to so I could experience it. But they died off right after I was born."

"I think it would be so cool. A little scary, but pretty cool," I smiled at him, and leaned in.

He kissed me passionately, his lips soft against mine.

"I'm right here, you know," Zorath said. I pulled away and laughed.

"What?" Knox asked.

"Zorath just keeps talking to me, and I don't think he wants to hear or see us being . . . *romantic,* so to speak." We shared a laugh.

Knox gave me a look that said, *I'd take you right here on this rock if I could.* I blushed.

"Actually," he started, "I may have a way for Zorath to grow faster, big enough for you to ride on."

My brows furrowed. "How in the world could you do that?"

"Let's just say I know some people. Maybe the best Master Alchemist in the realm." He winked.

"That would be incredible if it was possible." I looked back at Zorath, who had gotten up to drink from the pond. "How did the talk with your father go?"

Knox stiffened ever so slightly, as if he'd forgotten to tell me about it. "It went fine."

"Did . . . did you tell him about us?"

His gaze bore into me. "I told him that I wasn't going to marry Scarlet anymore. That the arrangement was over between us and Astria, and whatever needed to happen with her and Thorin, can happen. They can leave, they can stay, I don't care. But I told him how wonderful you were, how I've gotten to know you so well since you've arrived. I told him he had nothing to worry about with you and that he could trust you in his court however needed."

"Oh, that's nice." It was nice that he would go through the trouble of telling the King so many things about me. "Why would he be worried about me?"

A low growl escaped from his throat. "Let's just say that because of who you are, there is a special Illumae in you—ancient—and he suspects you may use it to *your* advantage and not his. But I told him that you haven't even used your powers here and that he had no reason to not trust you." His hand reached up to stroke my cheek. "But that's it. He's just being paranoid with all these things happening at once. He merely wanted to tell me some things about tomorrow. About what to expect." The tension in his face was apparent. Tomorrow could be big for him. If the stars decide his fate, he'd become the new High King. I would be anxious in his situation, too. Especially if I didn't want to rule.

I rested my hand on his, stroking the back with my thumb. His eyes flicked up at me and remained there. "Knox. You're going to be great. You're a great leader, whether it be an army or a kingdom, and I have faith in you."

He blinked away the tears forming. "Thank you, beautiful." Then he kissed me again.

CHAPTER THIRTY-NINE

The night of The Ceremony of the Stars arrived like a flood of glittering destiny, wrapping the kingdom in a shroud of opulence. The air felt extra thick with magic, as if the stars themselves were leaning closer to the world to be witnesses of tonight.

I stood before the mirror, watching as the final touches were made to my appearance. The gown, an exquisite emerald green—hand picked by Jules and Erika themselves—clung to my form with a delicate grace. The fabric shimmered under the candlelight, matching the hue of my eyes. The dress was structured yet fluid, flowing down in a gentle cascade of silk and satin, the bodice adorned with elaborate golden thread work that caught the light with every movement. The neckline followed the shape of my breasts like it was molded for me, with one inch straps holding it onto my body.

It was without a doubt the most beautiful dress I'd ever seen. Let alone, worn.

Half of my hair was pulled to the back of my head, curls framing my face and my neck. The last touch was a soft shimmer of pale gold dust along my collarbone, a subtle hint of magic that made my skin glow.

As the final touches were completed, I stood frozen before the mirror, seeing not just a girl from the wilds, but someone who belonged in this world—one that I may not fully understand, but knew I could find a home in. The weight of tonight pulsed in my chest like a second heartbeat.

Erika and Jules stepped back. "You look stunning, Lady Valora." Erika approved.

Jules nodded from behind me. "Absolutely beautiful."

"Thank you so much," I responded, turning to both of them.

"You'll be the most beautiful one on the floor," Jules smiled.

I grinned back. They've been there for me every day since being here, and they have made me feel like a new woman every time I'd gotten dressed. I couldn't thank them enough for dolling me up to the extreme for this big event.

I stuffed my father's dagger into its place between the mattress and the headboard. I'd taken it with me everywhere since I'd been here. But this was my time to be a Lady, a guest. A Girl of the Prophecy.

"You do look beautiful, Master." Zorath added in his approval.

"Thank you."

I walked slowly toward the door. My throat pulsed with a rhythm I couldn't quite place. Anticipation? Fear? I could only imagine how Knox felt.

I made my way down the hall, down the two flights of stairs, and down the long corridor that led to the Grand Hall.

When I stepped into the ballroom, the sheer scale of it almost took my breath away. The room stretched high above me, the vaulted ceilings draped in silver and white, with crystal chandeliers hanging like stars above the gathered courtiers. The floor was polished marble, a smooth expanse that reflected the golden glow of the lights. The walls were lined with tapestries depicting the kingdom's history: dragons, battles, and celestial alignments.

It was the same place I'd first come to, where I first saw Knox and Scarlet, but it had been altered to fit the theme for the ball. And it was *magnificent*.

The entire hall was alive with movement. Hundreds of people from all over the kingdom that Knox had spent all night and all morning welcoming into Velorum. Noblemen and women, richly dressed, all in their finest, swirled around in a symphony of colors and whispers. Music played softly in the background, strings and woodwinds weaving together in a hauntingly beautiful melody.

In the center of the room stood a large, round bowl. No—a fountain, filled with a dark blue water that resembled the night sky and rimmed with coins. The stone of the fountain was so pale it looked like it had been carved from the moon itself. Many people gathered around it in awe, its magical presence awakening.

Then, he was there.

Knox stood at the dais ahead, his black suit contrasting sharply with the golden light. He was speaking to his mother, but when his gaze scanned the ballroom and landed on me, everything seemed to slow. His eyes widened for just a moment, his breath catching as his posture stiffened.

The world shifted.

I'd seen Knox before. His dark and untamed beauty, the sharp lines of his jaw, his piercing eyes that were always a little too intense. But tonight, as I crossed the threshold of the ballroom, I saw him in a new light.

His eyes drank me in, searching me, pulling me closer with a single, weighted glance.

A warmth rose to my cheeks, my pulse quickening as I neared him, the eyes of the people now following me. Knox took a slow step forward.

The silence between us was charged. The soft murmur of conversations buzzed around us, but in that moment, it felt like the entire room had faded away. Only he and I remained.

Before I could make it any closer, he was swarmed by others, Scarlet being one of them. Her curls were unbound, wild, but beautiful. She was dressed in a ruby-red that sang through the air, adorned with detailed silver patterns and jewels. She laid claim to her beauty, and the fact that Knox still chose me, shocked me to every end.

"Attention," King Polaris's voice echoed through the hall. All eyes turned to him. "I'd like to introduce some important people tonight start-ing with our special guest, Lady Valora Emberlyn of The Prophecy." All eyes landed on me, and I could only fake a smile. Some clapped, others looked at me with disdain.

The King finished his speech, acknowledging all the important members of his court and everyone that helped with preparations for this day. I looked at the dais to see him raise his hand and flick his wrist. The gesture was small, almost imperceptible, but it held such power.

With a sound like a distant thunderclap, the roof of the ballroom began to open. Slowly, gracefully, the ceiling parted, revealing the vast, starlit sky above. The stars, thousands of them, burned brightly above us. There was no sign yet of the star's alignment.

The music continued, servants rushing around with trays of food and alcohol. After one look around at the unfamiliar faces, I accepted the first chance I had at a drink, and inhaled it in almost a single gulp. And then one more. I'd need it to get through the socializing of tonight, and whatever the stars may bring.

People mingled for a while, and I made my way around the ballroom, taking in every beautiful detail I could, slowly easing my way around to the dais where Knox was being held up by his father.

The music halted me. The song changed, a slower melody, and everyone started to make their way to the center of the hall with a partner.

"May I have a dance?" A familiar voice found me.

Thorin stood next to me, dressed in a coal gray suit that brought out his eyes. He offered his hand.

I hesitated, overhearing Scarlet next to Knox. "Come on, let's not make this breakup awkward. One dance. That's all." With a look at me, he hesitantly took her hand.

I took Thorin's. There was no need to make a scene in front of everyone in the palace. Not when they all thought Knox and Scarlet were to get married, and Thorin was to be promoted here in Velorum.

My hands rested on Thorin's shoulders so lightly, I hardly touched him. My focus was elsewhere.

Knox and Scarlet danced, her arms locked around the back of his neck, purposely keeping his gaze away from me.

"I'm sorry for how I acted the other night," Thorin said, and I finally looked at him, noting the swelling and bruising on his eye had been covered up as best as possible with makeup, yet not enough to hide the horrible person underneath.

"Don't apologize," I replied.

"No, really. I—"

"Don't," I stopped him. "You are who you are, and I'm not going to change you. I don't *want* to change you, and I don't want anything to do with you."

The color drained from his face.

"And after this dance, you will *never* touch me again."

Thorin's lips turned white as a ghost.

The song changed, and Knox immediately released himself from Scarlet's grip and eased over to me. "Off," he snapped at Thorin, taking my hand and pulling me to him. Thorin didn't argue.

The room seemed to hush, as if the music grew quieter, the light brighter, and the air thinner. His fingers were warm against my skin. I was acutely aware of his every movement. The way his fingers brushed against the small of my back as he kept me close, leaving no distance between our bodies.

"You are radiant, Valora." He smiled down at me.

"Thank you, Knox. You're quite dashing yourself," I winked flirtatiously. He was the most beautiful man I'd ever seen.

He held me gently, carefully. There was a rawness to his touch like he wouldn't ever bear to let me go.

"Happy birthday, my fire." He was the first to tell me, the first that seemed to remember.

The entire ballroom swirled around us, a whirl of color and light. Knox's eyes never left mine, despite the storm that lay behind them.

"I have a gift for you, it's just not ready yet," he purred in my ear, his grip on my waist tightening.

"You didn't need to get me a gift. I've never even had a birthday gift." I blinked away the moisture from my eyes.

"I know I didn't need to, but I wanted to." His forehead reached mine, and though I knew every eye was upon us at this very moment, I didn't care. It didn't matter what people thought about us. He was possibly about to be their king. "I am yours," he whispered so softly I almost couldn't hear it.

"I am yours," I replied.

"And tonight, I can't wait to pleasure you with a *special* gift." His lips curled upward as his eye contact held firm, and I knew what he meant. Blood rushed to my cheeks at the thought. He'd wanted it to be special for me, a gift for me on my birthday. Gods, the way I felt about him . . .

"My lips have been starving for you all day," he murmured, our breath intertwining between us.

"Mine have too, my wolf," I responded, smiling at the nickname I'd given him, knowing it was terrible.

For a long moment, we simply danced, moving as one, swept away by the rhythm and the weight of everything revolving around us.

Once the song was over, masses of people made their way to the fountain. One by one, each member of the court took a coin in their fist and closed their eyes. A gold light shined through their hand until they released the coin into the fountain, which landed in the water with the flying of gold sparks.

It was just as Knox described, yet so much more magical to witness in person. We watched a while longer as dozens of people contributed, sipping the drinks we'd recently snatched from a nearby tray at the side of the hall.

"Would you like to contribute?" Knox leaned into me.

"Am I allowed? I've never done anything like it before."

"Of course you are," he said, placing his free hand on the small of my back. "Come on."

He led me forward, and the tingle of Illumae pulsed through the room as we grew closer.

Along the edge of the fountain was written *The Pool of Cosmos*.

"Here," Knox picked up two coins from the edge of the fountain, handing me one. "Hold it firmly in your fist, feel the magic within you flow through your veins into your palm. Into this coin. Once it has been transferred," he opened his hand, a glow of light falling into the water, "release it into the pool, and then you have contributed the essence of your Illumae to the stars."

I did exactly as he explained. I shut my eyes, feeling the magic coursing within me. The dragonblood in my blood. A shiver ran down my spine as I felt the weight of my power transferring to my hand. My fingertips began to tingle. Burn.

"Valora, open your eyes," Knox said, his voice urgent. So, I did.

My hand was glowing green, not gold. I let go of the coin, and it hit the surface with a puff of smoke. The crowd fell silent. Where the coin had fallen, a green flame appeared, and it quickly rimmed the inside edge of the fountain before it disappeared.

Silence filled the room.

Knox wrapped his arm around my waist and pulled me back with him, away from the fountain. A light lifted from it, meeting with the light of the stars and moon that began to shine down. A silver light bridged between the fountain and the constellations above.

"I've never seen that happen," Knox's voice drifted off.

"Seen what?"

"I've never seen the stars take the Illumae so quickly into the ceremony. You just fed it all of the Illumae it needed . . ."

For a moment, everyone stood to watch the light, the transfer of magic into the air. You couldn't just see it—you could *feel* it. I looked around and found the King and Queen, their faces a hardened expression on me. As if I'd ruined their night by adding my coin to the fountain.

Within a minute, the fountain disappeared, but the beam that cascaded down remained as the stars aligned above us. The light grew. It narrowed.

Until it fell upon me. Upon Knox. We were bathed in its glow.

A collective gasp rippled through the hall. Every eye was on us.

For a moment, it felt like the world held its breath. The magic in the air was palpable, and in the midst of it, the weight of destiny closed in on us.

Knox turned to face me, pulling me in as if we were about to dance again. As the light bathed us, Knox's grip on me was unshakable.

"No matter what happens, stay with me, Valora," he pleaded.

"Always," I assured him.

We looked over to the dais as a man with a handful of parchment scrambled his way up to the King's ear and whispered.

I didn't think King Polaris's face could get any darker, but somehow it did. Light crackled under his hands as he stood, gesturing for Knox to come to him.

We eased toward the dais.

"Leave her there," he ordered Knox. I stayed, watching his every movement as he approached his father.

He spoke to him in a whisper so low I couldn't make out what they were saying. The King's head nodded slightly to the side.

A flash of red appeared to my left, shifting my gaze to Scarlet.

"I really hate to do this, but it's for the best."

My eyes flashed back to Knox as he whirled around, eyes widened. "Valora!" He called.

But something had been draped across my face, soft, yet thick, and laced with a strange, heavy scent. The cloth settled over my mouth, and within moments it felt like the world was tilted out from beneath me. Darkness edged the corners of my vision, my limbs growing heavy.

Scarlet's presence was still there, and Knox's voice called out once more. But this time, he was screaming. Struggling.

And then the world went black.

CHAPTER FORTY

Cold. It was so cold.

It wrapped around me like a suffocating cloak, gnawing at my skin, seeping into my bones. I jolted awake, gasping for breath. My vision blurred, and for a moment, I couldn't tell if the darkness was inside me or around me. I blinked, forcing my mind to focus, to shake the fog from my thoughts.

The weight of the moment hit me like a hammer: I was no longer in the ballroom. I was not surrounded by the kingdom's people, the music, the shimmering jewels and the flickering of candles.

I looked around, forcing my eyes to adjust to the dim, flickering torch mounted outside of the room I was in, a set of bars between us. The walls around me were damp, coated with moisture and grime like they'd never seen the sun. There was no warmth here. Only the harsh reality of stone, steel, and cold air.

I tried to move, but the sharp jangle of chains halted me. My wrists were bound tightly, the cold metal digging into my skin. The chains were fastened to a freezing stone wall, and I realized with a sinking feeling that I couldn't escape.

Panic surged in my chest, and I tugged at the chains instinctively, but they didn't give. The sound of metal scraping against stone echoed in the empty space.

A bucket sat in the corner on my left, which I assumed was left for me as my toilet. A pile of hay was to my right, like I was a horse in a stall.

My gown, once a beautiful emerald, was now stained and torn, the fabric filthy from the grime of the floor.

I wanted to scream. I wanted to fight, to claw my way out of this prison, but the chains would make it impossible. My breath quickened, my pulse growing to my throat.

Someone groaned in the cell across from me, the sound of chains echoing from their walls. I gave it a moment before I said anything.

They groaned again, and then the voice was more familiar. "Knox?" I strained out.

"Valora?" He said, his voice hoarse like mine.

"What's going on?"

He eased himself forward, closer to the torchlight where I could see him. I did the same, though my muscles were weak as I pulled myself forward. "Valora, I'm so sorry we're down here. I have no idea what happened."

"Well," I said, my tone sharper, "it doesn't look to me like you're going to be the king, so *something* is going on."

"I—" Knox started, but was interrupted.

Footsteps. Down the hall.

Not the heavy clanking sound of a guard. Lighter, almost fluid.

Then a figure appeared between the two cells, and my breath caught.

Jameson.

I blinked, my heart stopping for a moment before the anger and confusion flooded back in. He smiled between the two cells, his gaze shifting to both of us.

"Hey guys. It's been a while." His smile was cold, a distant expression, nothing like the warmth I'd once seen in Solaria. "I'm glad to see you two are finally conscious. I didn't think you would be knocked out for three days straight."

Neither Knox or I said anything. I wanted to lash out, to demand answers, but the words stuck in my throat. And my hunger, the pang in my gut, told me he wasn't lying. I was so lost as to what was happening.

"Jameson, you bastard," Knox finally broke the silence.

"It's good to see you too, brother."

"Wait," I looked at Knox, his eyes meeting mine. "*Jameson* is your brother?" There was a bite in my voice.

"She didn't know?" Jameson turned to him.

I stayed silent. Knox seethed through his teeth, "Why are we here, Jameson?"

"I'm afraid this may have been the plan from the very beginning, Knox, don't you remember? When our father brought us into his council chambers to tell us about 'The Girl of the Prophecy'?" His eyes shifted over to me. "I wasn't some charming commoner who happened to cross paths with you in Solaria, Valora. I didn't just *happen* to show up at your father's shop one day hoping for an apprenticeship. My father sent me to get close to you. He heard of the prophecy, and with The Ceremony that was approaching this year, he wanted me to test you. Feel you out. Lead you here."

The words hit me like a blow to the chest. I didn't know if I wanted to scream, cry, or collapse. The anger boiled within me, but I was too stunned to do anything but stare at him with utter loathing.

"You *used* me," I said through clenched teeth.

Jameson's expression didn't falter. He didn't flinch at the accusation. "In a way, yes. I let you think I was your ally while I gathered information. I had to make sure you had all the right opportunities to lead you here. That way, my father could see you for who and what you are and determine for himself what you would do to his kingdom."

I shook my head, the weight of realization sinking in. I was truly in an enemy's fortress.

"I found out what meant the most to you: your family. I knew that was the way I'd be able to get in touch with you. To see you.So, I started working with your father, not even knowing that you'd come to work with him too, though that only allowed the plan to unfold sooner.

"I grew close to you and asked the questions I needed the answers to. Do you remember that cottage we went to? With the help of our magic, I created that for you. I placed that large green tome there on purpose, because in order for the prophecy to come true, it had to be read aloud. By *you*. Then everything could fall into place. Those three men that you killed, they weren't ordinary commonfolk. Not entirely. They were regular, terrible men when you told me about them, but then they were my pawns. I found Judah in misery, healed him just enough right after you stabbed him, and had all three of them placed under a spell. When you read the prophecy, they'd be summoned, and I could truly see your power. Truly see what you were capable of doing."

Jameson stopped and stared straight down the hall, a breath heavy in his lungs. "It was a shame how those three had to die, but we needed to know. I was shocked at how well you held your own against them, by the way." His grin cut through me like a knife.

"So, you're the reason that I'm here, that I was summoned to this foreign land and now locked in a dungeon." I blinked away the sting in my eyes. "You let me believe I could trust you. You . . ." I shook my head at the memory of my attraction to him. The time that we almost . . .

"That was all part of it. You were always a pawn, too. I did what I had to do for my family, for my kingdom. The prophecy is too important to us. To my father and to the realm. The King was right to take measures after hearing what you could do. Then seeing *The Pool of Cosmos* vanish after only a drop of your power . . . we can't risk you ruining his reign. Either of you."

"Did you know about this?" I turned to Knox.

He only sighed.

"Did you *know* about this?" My voice grew louder.

"I suspected my father would do something to keep you under his guard. When he met with us, he was worried about what you'd do to his reign, and if you'd actually be able to help him when he needed it most. He had told me he didn't trust you, and what you could do to his kingdom, but didn't tell me why. That's why I went to talk to him the day before the ceremony, to convince him that you were good and you were trustworthy. I thought he'd believed me . . ."

"Clearly he didn't," I snapped. Knox didn't retort.

"Sorry to come between your little relationship here, but it's what had to be done." Jameson's tone was laced with poison. "How was I supposed to know, brother, that you'd end up falling for her?"

"Jameson. I will *give* you the throne if you let us out. You know I don't want it." Knox pleaded.

"Mmm, I can't do that. Father's orders. When the stars' light shined on you, father raged. He will take the consequences of disobeying the stars over giving up his throne now, especially to you, since you and Valora grew so close. You're a threat to him now. Besides, if I don't let you out, you still *can't* be king. So, it doesn't matter either way." He turned on his heel to exit, but stopped short. "Oh . . . and the cloth that was used to cover your mouths was enchanted with magic that suppressed your mind and your powers. Once that wears off, the dungeon was also warded against magic, so don't even think about using your powers to escape because it won't work."

Knox growled, "You evil bastard. Fuck you."

"Love you too, brother." In a single blink, he disappeared out of thin air with a *whoosh*.

I stared in disbelief at Knox, whose anger even in the dim lighting, couldn't be more apparent on his face. "I'm sorry about this." He hung his head.

I didn't say anything. I couldn't. I was so angry, so mentally drained, that I didn't know what words could help in this situation.

I tried reaching out to Zorath through our mental link. No answer. I tried again. Silence. It's like that shimmering thread that bound our souls had been severed, and our communication was lost.

Too many thoughts ran through my head. The truth was more complicated than I ever thought, and I wasn't sure how to feel about it.

CHAPTER FORTY-ONE

Time felt as though it no longer existed. Only the steady drip of water from the stone walls and clinking of chains as Knox and I shifted uncomfortably in our cells. I couldn't remember the last time I saw the sun, except for the small ray of light that would beam in through the tiny window at the top of the wall behind me. The air was thick, stifling, and my thoughts felt trapped in the same confined space as my body.

I had hardly spoken to Knox in days. Not since Jameson came down to talk to us. It was hard to face him. The man I thought I knew, that allowed me to feel comfortable here, was imprisoned with me. I was betrayed, and I wasn't sure what truths he'd hidden from me, too.

And then I cried. Silently, at first, but then it was uncontrollable.

"Valora . . ." Knox whispered, easing forward into the light of his cell.

I sniffled. "Every time I close my eyes, I see your brother's face. He manipulated me, used me, when I thought I had a friend in him. He gave me the sword, the first sword I'd ever made, as a gift. I lost it the day after I killed those men . . . the day that Jameson left. All I feel is betrayal. The walls feel closer every day. I'm suffocating." My voice broke and I wept harder. "And you're here suffering with me."

"I want you to forgive me. For letting this happen to you. To us. I swore I would protect you, and I failed." His words weighed heavier than the chains that held me here.

I looked up and found his eyes, pleading for mercy. For forgiveness. He'd broken off a royal agreement to be with me without anyone's blessing. He'd assaulted another royal family member that assaulted *me*. "You really tried to protect me, didn't you? From everyone. From your father."

He nodded. "My father is a dark man. He's had his intentions from the beginning, and I tried to ignore them and change his mind. I tried to show him your good side. When I went to him that one morning, I swear I thought I did everything I could. I thought everything would go well at The Ceremony, now that I could be with you. But . . ." he stopped himself and sighed, "he wants to use your magic, your Illumae, to restore Velorum to its full potential. He wants to use it for his own gain, and become as powerful as he used to be when he had a dragon by his side. I thought, as long as he was convinced you wouldn't do any harm, that you trusted me, that everything would be alright, and you'd be able to help the kingdom without him trying to use your power for his own gain. But I was wrong, and I apologize for it."

I pondered over everything he'd said before responding. "He'd told me one day in the halls to find a way to restore Velorum's Illumae since there was an ancient magic within me. He even said that I was a mystery, so it's evident he really didn't know what to think of me or my power." I paused. "What did he say to you at the dais? Right before we were taken away?"

His eyes flared. "He told me that he tried to believe me, but it was evident that you were too powerful, therefore, I could no longer be trusted. Because he couldn't trust you to use your magic against the kingdom. That's when I turned to see Jameson appear out of nowhere, covering your face, and then the same happened to me, and I knew I'd failed you."

I only looked at Knox. At the broken man before me as he lowered his head, a tear streaming down his face. "I forgive you." His eyes lit up, like hope blossomed in them for the first time in days. My brain began to work. "Do you think we will ever make it out of here?"

Knox gulped. "Valora, you are everything I have ever thought about. Everything I've dreamed of. You are everything I was missing in my life, my support, my strength. I will do everything in my power to get us out. Die if I must."

"And what of my dragon? I need him, and he needs me. He needs to get out."

Knox sat in thought for a moment. "We will figure it out. We will get out of here. Together."

I huffed. "Is there a way to disarm the wards that keeps our magic suppressed?" The fire that I could normally feel tingling in my veins hadn't been present since the ball.

Knox shook his head. "If my father used a spell of his own design, then no. The only one that can break the ward is the one who created it."

I gulped. "He's *that* powerful? To create his own spells?" And King Polaris saw *me* as powerful . . . saw *me* as a threat.

Knox's head bobbed. "In his younger years, he told me he did drastic things to strengthen his own powers, though he never clarified what. Some believe he delved into forbidden magics that aren't dared spoken of now. But whatever he did, it worked. No one then, even while all the dragons were alive, had ever seen an Illumae channeled with such intensity." He paused, his gaze distant. "He *did* bond one of the rarest dragons to ever live, and their connection was supposedly legendary. Unbreakable. Lucia amplified his abilities far beyond anyone else was capable of. So, it makes sense that he's able to wield such power."

I sat back against the wall, the fabric of my dishevelled dress rustling against the cold stones. Was there any hope for us to get out of here if the King had such power?

I stared at the iron bars ahead of me, at the way the chains hung from my wrists, bolting me to the cell. I was contained. My powers were contained, not gone entirely.

"There's something that just doesn't sit right with me." I didn't look at Knox.

"What do you mean?"

I let out a slow breath, finding the words that were wrapped around my brain. "If your father truly thinks that I could be dangerous, that I'm too powerful to be trusted, why hasn't he done more than just keep us imprisoned? Why hasn't he just . . . drained me of my Illumae and been done with it? He's suppressing our magic to keep us from escaping, yet he won't simply take it away entirely?"

Knox's jaw tightened in thought. "Maybe he doesn't know yet how to extract it from you."

"Perhaps," I murmured. "But, he is the High King—a man that created his own spellcraft. He made the wards that surround us. He dabbled in magics that we don't understand. Yet, he can't figure out my power . . ."

"What are you saying, Valora?"

"I think this is his way of holding us down. The cell. The chains. Everything he's done so far. I don't think he *knows* how to channel my Illumae, or my dragon's, let alone if it's even possible. And I think . . ." I trailed off, finding the right words. "I think the longer he goes without being able to take my power, the more afraid he'll become that he can't do it."

Knox's eyes flared, but he said nothing.

"You told me during the first conversation we had that the power within me, the dragonblood, is something the people have never seen. A magic the King may not know how to handle."

Knox nodded slowly as though he were searching for the memory.

"You told me that you think I'm more powerful than I lead on because I'm not a Polaris, and because I bonded the last dragon."

Knox's expression softened. "How do you remember me saying that?"

With a rustle of chains, I tapped my temple. "My strong memory that comes with my powers."

He stayed silent. "So, what do we do?"

"Well," I started, my gaze drifting to the flickering of torchlight against the hallway, "if the strength of my memory is still intact, then that means there's dragonblood still flowing through me. Meaning my fire still flows through me, it's just not awakened."

I shifted my focus back to Knox. The way he stared at me with awe like I was a storm rolling over the mountains made my breath catch.

"So," I lifted my palm, imagining the flame that was once ablaze there, "we pray to Aesis and Tyche for hope and luck to find a way out of here."

I closed my fingers into a fist, meeting Knox's gaze once again.

"And I'll pray to Phobos, God of Fear, and Helum, God of Death, that King Polaris sees me coming for him."

CHAPTER FORTY-TWO

THE FOOD THE GUARDS brought us with every passing day was hardly enough to keep us alive. Knox's skin was growing more pale, his face sinking in. My bones were sore from lying on the stone floor. My dress no longer clung to my skin. I couldn't sleep. I could hardly think. The hope I'd had so many days ago of regaining my power, was slowly withering away.

We were withering away.

"Knox . . ." I called out, my voice hoarse. I was dehydrated, no doubt. Chains shifted across from me as he stirred. "I'm losing hope."

He crawled forward, pressing closer to the bars. "My fire," he said softly, "you have to stay strong. We *will* get out of here, I feel it. Just stay with me."

I wish I could believe him this time.

But then footsteps echoed through the dungeon, growing louder by the second. Quick, light footsteps. Not the thud of armored boots on stone.

My heart stuttered.

From the shadows emerged a figure, and Jules stood before me, her silver hair contrasting her dark skin.

"Jules," I said through clenched teeth, forcing myself to my feet. My legs trembled under me. "What are you doing here? If you get caught . . ."

"I know the risk, my dear. I've worked for the man long enough to know. I've heard things throughout the castle, and I finally found out where they'd taken you." Her eyes darted over to Knox behind her, then back to me. "What do you need?"

My eyes widened. "Food, water, and most importantly the keys to these damned cells." I managed a weak smile.

"I will see what I can do," she turned to Knox, offering him a small bow. "My Prince, I am sorry for what has happened. I love Miss Valora, as she has been nothing but kind to me. You both deserve your freedom. I will try to help however I can."

"Thank you, Miss Jules," Knox stood at the gates of his cell. "I'll tell you what you can do for us." He gestured for her to come closer, so she did.

And then he was whispering inaudibly into her ear. When he finished, she pulled back, her eyes brightening. "I'll see what I can do." She faced me again. "I will be back for you." In a moment, she was gone again. I met eyes with Knox. "What did you tell her?"

The corners of his mouth rose, just barely. "It's a surprise."

I frowned. "I don't believe now is the time for surprises, Knox."

He grinned, "Then let's call it . . . hope."

His "hope" was beginning to fade as the days blurred together. I'd had hope, I really did. But each day that passed was a gray reflection of the last. Time had no meaning. There was only the sound of our breath, the rustling of straw beneath us, and the sharp clinking of chains whenever we moved.

Hopeless. That's what this place was.

And I hated that Knox had to suffer through it with me. It wasn't really his fault. It was my own. He wouldn't be here if I hadn't encouraged him to stand up for himself. He broke it off with Scarlet because of me. He told his father about it because of me. If he hadn't, maybe I would have had a fighting chance of escaping this place. But he was stuck in the same position I was, just a few feet across from me.

I missed Zorath, the bond we shared. Not hearing from him, not feeling his magic, had created a hole in my chest. He was probably just as alone as

Knox and I felt down here, locked away in his sanctuary.

If he was still alive.

I couldn't bear the thought of losing him, not after everything we've been through. I felt like nothing without him. Without my powers.

But the pain of Zorath's absence wasn't the only thing that gnawed at my soul.

"I miss my home. Solaria." I blurted, drawing Knox's attention. "It was the only place that I really knew before now. I miss the open ocean that waited for me whenever I needed to clear my head, the salty sea breeze that washed over me. I miss the blacksmith shop that I used to work at with my father. I miss the way the sunlight felt on my face as I walked the dusty roads that lined the streets. It was a simple life I had before this nightmare began. Before I'd been stolen away from everything I knew."

Knox let out a loud sigh of defeat.

"Most of all, I miss my parents," I shook my head in disbelief. "I don't even know if they are still alive."

"How come?" Knox's voice perked.

"The Eclipse Guard had kept them back when they took me away. I remember their faces, my mother's eyes filled with tears and my father's anger and helplessness as they were forced to watch me go." I blinked away the sting in my eyes. "The last thing I remember was seeing my mother hovering over my father after a guard struck him down and continued to beat him. I never had a chance to say goodbye, never got the chance to tell them how much I loved them."

"I'm sure they are still there, waiting for your return. They know how strong you are, Valora." His eyes softened.

I sniffed. "They could have died trying to protect me, for all I know. Each time that I wonder about it, I imagine the worst. I've lost everything."

His eyes wandered, searching the cell for the right things to say. "You haven't lost me."

My eyes darted to him to see the hurt in his eyes. There was hurt in his voice. In his posture. "They would love you." I shook my head. "I shouldn't be complaining. You've lost things too."

"I've been damned by my father, something I'm unfortunately used to. You were taken away and shoved into an unknown hell. There's a difference, and you have every right to feel the way you do. But remember who you are. Don't lose yourself in the process of grieving."

He was right. There was so much pain swelling inside me. The uncertainty weighed heavy in my chest. I wanted to scream. I wanted my scream to break down the walls of this place and allow me an escape.

We'd spent weeks locked away down here, pacing in circles. The prophecy, The Ceremony of the Stars . . . it didn't matter anymore why I was here. I was nothing.

It was all too much to think about. It was too much weight to carry. It was breaking me, and the deeper I sank into my thoughts, the harder it became to find a way back to the surface.

Remember who you are.

Don't lose yourself.

But I hated myself. I hated the girl I'd become that put myself in this situation.

Tears burned in my eyes, and for the first time in a long time, I let them fall freely.

"Valora . . ." Knox's voice called out.

The sound of my sobs echoed through the dungeon, bouncing off of the cold walls. My body trembled, and the stirrings of a wild, untamed fury rose in me.

I wanted to tear down the walls of this place that destroyed me, and destroy *it*.

Heat rose to my chest, my heart thumping hard and loud. The power of magic stirred in my veins. The air around me crackled with energy.

"Valora," Knox's tone sharpened. "Hold it together."

But it was too late. The flames inside me had already ignited.

My hands slammed into the stone floor in front of me without hesitation, a desperate, uncontrolled motion driven by my fractured mind.

A pulse of green light flickered from my fingertips. The energy surged through my arms, crackling as flame rose from my fingers to my hands. From my hands to my wrists.

Then, the chains that held me were ablaze, the fire growing wild and untamed as it travelled along the iron, melting it onto the floor.

It reached the wall, where it stopped and simply danced around me.

"Valora . . ." Knox breathed across from me in disbelief. He'd never seen my power until now. Not really.

A strangled cry left my lips as I collapsed to the floor, my fingers trembling as the metal melted off of my body. It didn't burn me, but the power flowing through me was there, alive, and so much stronger than I remembered.

Just as quickly as it had come, the fire around me sputtered and died, leaving nothing but charred stone and liquid metal around me.

Shadows swirled around Knox, emerging from his back like a set of wings. Then they were gone, disappearing under his will.

I broke the wards.

CHAPTER FORTY-THREE

THERE WAS A FIRE in my chest now. A fire that hadn't been there in weeks. My heart felt heavy, but the weight was no longer crushing me. No. It was heavy with determination. It was ready for escape.

It had only been a few hours since I'd broken the wards. A few hours of sitting with our thoughts and finding a way to escape.

"Valora," Knox's call dragged me from my thoughts. "What if we've had it all wrong?"

I cocked my head. "What are you talking about?" I stepped toward the bars holding me back from him.

"What if the stars weren't shining on me at the Syzygy to claim *me* as king? What if . . . the reason my father has us both here is because the stars called out to both of us?"

"I don't understand. I thought we'd established why we're here. Your father wants my rare Illumae."

Knox shook his head. "He does, yes. But if we were both meant to rule? Together."

"No. I'm not made to rule."

"You may not be, and neither am I. That's why the stars chose us together. I'm not sure what the Master Astrologist told him once they aligned, but it could very well be that they chose you, too."

And then, it all made sense. He didn't want to rule on his own, and I have no royal lineage. The stars not only chose him, they chose me to stand alongside him.

Because he was mine, and I was his. And we were written in the stars.

"Valora, I'd give up every title I could ever have to stand by your side. Ruling a kingdom or not." His eyes bled into my soul. "I—" He lowered his head.

"You what, Knox?"

"You know how I feel about you, Valora. You must."

The sound of my heart rang in my ears. I knew what he meant. Because I felt the same way.

"I know. I can feel it." I smiled, fighting back tears. "I feel the same for you."

Knox's dark eyes brightened, a new light behind them. "You are the flame that lights my darkest shadows."

For a moment, we felt like the only two people in the world. I couldn't help but smile knowing he reciprocated the same feeling I had for him. My person. The darkness to my light.

Footsteps sounded from down the hall. I backed up to the wall, hiding my now freed wrists behind my back. If it was a guard, they couldn't know that I'd freed myself from the chains. Not until I knew how to escape the cell.

But it wasn't a guard that appeared before me. It was Jules.

"I'm sorry I couldn't make it here sooner," she spoke, her breath shaky as she stepped into the light, an oversized satchel hanging over her shoulder.

"No need to apologize, Miss Jules." Knox stated. "What do you have for us?"

"Everything you requested, my Prince," she reached into the bag, and I stepped forward for a better view as she handed me an article of clothing through the bars.

Not *any* clothing. A set of armor. Dark green armor, its scales glimmering faintly in the dim torchlight. Perfectly crafted, sharp-edged. I looked between her and Knox, only to find Knox gleaming with joy.

"Happy birthday, beautiful. I had it made custom for you from the scales of a Diamondtail, then colored to match your eyes—and your fire. I'm sorry that it wasn't ready for your birthday."

I stood in awe, staring at the armor before me. *My* armor that was made for me. Thanks to Knox. "Thank you," I breathed.

"There's more," Knox said, bobbing his head at Jules. She took out a sword from the satchel. A blade shorter than most swords. Its hilt was solid black and its cross-guard and pommel glistened with gold, adorned with a small green orb in its center. *My* blade. I reached out for it.

"How did you . . ." I mumbled.

"I entrusted Jules with retrieving your sword from Jameson's room, if it was there. Turns out it was." He turned toward her as she handed me a pair of boots, the boots I'd come here with.

"One more thing, dear," Jules started as she pulled out my father's dagger and handed it to me. "I knew where you hid it. I know how much it means to you."

It took everything in me to not sob then and there. I had no words for how thankful I was.

"Did you see Zorath?" Knox asked.

She nodded. "Yes. It should be done now."

"You've seen my dragon?" My voice raised a little louder than I intended. I reached out through our bond, finding that shimmering thread connecting our minds. *"Zorath?"*

No response.

"He may be sleeping, my dear," Jules started. "The Master Alchemist gave him a potion allowing him to grow, and it was a tiring procedure. He should be waking up soon."

Knox winked at me. "Told ya I could get it done."

"Thank you, Knox, and Jules. Thank you."

"You're welcome. I must go before the guards return. Good luck to both of you." She disappeared down the corridor, her shadows dancing along the walls.

"Now put on that armor, and let's get out of here."

The armor was flexible enough to move in, but it fit like a glove. I tossed the dress that had been my only cell companion for weeks into the corner with the hay, and sat down where my chains used to be. My dagger was strapped to my hip. My sword laid next to me. Waiting.

It wasn't long before the guards came to give us our meal.

Just one. One guard. A large man.

I could do this.

He slid Knox's bowl to him, then turned to me, his armor glistening in the fire's light. He wore no helmet—he wasn't expecting a fight.

His expression changed when he met my eyes, then noticed my change of clothes.

"What the hell?" His gaze darted to the sword next to me. "Who the fuck gave you *that?*"

I stood up, grasping the sword with a familiar comfort. "Do you want to come take it from me?"

He growled. The guard simultaneously unsheathed his blade, and took the keys from his belt. The door of my cell opened for the first time in weeks. He stepped through.

Only one obstacle left.

He marched in, lifting his blade in the air in prep to strike.

Spinning low, I swivelled behind him, slashing the back of his knee. The sound of flesh tearing rippled through the air, and blood dripping on the ground.

He crumbled, roaring in pain, swinging the sword blindly in an attempt to hit me. I ducked and pivoted out of reach. He twisted, struggling to stand, but his leg gave out once more.

He panicked.

"Are you going to take it from me, or what?" I spat. I was *done* playing games with these people. With this kingdom.

He slashed upward. I blocked him, sparks flashing as our blades met with a sharp *clang*. With a fluid motion, he stood and lunged on the weight of his good leg, aiming for me.

I sidestepped, letting him stumble forward, the keys landing on the stone floor in front of me. His sword flew forward toward the hay. His hands scrambled across the floor, searching for *something*.

"Oh no you don't." I kicked the keys away from his grasp, and stepped behind him, pressing the tip of my blade against the back of his neck.

He grunted as I drew blood.

"You're going to regret this, *dragon girl,*" he spat.

"Huh," I laughed, "Will I though? Or will you?"

He flipped onto his back with a swift motion, reaching for his sword in the process. But my blade pushed forward, driving itself into his neck, blood spewing from every hole.

Until his body was no longer moving.

I removed the blade, fire coursing in my veins.

The silence that followed was deafening, and it was hard to not take my eyes off of what I'd just done. What I'd done to this man that was only doing his job.

But he deserved it for keeping us down here.

I picked up the keys with a trembling hand, and turned toward Knox's cell.

He was already waiting at the bars, eyes wide with something between awe and relief.

"Val, remind me never to get on your bad side," he murmured with a smile. "You're so . . . fierce." His voice was thick with admiration as I unlocked the door.

Before it had completely opened, his hands were around my jaw, pulling my lips onto his. I couldn't stop myself from responding, from deepening the kiss. I dropped the keys and reached around his back, tugging him closer.

He pulled back slightly, resting our foreheads together, his breathing ragged. "Valora, I lo—"

"Don't," I interrupted. "Don't say it. Not until we are out of this place. Together."

He cradled the back of my head, leaning in close to my ear, breathing me in. "My feisty girl," he said, a warmth in his voice. He left a kiss on my neck, then on my lips, then pulled away. "Let's get out of here."

He ran into my cell and claimed the guard's sword that laid in the hay.

"Good thinking," I said. "Might need that."

"Hopefully we can get out of here without them knowing we've escaped."

Horns sounded outside, loud and with warning.

"Nevermind. I think they know," he said as he led me down a hall. "This way."

I sheathed my sword as we moved swiftly down the corridor, our footsteps light but purposeful.

We passed unwary guards down a hallway without incident. The castle was such a vast expanse of passageways, and I'm glad Knox was here to guide us.

But then, we ran into a patrol. Three guards, their armor gleaming in the flickering torchlight.

I didn't hesitate.

With a fluid motion, I drew the sword from my side and lunged at the nearest one, striking him down before he had time to react. The others rushed toward me, but Knox was right there beside me, his movements like lightning.

He knocked one guard aside with a powerful blow to the chest, then took the final one down with a swift, deadly strike to the throat. We stood breathless, the echo of swords filling the stone halls.

"We need to keep moving," Knox said, his voice low but urgent. "They'll be on us soon."

We ran down the corridors, our path growing increasingly dangerous as more guards appeared. We fought our way through, side by side, the sound of clashing metal and the rhythm of our breaths filling the air.

Then, as the way out of the dungeons was just in sight, a large group of guards appeared at the end of the hall. Too many. Way too many.

I froze for a moment, panic rising in my chest. We wouldn't be able to fight them all in this narrow corridor. There were too many of them. They'd swarm us. Trample us.

Knox must have seen the fear in my eyes.

Without a word, he grabbed me by the shoulders and pulled me into a kiss. His lips were desperate against mine, his hands cupping my face as if trying to pour everything he felt into that one connection.

"You have to go. Down this hall. You need to escape."

"I can't leave you here. I won't." My eyes burned.

He raised his hand toward the guards, and everything in front of them turned black. Shadows covered them. Hiding us from their sight. "I will hold them off. I will catch up to you. I promise. Go find Zorath, and I will find you. Your flames aren't that hard to spot," he winked, and then he was gone, disappearing down the hall as the sound of guards grew louder.

With one last look, I ran.

I didn't stop.

CHAPTER FORTY-FOUR

I TRAVELLED DOWN A nearby passage and up a flight of stairs. The clanking of swords rang out behind me, the echo of barking and growling following. I tried not to think about it.

I had to find my dragon.

"Zorath," I called out, *"please be awake."*

"I am ready, Master." His voice was deeper, like he'd aged years since I last heard him.

It felt like I'd been running forever. The muscles in my legs quivered. Lack of sustenance had really taken a toll on my stamina. But I had to keep going. I couldn't stop. Adrenaline had to keep me going.

Every breath felt like the last one I would ever take. Every heartbeat raced through my neck, through my heavy arms. The labyrinth of passageways twisted around me like a maze. Every shadow that flitted in the corners of my eyes, every crevice in the stone beneath my feet was only a reminder that I was travelling far from the prison that held me just moments ago.

But I wasn't free. Not yet.

I finally reached a grand hallway. Ahead, the doors to the outer world beckoned to me like a faint promise. As I went to take another step, a fresh wave of guards turned the corner ahead. Their armor shined like cold steel, their weapons sharp at the ready. They began to close in.

There were so many of them. Too many to count as they pressed in. I was alone on my end, but there was nowhere I could run unless I turned back. I couldn't go back. I had to fight.

My heart beat in my ears, drowning out the clanking of their armor drawing near. My sword was still heavy at my side, but it was my only option besides a dagger, and I doubted that a dagger would help me against these guards. I channeled my breath in and out, until I could feel my power. Power coursed through my veins, angry and determined.

I will win. I will win.

I stood tall. They grew closer. Closer. Then I felt it, and the world seemed to still. The spark deep within. That flicker of energy from the very core of my being.

The dragon inside me.

I raised my sword, closing my eyes for only a moment, letting the power grow. I called upon everything I was, everything I had fought for.

The flame was within me, burning. Green light pulsed from my fingertips. A flicker at first. Then a roar as loud as a dragon surged through me. My sword hummed, a low dangerous growl, and I could have sworn the guards slowed their pace.

But it was too late for them. The green flame erupted from my blade like a wild inferno. It ignited with power. With a single slash, I cut through the front lines of the guard. They staggered back, screaming, as their armor was set aflame, melting to their skin with every second passing.

The second wave came at me, determined to stop me despite the previous guards cowering in fear, burning alive. But I would escape. I struck again, the flame growing higher. Brighter. *Hotter.* The air grew thick with smoke and the scent of burning metal—soon to be burning flesh. Guards fell, their weapons now useless against me.

I moved forward, not looking back.

I pushed through the final set of doors, emerging into the night air. The moon hung high overhead, casting pale silver light over the landscape.

I was lucky I recognized where I was. I ended up at the North Door. This would lead me to the dragon sanctuary.

There, in the distance, was my dragon companion. He sat waiting under a tree, hidden in the shadows.

My heart leapt at the sight of him. He was a great, tall beast now, easily twice my height, at the least. His iridescent scales shimmered as he stepped into the moonlight and lowered his head for me to greet him.

"Master, I've missed you," he growled under his breath, a sound of joy.

"I've missed you buddy," I replied, hugging his snout.

"What shall we do?"

Escape. Leave this forsaken kingdom to rot in its evil.

Still, there was one more thing weighing on my mind. Something I couldn't *not* do before leaving.

I stood still in the darkness, touching my fingertips together. I closed my eyes, reaching back into my memory for a conjuration spell I read in the cottage.

Memory, don't fail me now.

I trailed back into my mind until I could recite the incantation. "By the stars and moon so bright, weave the thread of day and night. From the stars, bring forth might, a bag of magic, deep and light."

A cloth bag rested in my hands upon opening my eyes.

"What is this?" Zorath asked, nuzzling closer.

It looked ordinary on the outside, then I reached my hand inside, never touching the bottom. It was a bottomless pit in a bag.

"A way to carry our belongings," I said, tossing the satchel over my shoulder.

Nearby were the gardens. We hurried. Through the gardens, through the trees, and to the hidden entrance to the dragon hatchery in the hill.

As we approached, I heard the rustling of guards.

Fuck. How did I not think they'd be guarding it?

I pressed my fingers together again. "By string of moon and light, form a weapon sharp as night. Branch of the wild, talon of the sky, bow in my grasp, I'll let the arrow fly."

With little effort I was holding a bow and a quiver of arrows that I slung across my back. I readied the bow, and nocked an arrow, drawing closer. The moment they laid eyes on me, I drew back, green light extending into the arrowhead. I shot twice, both straight into their hearts, lighting them aflame in the process. They fell backward, one running into the hatchery as he panicked.

"Oh no." My heart dropped. The tables inside were now on fire. The cradles were burning. Everything ahead of me inside began to ignite. I had to get these eggs out *now.*

I moved quickly, snatching as many dragon eggs as I could and stuffing them into the magical bag.

Horns sounded again outside. Loudly. Heavy doors opened in the castle. They were coming.

I secured the eggs in the bag and ventured back outside into the clearing where Zorath waited, where ahead I saw guards funneling out of the gates. Dozens and dozens of them. They'd be here within minutes.

Zorath turned toward me, his eyes inquisitive. *"Where is Knox?"*

I rushed to his side, slinging the bag around in front of me and securing it around Zorath's neck. "He told me he would find me." I felt the army's presence growing closer and closer.

The moment was now.

I faced the castle once more, my pulse pounding in my throat. The heat of my power burned inside me, swirling like a storm, ready to break free.

As I looked back at the looming structure, once a place of allure, now a symbol of everything that imprisoned me, the anger that had simmered below my skin erupted.

"This place took everything from me," I growled to myself. The guards grew closer, dozens and dozens of them, but it no longer mattered. Power rose wildly in my blood.

I stretched out my hands to my sides, feeling heat crackle at my fingertips.

"This kingdom is a poison. A prison."

My anger, my pain, my heartbreak, it all swelled up.

"I am unburnable. I am powerful."

In that moment, I knew what I was capable of. It all surged through me.

"I am the Master of Flame."

The words rang out like a war cry, and with a roar, I unleashed everything.

A blast of green fire erupted from my palms, from my being, tearing through the night. Zorath followed suit, breathing fire in every direction I wasn't.

The ground beneath us trembled as soldiers scattered, their armor igniting as they fell. They screamed in terror, a familiar sound.

But I didn't stop.

The fire spread, feeding on my fury, feeding on everything in its path. I cried out, releasing even more power. The ground quaked again, and the castle walls ahead seemed to groan in response.

The flames began to spread. Quickly. So quickly. As if they had been waiting impatiently for me to unleash them. We were too close to the castle, and it was just about too late.

Windows shattered ahead, bricks crumbled under the weight of my fury. The fire spread like a living thing, consuming the castle with a destructive wave.

Like a wild beast unleashed.

I stopped the release of my flame and so did Zorath. The air was thick with smoke, the heat beginning to rise. Power hovered in the air, crackling around me, out of control.

My mind raced. Knox said he would find me. But what if he was still inside? Trapped. It would be my fault that he didn't escape if he was trapped behind my flames.

Or he could be dead.

I couldn't know. The hope of going back for him was gone the minute the castle was set ablaze.

And then, I heard it. The thunderous rumble of not just dozens of guards, but an approaching army. Large and ready. They marched out from either side of the castle, and would soon surround me.

I couldn't wait around for Knox. He was strong. He was smart. He was still a prince. My time was up. If I fought all of them with flame, I would crash. My energy levels were growing weaker by the minute.

"We have to go, Zorath."

He grumbled, but leaned down for me to climb.

I seated myself onto his back, my heart racing as I clenched my thighs against him and wrapped my hands around the spines on his neck for stability. The clanking of armored footsteps grew louder behind us.

Zorath spread his massive wings, and with a single, powerful thrust, we were airborne.

The wind whipped through my hair as we soared higher and higher into the night sky. Below us, a sea of green—a glow that cascaded over all of Velorum.

I turned to take one last look, my heart heavy with loss. *Knox . . .*

I wiped the moisture from my eyes, trying to steady my breath. I never got to say those three words to him. But he'd still let me go. He'd let me live.

Explosions rang in the distance as an inferno of light and destruction raged behind us. Flames danced around the city.

I'd destroyed the kingdom, just like the prophecy predicted.

I looked ahead, at the vast expanse of stars that stretched out before us. The ground fell away beneath us.

Anger boiled within me as I realized the war was only just beginning.

ACKNOWLEDGEMENTS

To start, I am incredibly grateful for my editor, Lauren, with Tea & Tales Press for reading my manuscript thoroughly and helping me refine it in a timely manner. Not only did she treat me professionally as an author, she also hyped up my book as a friend, and I enjoyed working with her.

I appreciate all of my beta readers and everyone who has been interested from the beginning. In the early stages of my drafts, they gave me the feedback I needed and that encouraged me to keep going so early in the process.

I want to give a special thanks to Angie and Sarah for offering to be truthful readers for me. They gave me honest thoughts about my story, and kept me looking forward to the next step.

Thank you to my parents for reading my very first draft ever written and telling me that it was good, when it was, in fact, *not* good.

A huge thank you to Hunter, my wonderful and loving husband that never judges me for writing, always gives me time to work and think about my projects, and supports me every step of the way. You are my rock. I love you so much.

And finally, I appreciate my readers. The ones who found me either at a bookstore, through social media, or even at work. Your encouragement keeps me going, and it inspires me to do even more. I hope this story brings you as much joy as it did for me to write it. Thank you.

ABOUT THE AUTHOR

Kennedy Anderson is from south Mississippi, where she's lived her entire life. She is also a wife to her loving husband, Hunter, who has supported her through every step of her author journey. Kennedy's favorite TV shows are Game of Thrones and Friends. She is a fan of anything that involves dragons, magic, or romance. Her drink of choice is a good IPA beer.

Though she works full-time in healthcare, she has always found a passion in creativity—specifically in music, art, and writing. She spent her middle school and high school years in band, playing on the drumline and learning every other percussion instrument she could put her hands on. That's where she thrived.

Kennedy grew up appreciating art and writing with her grandmother, who has since passed, but the memories of writing short stories, drawing, and painting together live on. She writes not only for herself, but for her Mamaw.

When she isn't writing, she is working at her full-time job, reading, or riding the motorcycle with Hunter.

Follow Kennedy Anderson on social media for more information on upcoming works.

TikTok: @k.anderson.author

Instagram: @kennedy.anderson.author